Praise for *Fast ——*

"*Fast Track* is one of those rare novels that you simply can't put down. I was hooked on page one and it was non-stop until the very end—an emotional roller coaster."

Wolf Blitzer
Anchor, CNN's "The Situation Room with Wolf Blitzer"

"John DeDakis has penned a story so real it rivals real-world scenarios. As a psychiatrist, I have seen and treated many Lark Chadwicks—complex, heroic women who somehow reach down through their traumas to find a foothold of resilience in their shrewd intellect. Nobody writes like this without it being real."

Dr. Paul Dobransky
Psychiatrist

"I was so interested in what happens with Lark I couldn't put it down. It's an awesome book—a fun read. Intrigue, humor, emotion—what more do you need?"

Carol Costello
Former CNN Anchor
Journalism Lecturer, Loyola Marymount University

"*Fast Track* is a page-turning thriller that you simply won't be able to put down from start to finish. The suspense is palpable, the characters unforgettable and spectacular, the plot ingenious and masterfully crafted."

Barbara Casey
Author and Literary Agent

"I've known John DeDakis as a dedicated and skilled journalist since 1975 when I was a White House reporter for United Press International. Then, as a journalism professor, I appreciated all the more John's commitment to bringing to life ethical journalism and mentoring relationships. He knows about the roller coaster of life's experiences and he demonstrates that in *Fast Track*. IT'S A MUST READ."

Wesley G. Pippert
Former Director, Washington Program
University of Missouri School of Journalism

"John DeDakis has been a friend both professionally and personally for over thirty years. His artistry with a story flows in a captivating way. Warmth, modern struggles, and life's realities blend into a book one reads and immediately recommends to others. This is vintage DeDakis. I first knew him in the midst of tragedy. Hope followed."

Lowell H. Mays
Corporate Psychologist
Former Consultant to Sheriff & Coroner's Offices
Dane County, Wisconsin

"Another Hemingway, but better. John DeDakis writes with clarity, sensitivity and passion. Clearly, he knows what he's describing on a very deep level."

Patricia Daly-Lipe, Ph.D.
National League of American Pen Women
President, Washington, D.C. Branch

"John DeDakis carefully combines the meticulous detail of a journalist with a compelling story line that puts him in the forefront of mystery writers. The result is a most satisfying read—rich in vivid detail, riveting in its plot development, and moving in the way it dissects the lives and motives of his characters. With this breakthrough work, DeDakis has established himself as a top mystery writer as well as a journalist of the first order."

James Hoyt, Ph.D.
Former Director, School of Journalism
University of Wisconsin, Madison

"Fast Track sucked me in and kept me up half the night."

Judy Boysha
AP Radio

"In *Fast Track,* John DeDakis gives his readers appealing characters who jump off the page and a plot with delicious twists and turns."

Mindy Ratner
Minnesota Public Radio

"DeDakis crawls inside the mind of a twenty-something female, authentically capturing her character, curiosity and self-expression in this can't-put-down thriller."

Kris Kosach
ABC Radio

"If the book were a meal it would be a gourmet's feast. *Fast Track* is an emotional roller coaster that twists and turns the reader through an odyssey of suspense and mystery. Give yourself time when you pick it up, because you won't put it down until the final page. John DeDakis, the accomplished journalist, has revealed other skills as a master storyteller."

Herb Glover
Program Director
American Forces Network Europe, Retired

Praise for *Bluff:*

"Lark Chadwick reminds me of me in the early days of my career, driven by curiosity and the need to unravel true and compelling stories. It's no surprise that veteran journalist John DeDakis so accurately depicts the life and work of a reporter, but how he can so accurately write from a woman's point of view—with all the intrinsic curiosity, emotion and passion—is nothing short of astounding."

Diane Dimond
Author and Investigative Journalist

"I raced right through it. John DeDakis is a masterful storyteller who has adroitly woven several story lines into this fast-paced page-turner. With true-to-life characters and an insider's knowledge of the world of journalism, the second of DeDakis' Lark Chadwick mysteries will not disappoint fans of *Fast Track.*"

Charlene Fu
Former Foreign Correspondent for the Associated Press

Praise for *Troubled Water:*

"As a young female journalist, I spent most of this novel wondering how John DeDakis got into my head. *Troubled Water* is sharp, suspenseful and—most importantly—utterly believable."

Jenna Bourne
Investigative Reporter
10 Tampa Bay, WTSP-TV (CBS)

"What happens when you pair a cub reporter with murder, mayhem, and a handsome bad boy? A great read. Once again, John DeDakis proves he knows how to write a gripping thriller. I loved it."

Jillian Harding
Former Producer
CNBC, CBS

Praise for *Bullet in the Chamber:*

"*Bullet in the Chamber* manages to capture all of the intensity, grit and breathlessness of covering the presidency in an age of nonstop news and fierce competition. Lark Chadwick stands out as a protagonist who is at once compelling and compulsively true to form. John DeDakis gets inside the head of a modern-day White House journalist who has no idea what's in store for her when she begins this rollercoaster of a ride."

Josh Lederman
Former Associated Press White House Reporter

"John DeDakis combines the heart-stopping and heartbreaking in a story of drugs, drones, corruption and politics. Lark's latest adventure is entertaining and harrowing. And always riveting."

Henry Schuster
CBS News "60 Minutes" Producer

"I've been there. So has John DeDakis. Lark Chadwick's first days as a White House correspondent are spot-on. DeDakis kept me turning pages well past two o'clock in the morning."

Carolyn Presutti
Voice of America (VOA) TV Correspondent

Praise for *Fake:*

"Fake, by John DeDakis, is a stunner of a mystery, the kind of book that hooks you at the first page, and then won't let go. DeDakis tells this story of betrayal, tragedy, and political posturing with an insider's view of Washington's under-belly that is so vivid and feels so real that he resets the bar for inside-the-Belt-way thrillers."

John Gilstrap
Author of Total Mayhem and the Jonathan Grave thrillers series

"A gripping, topical tale about the difficulties of discerning the truth in the new world of fake news."

Kirkus Reviews

Fast Track

A Lark Chadwick Mystery

Books by John DeDakis

Lark Chadwick mysteries
Fast Track
Bluff
Troubled Water
Bullet in the Chamber
Fake

Fast Track

A Lark Chadwick Mystery

John DeDakis

SPEAKING VOLUMES, LLC
NAPLES, FLORIDA
2020

Fast Track

Copyright © 2005, 2020 by John DeDakis

Cover design by Hannah Linder

ISBN 978-1-64540-375-3

To the memory of my sister
Georgia Ann
And our parents
N. George and Ruth DeDakis

Author's Note - 2020 Edition

Fast Track was originally published by ArcheBooks in 2005 and remained in print until the company went out of business in 2019. My thanks to Kurt Mueller of Speaking Volumes for coming along just in time to keep alive *Fast Track* and *Bluff*—my first two novels in the Lark Chadwick mystery series. Thanks also to my agent, Barbara Casey, for being my champion from the beginning.

And thank you to Dennis De Rose of MoneySaver Editing for his eagle-eyed catches of mistakes in the 2005 edition and generous reviews of my first five novels.

Finally, a big hug to my wife Cindy. You were with me twenty-five years ago at the start of this odyssey, and again as a reliable proofreader for this edition.

I tell my writing students, "Write what you know," and I practice what I preach. I know journalism—and I know grief.

The first chapter of this book is ripped from reality, October 11, 1980, the day my sister Georgia took her life. I was on the scene that day. Writing about it was cathartic, but *Fast Track* is not Georgia's story. Nor is it entirely mine. Yet my protagonist, Lark Chadwick, is the kind of person I wish my sister had allowed herself to become—tough, resilient, resourceful, not a victim, and not allowing herself to be defined by some guy.

But, as you'll come to see if you read my other Lark Chadwick novels, Lark also has plenty of struggles and shortcomings. Lark's journey might be a lot like yours, with many unexpected twists and turns along the way, but with innumerable opportunities to change and grow, as well.

Thank you for coming along. I hope you enjoy the ride.

Chapter One

It was just past midnight, the end of another on-my-feet marathon, waitressing the dinner shift. I hustled through the steamy kitchen on my way to the back door, trying not to slip on the grease-slicked red tile floor. As I skated past Tommy, the baby-faced high school kid who always does a great job busing my tables, I slapped twenty-five bucks of my tip money into his palm.

"You're the best, Lark," Tommy called over the hiss and clatter of dirty dishes and a growling garbage disposal. "Hey! When are you gonna ditch this joint and run away with me to Costa Rica?"

"Next year, Tommy. I promise. I'm too old for you right now."

It was our running joke. But tonight it struck me as particularly ironic—and sad.

I really need to talk with Annie.

When I last saw her before I left for work she was already on her second rum and Coke.

Maybe we can help each other laugh again.

The lights of our modest split-level house on Dale Drive were still ablaze when I wheeled into the driveway. As I got out of the car, a biting breeze off nearby Lake Mendota blew my hair in my face. I shook my head and the wind shoved the wild strands aside. The October sky was bleak and overcast. It felt as if snow was in the air.

When I pushed open the unlocked front door, a strong noxious smell assaulted me.

"Annie?" I called. "Annie? What's that smell?"

I heard Annie's car running in the attached garage.

"Annie?" I stepped into the house.

That's when I saw her.

"Oh, my God...ANNIE!"

She was sprawled on her back, arms outstretched, legs sticking through the open hallway door into the garage. She wore a gray woolen warm-up suit and tennis shoes, exactly what she was wearing when I left for work. Her Nissan continued to spew carbon monoxide into the house.

The rest is a panicked jumble: I remember darting into the garage, turning off the ignition with quivering hands, throwing open the garage door, making a frantic 911 call, and covering her lips in a desperate attempt at mouth-to-mouth. Her clammy skin felt like cool putty.

"Oh, God...Oh, God." My heart galloped.

In the distance I heard the whine of sirens, but kept working on Annie, blowing air into her lungs, watching her chest expand, relax, then stay that way.

"Come on, Annie. Come ON. BREATHE!"

Her ashen face remained blank, eyes gazing indifferently past me at the ceiling, raven hair splayed against the floor's polished wood. Her face was vacant, impassive, so unlike the beautiful, radiant, gregarious person she'd once been.

The sirens grew louder. I glanced out the open door behind me and saw a fire truck. Seconds later, an ambulance and a police car screeched to a stop in front of the house. A man wearing a bright orange windbreaker and carrying what looked like a huge tackle box dashed in. Kneeling next to me, the man set the box down next to Annie's head, felt her cheek and pressed her neck.

I kept blowing into her mouth and pressing her chest.

"I think she's gone, ma'am," he said softly. "She has been for some time."

"No she's not," I cried. "There's still a chance." I kept blowing and pressing.

"There's got to be a chance. We have to keep trying…have to keep tr—" my voice trailed off and I buried my head on Annie's chest and sobbed. My tears made dark blotches on her gray sweatshirt.

After a moment, I sat up and, still crying, took her right hand in both of mine.

Her hand felt cool. I sandwiched it between my two warm ones, trying to transfer my heat to her, but her hand insisted on remaining cold. Tenderly, I stroked her cheek with the back of my left hand.

Cold. So cold.

"Lark!"

I turned.

Father Dan Houseman, the new priest at the nearby St. Stephen's Episcopal Church, stood in the doorway. He's in his mid-thirties and looks like a thoughtful version of the Marlboro Man—ruddy and a little scruffy in tweed, denim, and wire rims, his white priest's collar the only nod to ecclesiastical formality.

"Father Dan!" I jumped up. "What are you doing here?"

Quickly, he came to me and surrounded me with his arms. I let myself collapse against his shoulder. He smelled of Old Spice.

I backed away. "How did you know to come?"

"I was on call," he answered, not seeming to take offense at the skeptical tone in my voice. "I'm a volunteer chaplain for Dane County."

A year ago, when Father Dan arrived at St. Stephen's—and Annie learned he was single—she seemed to turn into a giddy schoolgirl, sometimes referring to him as "The Hunkatollah."

I admired him from afar, but knew I had no chance competing against Annie. She was the vivacious one; I'm the shy barn owl, always scoping things out from a safe distance. Part of me ached to be with him, because he seemed to be such a good person. But the suspicious side of me feared he was just another smooth operator—a sophisticated version of the drunken frat boys who used to try to paw me at parties.

Probably half a dozen firemen were in the house, opening windows and placing fans by them. Their whirring kicked up a chilly breeze.

"Excuse me, Miss." A middle-aged policeman with a concerned look on his clean-shaven face held a small notebook in one hand and a ballpoint pen in the other. "I'm sorry to bother you, but I need to ask you a few questions. Could you tell me your name?"

"It's Lark. Lark Chadwick."

"Age?"

"Twenty-five."

He scribbled. "And the name of the deceased?"

It seemed so weird, so clinical, to refer to what had once been such a vibrant, alive person as "the deceased."

"Anne Chadwick," I monotoned. My head throbbed.

"And your relationship to the deceased?"

"She's my aunt. My father was her brother."

"Was?"

"Both my parents were killed in a car accident when I was an infant. Annie raised me since I was four."

"Who raised you before that?"

"My grandparents—her parents."

"And how can they be reached?"

"They can't. They're...deceased." I smiled ruefully at how comfortably I could ease into cop-speak.

"Her age?" He nodded at Annie, lying prone on the floor.

"Thirty-nine."

"Marital status?"

"Divorced. Her husband ditched her twenty years ago."

"Any children?"

"No."

I went through the motions of answering his questions, all the while feeling like I was having an out-of-body experience.

"In the past few days did you notice if she'd been distressed about anything?" the cop asked.

"Nothing specific," I said, trying to remember. "She seemed preoccupied lately, but certainly not suicidal."

Suicide. The word stuck in my throat. I couldn't believe that Annie would even consider the ultimate rejection of life and hope. The ultimate rejection of family and friends. The irrevocable rejection of me. It didn't seem possible, yet there she was, lying dead at my feet, arms outstretched as if making an angel in the snow.

"It just doesn't make sense," I cried, turning to Father Dan. "Annie held the personality franchise for the entire Midwest. Why would she do such a thing?"

Father Dan shook his head slowly, sadly. His eyes were puffy and bloodshot.

I turned away. "This doesn't make sense," I muttered.

I stalked through the living room, stopping outside Annie's bedroom door, my arms folded tightly across my chest. "She wasn't depressed. She loved life. I just don't get it."

I glanced into Annie's room, looked away, did a double take—and screamed.

Chapter Two

Annie's room was a mess. An absolute mess. All the drawers of her desk were scattered on the floor, empty, their contents heaped onto her bed.

Father Dan and the policeman came running to my side.

"Her room's been ransacked!" I could barely choke out the words.

"Don't touch a thing," the policeman ordered. He grabbed me by the arm, stopping me as I began to stride into Annie's room. "This is now a crime scene!" he announced loudly enough to be heard over the whine of the fans. "No one is to touch anything until detectives and the coroner arrive. I'm ordering everyone to clear the area. Now!"

One by one the firemen and EMTs trooped outside. The policeman used his radio to ask for a crime scene detail, the coroner, and detectives.

I stood in the doorway, gaping in shock at the upheaval in Annie's bedroom. Suicide was a hard enough possibility to grapple with, but could someone else have been here in the house with her this evening? Someone looking for something? Someone who wanted her murder to look like a suicide?

"You done with her?" Father Dan asked the cop, pointing at me.

"Yes, sir," the guy nodded. "But the coroner and the detectives will want to talk with her when they arrive."

"Let's go for a walk." Father Dan took me by the elbow and steered me toward the front door.

In the hallway, I slipped from his grasp and turned to take one long last look at Annie sprawled on the hardwood floor. Her pallid lips would never again frame the toothy, ironic grin that preceded the arrival of some funny, sarcastic remark. Yet, even in death, she looked beautiful— at peace.

I knelt by her side. Her dull eyes stared, half-lidded, at the ceiling. I shivered.

"Why, Annie? What happened?" I whispered.

She ignored me.

I stood abruptly. "Let's go."

It was still overcast, but not as windy as it was earlier. We walked aimlessly in silence along Dale Drive, my quiet, tree-lined street.

"Why? Why'd this happen, Father Dan?" I asked, angrily. "You're the man with the answers. The man who knows God. The man Annie had all those cosmic talks with. The man who's supposed to be able to make sense out of the senseless." My voice grated with sarcasm, but I didn't care.

Father Dan absorbed my fury with a sigh. "She was a very needy person, Lark. She needed people, but there was a hole deep within her that not even people could fill. I think she must have felt alone and afraid."

"You'd talked with her a lot, hadn't you?"

"On several occasions, yes," he said.

"You think it was suicide, don't you."

He nodded.

"But you saw the room. Somebody'd turned it upside down looking for something."

"That somebody could easily have been Annie," he said gently.

"She was a neat-freak, Father Dan. I've never seen her room even close to that messy."

"You'd never seen her with the car turned on and the garage door down, either, had you?"

I stopped walking, buried my face in my hands, and sobbed.

"I'm sorry," Father Dan said, his fingertips gentle on my shoulder.

I stiffened and forcefully shrugged his hand away.

Undaunted, he fished a handkerchief from his sport coat pocket and held it out to me. "I shouldn't have been so blunt."

I snatched it from him and blew my nose. "So, you know, then, what was bugging her?"

"Somewhat."

"Then why can't you tell me?" I shouted.

"What a person tells a priest in private is strictly confidential."

"But she's gone now."

"True, but she still feels very much alive to me. Let me hold onto some of her secrets for now. Maybe, at a later time, I'll be free to tell you more, but not right now, okay?"

I sighed, not sure it was okay, but I decided to let it drop—for now.

We shuffled along the darkened street in silence.

After a few minutes he turned his head to me. "What will you do now?"

"My life's a mess," I said simply. "I've just been drifting and empty, but now I need to make some really basic decisions, like what I'm going to do with my life."

We turned right onto another elm-lined street. It led toward Midvale Park. We walked in silence awhile longer.

"I forget, are you working or still in school?" he asked finally.

"I dropped out my senior year to write the Great American Novel."

"Really? Did you finish it?"

"Yeah. Right. The first two years were filled with false starts and writer's block. Then came what felt like a fevered burst of creativity."

I kicked a stick off the sidewalk.

"And then?" he prompted.

"Got my first rejection in the mail today."

"I'm sorry," he said gently, touching my arm.

I shrugged. "The guy said he liked my writing, but called my book 'an angst-riddled screed that merely highlights your deep, unresolved anger and distrust toward men.'"

"Ouch."

"The jerk." I jammed a hand inside my jacket pocket and felt the letter, still crumpled where I'd stuffed it as I dashed out of the house for work. For an instant, my mind flashed back three years to the bachelor pad of my English professor—his eyes wild, face stern, his body pressed against mine as I lay helpless against the cushions on his sofa.

"Are you okay?" It was Father Dan. He tugged gently at my sleeve.

"No," I said, trying yet again to shake the awful memory from my mind. "I'll never be okay."

We passed the undulating wooded hills of Midvale Park on our left, then turned right onto Owen Street, heading toward Dale Drive. When we got to the corner of Dale and Owen, Father Dan stopped beneath a streetlight and turned to look at me.

His face was earnest in the stark light.

"This is going to be an extremely hard time for you, Lark. I don't think you should stay alone."

I considered this. My emotions were reeling, tempered only by the numbness that comes from shock and exhaustion. I knew I needed help navigating through what appeared to be an impenetrable gloom. Father Dan seemed the logical person to lean on.

"I don't know where I could go."

"Do you have a close friend you could call?"

"She's in Europe."

"A neighbor?"

I shook my head. "We all go our separate ways. I don't really know them."

He thought a minute.

"I could stay with you," I said timidly.

Father Dan shook his head curtly, as if being bombarded by a pesky horsefly. "I'd like that, but it wouldn't be wise."

"Why not? You're the only person I'd feel comfortable with right now."

He rubbed his chin, thinking. "There are some people I could call." He pulled a cell phone from the pocket of his sport coat. "The church has a grief ministry. I know a family who'd take you in on short notice."

I felt a sudden flush of embarrassment that I'd so audaciously invited myself into his private sanctuary. "That's okay. Skip it." I touched his arm to stop him from stabbing the buttons on his cell. "I appreciate the offer, but I'll be all right."

He studied my face. The long shadows cast by the streetlight accentuated his doubtful expression.

"Really. I will," I said.

He sighed. "Are you sure?"

"Uh huh," I lied.

Chapter Three

When Father Dan and I returned to the house, all the lights were burning and the entire yard was wrapped in yellow "crime scene" plastic tape. The fire truck and ambulance were gone, but several more police cars and a couple of unmarked sedans were parked on the street. As surreal as the scene was, I was relieved there were no flashing lights, no intrusive TV cameras, and only a few bystanders maintaining their vigil at a respectful distance across the street.

The clean-shaven policeman who'd interviewed me stood guard at the end of the driveway. "The coroner's inside. He'll want to have a few words with you, Miss."

He lifted the tape for us.

Inside, Annie's body was gone, but a faint exhaust fume smell lingered. I found myself listening for the familiar rustle of Annie's clothes, or the sound of her voice calling out to me from another room. Instead, a houseful of strangers meticulously inspected everything. A man and a woman were on their knees by the door into the garage, using a brush as they closely eyed the doorknob.

A portly man approached us from the kitchen. He looked to be in his late fifties, wore horn-rimmed glasses, a trench coat, and had oily, thinning hair slicked straight back.

"Evening, Padre," the man said, sticking a beefy hand toward Father Dan.

"Hi, Ed." They shook hands, then Father Dan turned to me. "This is Lark Chadwick, the victim's niece. Lark, this is Dane County Coroner Ed Sculley."

Sculley's fleshy hand surrounded mine like a hungry giant amoeba.

"I'm sorry about your loss, Miss…er, Mizz Chadwick," Sculley mumbled perfunctorily.

He seemed to have great difficulty preceding my name with "Mizz." It was as if he'd been scolded one too many times about being politically incorrect with members—especially younger members—of the opposite sex.

"I wonder if I can ask you a couple questions," Sculley said.

"Sure, I guess."

"Let's sit down where it's more comfortable." Sculley led us into the living room.

It felt odd being invited into my own house by a stranger. Father Dan and I sat on the sofa, our backs to a picture window which would have looked out onto the street had the drapes not been drawn.

Sculley's weight sagged into a chair to our left. Over his shoulder I could see into the garage where investigators hovered around Annie's car.

"I have to tell you straight out, Mizz Chadwick, this looks every bit to me like your average, everyday suicide."

"But—"

He held up his hands, palms forward. "I know. I know. You're going to say she wasn't suicidal…her room was ransacked. I know all that. And for that reason, as you can see, we're scouring the place for the possibility, however remote, that there was, indeed, some intruder. We're giving you the benefit of the doubt, Mizz Chadwick. But I'm willing to bet you that once it's all said and done, you're going to have to deal with the fact that your loved one just plain did herself in."

"Thank you for keeping such an open mind, Dr. Scarpetta."

"It's Sculley."

"Whatever." Obviously, he didn't get my sarcastic reference to Kay Scarpetta, the super-competent medical examiner in Patricia Cornwell's novels.

"Now, in the interest of keeping said open mind, Miss...er...Mizz Chadwick, is there anything more you can add that might lead to a conclusion other than suicide?"

Just then a bald man entered the room and stood next to the chair holding Sculley's bulk. "Looks like I got here just in time," the man smiled as he stepped toward me and reached out his hand. "I'm Detective Silver."

He shook my hand, and Father Dan's when I introduced them. The detective looked more like an accountant than all those rugged hunks who play detectives in the movies or on TV.

"Sorry to interrupt," Silver said. He took a nondescript black ballpoint and a small notebook from the inside pocket of his gray sport coat and opened to a fresh page. "Please continue your story." He clicked his pen into position.

I told Sculley and Silver what I'd told the first cop on the scene, earlier: Annie had never been suicidal, but had been preoccupied in the past few days.

"Tell us more about that," Silver said. "Did she give you any indication as to what it was that seemed to be weighing on her mind?"

"I've been wracking my brain trying to come up with something."

"Any seemingly insignificant little tidbit could be important," Silver said.

"Actually, I'd been a little concerned about her," I said.

"Go on," Silver prodded. He leaned closer. "What had you concerned?"

"I dunno exactly. She'd been acting weird lately."

"How so?"

13

"Hard to put a finger on it, but it started not long after Grampa died."

Silver scribbled something in his notebook. "Her dad?"

I nodded.

"When did he die?"

"About six months ago. Heart attack. Gramma died of cancer a few years back. Anyway, Annie'd been handling Grampa's estate—you know, putting the farm in Pine Bluff on the market, going through his personal papers and stuff. She'd get weepy, but then she'd dig in and get on with it."

"Uh huh," Silver said, scribbling.

"On Monday, Annie really seemed freaked about something. I tried to get her to tell me what was wrong, but she just said she found something of Grampa's that she had to 'check out.'"

Silver looked up from his notes. "Any idea what she meant?"

I shook my head helplessly. "I wish I knew."

Father Dan fidgeted and cleared his throat. "Um, maybe I can add a little something to that."

I turned to Father Dan. His face was flushed, beads of perspiration glistened on his upper lip.

"Annie came to me over the past few months and I, um, counseled her on several occasions," Father Dan said, looking at the floor.

"What was the nature of those counseling sessions?" Silver asked.

Father Dan looked at the detective. "I'm not at liberty to divulge that. The priest-penitent relationship is sacred. But pertaining specifically to your investigation, there is something I can add to what Lark has already said."

"Go on," Silver said, turning a page, writing fast.

"The last time I met with her," Father Dan continued, wiping the sweat from under his nose, "she came to me in a very confused state."

"And when was this?"

14

"Wednesday evening in my office at the church."

"She was confused?"

"Paranoid, actually. Her eyes were wide as she kept scanning the room for danger."

"And this struck you as unusual, given your past counseling sessions?" Sculley, the coroner, asked.

"Yes. On this occasion she seemed frightened."

"Did she say why she was frightened?" I asked, jumping into the interrogation.

"No," Father Dan answered. He avoided my eyes and continued looking at Sculley. "I tried to probe, but she was very guarded."

"Did she say anything about what it was that was bothering her?" I was sitting on the edge of the sofa almost leaning into Father Dan's face.

He turned to me. "Only that when she was going through her father's papers, she'd come across something she described as shocking." His voice trembled.

"What? What was it?" I nearly shouted.

"I don't know. She wouldn't tell me. I wish now I'd been more aggressive in questioning her." Father Dan looked sadly at the floor.

"Then why did she come to you if she wasn't going to tell you anything?" I pressed.

"She had what she called a 'hypothetical question.'"

"And what was that?" Silver asked, trying to regain control of the interview.

Father Dan looked past me at Silver and Sculley. "She wanted to know what a person should do if they came across evidence of a crime."

Silver again: "What kind of crime?"

"She wasn't specific."

"What did you tell her?" I asked.

Father Dan looked at me, his eyes wide. I thought of a deer and headlights. "I told her I needed to know more about it, but she refused to go beyond that cryptic statement, other than to say that the details were embarrassing."

"Embarrassing to whom?" I wanted to know.

"She didn't say. Wouldn't say."

"Did you give her any advice?" Silver asked.

"I advised her that if she believed a crime had been committed, she should turn the evidence over to the proper authorities."

"Did she?" Silver asked.

"I don't know, but I doubt it," Father Dan said. "She simply smirked and said, 'That's what I was afraid you'd say.'"

"How did you interpret her smirk?" Silver wanted to know.

"As cynicism. Annie was a rather bawdy, iconoclastic person. I assumed she meant that the authorities weren't smart enough, or weren't trustworthy enough to handle whatever evidence she had. It was the last time I saw her alive." Father Dan buried his head in his hands and sighed. "I wish I'd tried harder to find out what was bothering her," he said. There were tears in his ice blue eyes when he lifted his head and looked at me. "I'm so sorry, Lark."

Chapter Four

I awoke a little after eight o'clock Saturday morning, still groggy from only a few hours of fitful sleep. Father Dan had stayed until nearly four when the cops took down their crime scene tape and said it would be okay for me to stay. He left only after I'd assured him yet again I would be all right on my own.

My feelings for Father Dan were conflicted and confused. One side of me clearly wanted to be near him, but I was shocked when I realized for an instant that now Annie ("my chief competition") was "out of the way." When those words popped into my head, they horrified and disgusted me. How could I be so selfish at a time like this? I shoved the thoughts aside and quickly replaced them with doubts about Father Dan: had he really been on call, or were his motives more carnal? Were the two of them planning a midnight rendezvous?

I peeked out the window. Once again, the sky was overcast and depressing. The house had never seemed so empty, so cavernous, so quiet. It would have been tempting to wallow in self-pity, but I pushed the loneliness away before it could envelop me.

Restless, I dug my diary out of my backpack and began writing furiously. The ballpoint swirled rapidly across the page, leaving behind my neat, tight penmanship.

Writing always helps me focus. I felt compelled to recount the events of the past evening while the memories were still fresh, even raw. But more than the desire to remember was the obsession to understand.

As objectively as I could, I wrote down the facts favoring a ruling of suicide in Annie's death, but I also included Father Dan's cryptic observation that Annie appeared "paranoid," and had claimed to have found evidence of a "crime" she'd called "embarrassing."

I concluded my entry this way:

> *Granted, Annie had a decidedly mercurial temperament, but she loved life too much to kill herself.*
> *Or am I just too ashamed of suicide to face the truth?*
> *Suicide?*
> *Or Murder?*
> *I wish I knew.*

My cell rang just as I was putting the cap back on my Bic.

"I hope I didn't wake you up." It was Father Dan.

"That's okay. I had to answer the phone."

He chuckled. "You're wide awake, then?"

"I wouldn't say wide. Didn't sleep all that great."

"I held off calling for as long as I could. The first night's always the toughest."

I grunted, unconvinced.

"You hungry?"

"Yeah, I guess."

"How 'bout brunch?" When I didn't answer right away, he added, "My treat."

"Sure. I'm such a sucker when someone else is buying. When?"

"I can be there in ten minutes."

"Gimme at least half an hour. I need to take a shower."

After we hung up, I dragged myself out of bed. I really didn't want to go, even if it meant being with Father Dan.

I felt a little better after my shower. I put on a denim work shirt, jeans, a baggy sweater and was just lacing my hiking boots when the doorbell rang.

Father Dan smiled when I opened the door. He wore jeans and his I'm-on-duty priest's collar beneath a partially unzipped University of Wisconsin warm-up jacket.

"Morning," he said.

"You're wise not to have put good in front of it."

He lost his smile. "You okay?"

"I don't think I'll ever be okay."

"Let's just live one day at a time," he said.

"I wouldn't call it living, either," I said bitterly.

"Sorry. You know what I mean."

"Yeah, I do. I'm sorry, too. You're just doing your job," I sighed.

He took me gently by the elbow and walked me to his car, parked behind mine on the driveway. Father Dan drives a dark blue Toyota Corolla, nothing fancy. He opened the passenger door for me. A few minutes later, we drove up in front of the Dickerson Funeral Home, not a restaurant.

"Why are we here?" I asked.

"First, you need to make funeral arrangements, then you can eat."

"Mighty manipulative of you, mister." I tried to make it sound like a joke, but inside I was a little peeved at his presumptuousness.

"I had to lure you out of the house somehow. Tell me honestly: would you have come if you'd known we were going to stop here?"

"Probably not."

"I rest my case."

"You win," I shrugged.

A moment later we were sitting in a quiet and plush office where a small, somber man with heavy, black-framed Buddy Holly glasses took down the bare facts about Annie's life for her obituary, and then got me to nail down the funeral arrangements.

Somehow I got through it.

"Where do you want to eat?" Father Dan asked as we left the funeral home an hour later.

"We could go to The Lamplighter. I'm supposed to work tonight. I can tell my boss why I won't be coming in. He's got the personality of an adder, so his reaction should be interesting. Glad I've got a prayer warrior on my side." I punched Father Dan playfully on the shoulder.

He laughed.

The Lamplighter was only a few minutes away near a shopping center on a busy four-lane boulevard divided by a tree-lined safety island. The breakfast rush was just ending when we arrived.

My boss, Mr. Green, a bald, humorless man in his fifties, was manning the cash register.

"Hi, Lark," he glowered. "I need you to work the lunch shift and the dinner meal, too." It was a statement, not a request. "Janie called in sick. She's probably just hung over from a hot date last night."

My anger began to build, but I kept it in check. "Gee, I can't, Mr. Green," I said sweetly. "I'm sorry. In fact, I was just going to tell you I can't work tonight, either."

He grimaced.

"My aunt died," I said.

He rolled his eyes. "You know the policy, Lark," he said condescendingly. "You can only get time off if the death is in the immediate family." He rattled off the line as if quoting verbatim from a policy manual—a policy manual he usually made up as he went along.

I felt my blood pressure spurt. In the past, I would always take a deep breath, die inside, then agree to do whatever he wanted. Today, I was ticked. Real ticked.

"Mr. Green," I said coldly, "my aunt has been like a mother to me." My eyes were narrow slits. "She's raised me since I was a baby, when my parents were killed in a car accident." Slowly, my voice rose in intensity. "Let's just say my mother killed herself last night. Does that fit into your policy?" I was almost yelling and near tears.

He looked stunned. His eyes darted around the room to see if anyone was listening.

People nearby had stopped eating and were looking in our direction. I don't think any of his galley slaves had ever had the nerve to stand up to him before—not to mention publicly.

He looked at Father Dan.

"It's true," Father Dan said, clearing his throat, uncomfortable. "We just came from the funeral home."

Mr. Green glanced at Dan's white priest's collar and made an instant calculation that maybe this wasn't merely a creative plot on my part to duck responsibility.

I continued to seethe inside, awaiting his verdict.

"Okay," he sighed. "I suppose we'll manage." He stabbed angrily at the cash register keys, trying to make me feel guilty. This time it wasn't working. He looked at me challengingly. "When you gonna be back to work?"

"Rigor mortis has barely set in," I exploded. "How am I supposed to know?" I thought for a second. "Next weekend," I heard myself say in a moment of weakness, then thought better of it. "No. Better yet: Never. I quit!"

Turning blindly, I pushed past some customers who'd just come in, and blasted through the doorway, leaving behind a stunned Father Dan.

Chapter Five

I stalked to the Toyota and, fuming, planted my back against the passenger door, arms folded across my chest, waiting impatiently for Father Dan to catch up with me.

When he unlocked my door, I dove into the passenger seat, replaying in my mind the tongue-lashing I'd just given Green.

"You were right, Lark," Father Dan said as he slid behind the wheel, "that Mr. Green definitely has adder tendencies." He stuck the key into the ignition and started the engine. "Is he always like that?"

"No. Today he was laying on the charm a bit thick." Putting my thumb to my mouth, I snagged a piece of dry skin between my teeth and gave it a yank. The pain made me wince. I looked out the window, trying to keep my eyes away from Father Dan's, but I could feel his gaze hot on my left ear. "I was stupid to quit, wasn't I?" I studied the small amount of blood pooling along the side of my thumb.

"It probably feels good right now," he said calmly, "but it has created a new problem. What are you going to use for money?"

I shrugged.

He turned on the heater and warm air whooshed in. "Where should we go to eat?"

"I'm not hungry anymore. And I'm feeling claustrophobic."

"I've got the perfect antidote," he said, putting the Corolla in gear.

A few minutes later we were on the prettiest part of the University of Wisconsin campus strolling through the woods on a path that snaked along the Lake Mendota shoreline between the student union and the Lakeshore dorms. The trail is a popular place for bikers, joggers…and lovers. The sun had come out and the remaining leaves on the trees were brilliant yellow and crimson.

"How're you feeling?" Father Dan asked after we'd walked for a while in silence.

I shrugged.

"Numb?" he probed.

"Numb fits." I picked up a stone and tossed it into the lake.

"She had her whole life ahead of her," Father Dan said as he watched the ripples expand from where my rock hit the water.

"Why would she do such a stupid thing?" I asked.

"Maybe to Annie it was the most logical thing in the world, at least at the moment."

"What do you mean?"

"Moments change. An impulsive act doesn't allow time for reflection."

"But maybe she wasn't acting on impulse. Maybe she'd been building up to it. I'll bet a lot of people who kill themselves feel as if their suffering will never end," I said, perhaps speaking as much about my own emotional turmoil as about Annie's.

Father Dan shook his head. "Does that sound like the Annie you knew, Lark?"

"Not really. She was like me—act first, think later. My biggest fault."

Father Dan nodded and sighed. "Taking drastic action based on feelings can be as precarious as building your house on shifting sand."

Just then a jogger, ponytail wagging, bounded past us from behind. She came to a sudden stop about thirty yards ahead and bent over to retie her running shoe. Dan stopped to look out over the water, but I noticed him glancing over to memorize every curve of her Spandex-sculpted behind. After a moment, her task complete, the woman bounded off like a graceful doe. After the woman was nearly out of sight, Dan turned his attention to the water and began whistling a tune I'd heard on the oldies station Annie used to listen to.

"Dock of the Bay, right?" I asked.

"Uh huh. Otis Redding. Did you know he died out there?" Dan pointed past Picnic Point, a spit of land jutting into the lake.

"He did?"

"Yep. Plane crash back in '67 or '68."

I shuddered. "Ugh. More death. Let's change the subject."

We started walking again.

"What was your major when you were in college?" he asked.

"English. Had a scholarship and everything. I love to read. And I write like a fiend, but now it's mostly scribblings in my journal."

"Why do you like to read so much?"

"I was lonely growing up. It was a way to pass the time. I always felt different from everyone else."

"Any idea why you felt different?"

"About the time I started school, I realized all the other kids had mothers and fathers. I had a gramma and grampa, but the big person I lived with I'd always called Annie."

"Did I hear you tell the cop you were four when you went to live with Annie?"

"Yeah. She was nineteen. Gramma had gotten too sick to take care of me. Annie'd gotten married the year before to some construction worker. When he dumped her, she changed her name back to Chadwick. Said he was a jerk."

"But the two of you didn't move back in with your grandparents?"

"Nope. Annie told me years later she had to get away from what she called the 'doom and gloom' atmosphere of living with them."

"Doom and gloom?"

"Yeah. After my mom and dad were killed, Annie said her parents were never the same, especially Grampa. They became morose and withdrawn. Annie said she had to get out or she'd suffocate."

"Did you ever ask her about your parents?"

"Oh sure. I remember the first time really well, even though I was only five or six. We were driving to Gramma and Grampa's farm outside Pine Bluff."

"Where's that?"

"About thirty miles southeast of here in Bluff County."

"Right. I've been through there. Very quaint."

"Anyway, we were stuck behind a slow-moving trailer truck on a hilly stretch of two-lane road. I remember suddenly blurting out, 'Whatever happened to my mommy and daddy?' There was this long pause. I studied the truck's mud flaps and waited. Finally, Annie said, 'They died in a car accident. You were just a baby. Your father was my brother.' It all came out of her in a burst of words."

"What did Annie say your folks were like?"

"She'd carry on about how wonderful and vivacious Lila was— that's my mom. Said my dad was cautious, friendly and had a good job at the bank as some sort of up-and-coming official. But y'know? I've never had a very good feel for what they were really like. And whenever I'd press Annie or my grandparents for more details, they'd always brush me off."

Father Dan turned to look at me, and stopped. "Maybe now's the time to find out about your past."

"What do you mean?"

"Take some time and try to learn about your parents. Maybe that will fill in some blanks, shore up your foundation, give you a direction for the future."

"I wouldn't know where to begin. The people who had all the answers are dead, and they weren't saying a whole lot while they were alive."

"You could go back to Pine Bluff. It's only a half hour drive from here. Chances are a lot of folks knew them. Take a couple weeks, maybe a month. See what you can learn. The process might give you the answers you'll need for your next step."

"I just quit my job, remember? What am I gonna use for money?"

"Tell you what: I've got a discretionary fund I can dip into to help pay your bills and maybe the next rent payment. In a month, we'll take stock and see where things stand. This is a difficult time for you, Lark. I want you to be able to do your digging without a lot of other worries. What do you say?"

I couldn't say anything because of the lump in my throat. Impulsively, I threw my arms around Father Dan. Was this what joy felt like? Or love? I'd never known.

Chapter Six

At nine-forty-five on the morning after we buried Annie, I drove Pearlie east along State Highway 58 toward Pine Bluff. Pearlie is my canary yellow, rattletrap VW bug. This particular stretch of road is new, perfectly straight, flat, and relatively free of traffic. But even as my mind raced ahead, excited about the launch of this search-and-discovery mission, regret kept tugging me back like gravity. One moment I'd be planning my day, the next I'd be wallowing in thoughts of Annie, how much I missed her, and how alone I felt.

The day was intensely bright, but windy—more like March than late October. As I continued to drive toward Pine Bluff, I felt a shiver of nervous expectation. *What if I can't find any answers? What if I discover I'm just wasting my time? What if? What if? What if?*

My plan was simple: Find the newspaper office and see if they have a back issue that might have an account of the traffic accident that killed my mom and dad. If that didn't work, I'd go to the bank where Dad had worked and see if anyone there remembered him. I assumed one of those options would at least begin to yield some answers.

My eyes strayed from the gray concrete to the black and brown fields bracketing the road. There were occasional farms in the distance and every now and then I'd pass a house with bales of hay snugged around the foundation to act as insulation during the fast-approaching winter.

The last few days had been an exhausting blur. On Monday, I'd found Annie's will in a small safe she kept in the basement. I took it to

Nicholas Davis—a probate lawyer who attended St. Stephen's. Father Dan recommended him, but I also knew who he was: a short, dapper man in his sixties who always sat with his wife, a retired elementary school teacher, in the third pew from the front on the left side.

The will was short—two pages—and consisted of mostly legal gobbledygook that left "the rest, residue, and remainder" of her estate to me and named me as executor.

Annie's safe also contained a key to her deposit box at a Madison bank. Mr. Davis said he'd arrange to get a document appointing me Annie's personal representative so I could gain access to her bank deposit box and inspect its contents for him as soon as possible.

Annie's obituary was in the *Wisconsin State Journal* Monday morning. In addition to being short, it bore the indignity of a typographical error, misspelling Chadwick with an H instead of a K.

In his eulogy, Father Dan talked lovingly of Annie. Tears shone in his eyes and dampened his cheeks as he spoke. He called her "beautiful," and "my special friend."

And he referred to her as "a very funny person." I had to nod in agreement with that.

Annie'd always been outgoing, with a strong streak of irreverence.

Father Dan's reference to Annie's sense of humor prompted a memory:

It was during church one summer when I was about fifteen. Annie sang in the choir, which sat in pews at the very front between the altar and the congregation. I sat alone near the front of the congregation where Annie could keep an eye on me. But her behavior that morning made me realize it was she who really needed the watching.

It happened during the part of the service when the priest is preparing for communion—a traditionally solemn and introspective moment. The day was stifling and St. Stephen's was not air-conditioned. A large floor fan stood dormant between Annie's seat at the far end of the front choir pew and the altar where Father Vincent stood. (Father Dan replaced the stodgy, but beloved Father Vincent who retired last year after a thirty-year reign.)

Sweat glistening on his forehead, Father Vincent caught Annie's eye and subtly gestured toward the fan. Annie had been out late drinking the night before and was still hung over. When she realized that Father Vincent wanted her to turn on the fan, she got up from her kneeling position, went to the fan, and, unfortunately, switched it on high. The sudden gale caught a pile of communion wafers Father Vincent held in front of himself on a silver plate and blew them into his face. The thin discs of bread, the consistency of very light cardboard, looked like confetti as they fluttered onto Father Vincent's hair and to the floor.

Several people gasped, but Annie burst out laughing. She quickly tried to stifle it, which only made matters worse. Her whole body bucked in spasms of smothered guffaws and her face turned red; Father Vincent's turned purple.

I cringed with embarrassment as the acolytes scrambled to pick up the light brown wafers that polka-dotted the marble tiles at Father Vincent's feet. Years later, Annie was still telling the story, always ending it by laughing so hard she could barely catch her breath.

In his eulogy, Father Dan also talked about how guilty he felt that he "wasn't sensitive enough" to have prevented Annie's death, because, he confessed, "As her Rector, I saw her pain because she let me see it. It was deep," he said, "so deep it eventually overwhelmed her."

A drive-by doubt-pang assaulted me when Father Dan talked bluntly about suicide. He called it a "selfish act—a kick in the gut to those who are left behind." But he did raise the possibility Annie may have been murdered:

"I know there are some who believe Annie died under mysterious circumstances—that a person or persons unknown were also involved. Perhaps. And the authorities are looking into it. But the question we all face at one time or another is finding the will to face life as it is."

Frankly, life as it is sucks.

I thought back to the night before the funeral. Father Dan had taken me to the funeral parlor about half an hour before the official start of the visitation period. Annie looked peaceful as she lay in the cherry wood coffin, but death had transformed her usually radiant face into a wax dummy. Her skin was cold and hard, like pottery. Her mouth was drawn and sagging. The rouge on her cheeks looked unnatural, almost clown-like.

She was gone.

I knew it.

I accepted it.

Then, as I'd stood looking at her, I suddenly came apart completely. Emotion, with an intensity I'd never experienced, wretched from me like a sudden case of stomach flu. I sank to my knees, sobbing.

Annie was dead.

Her body was there, but the spirit that had animated it, given it life, was gone.

All that remained was a shell, and no matter what heroic measures had been attempted by the Somber Buddy Holly Funeral Man, nothing could be done to prettify the stark, cold, empty reality that Annie Chadwick was dead.

I must have wept a good ten minutes that night. I remember Father Dan's gentle touch as he lightly stroked my back with his fingers. He didn't try to stop me from crying; he just let me go. When I'd finished, it felt as if a huge weight had been lifted.

Yet, as I sat listening to Father Dan's eulogy—and now, as I drove toward Pine Bluff—fresh tears rolled down my cheeks as I wondered for the millionth time why Annie was dead.

Chapter Seven

The Pine Bluff of my childhood, population 21,303, seemed relatively unchanged: Red brick, two-story buildings lined both sides of the street. Numbers carved into the stone at the top of the structures noted when they were built. Most of the buildings dated back to the 1880s.

Because yesterday's funeral procession had bypassed downtown, I decided to drive slowly through the business district before circling back to the newspaper office. As Pearlie and I crept through the middle of town, my head bobbed as I looked first to one side of the street and then the other. To anyone on the sidewalk, it probably looked as if I was watching an imaginary tennis match.

"That's where my father used to work," I told Pearlie as we cruised past the forbidding stone and marble edifice of The First Bank of Pine Bluff. "And that's our ultimate destination," I informed my car, as the store front for the *Pine Bluff Standard* went by on our left.

Across the street, I saw a sign for The Korner Café, which was in the middle of the block between the unmajestic Majestic movie theater and the Skoldvig Bakery. I'd always gotten a kick out of the contradiction.

I kept driving, head bobbing.

At the far end of the business district, on the right, loomed the tall, turreted sandstone Bluff County Courthouse. A couple police cars were parked in the back lot.

Next to the imposing courthouse was the smaller, but more modern, City Hall that seemed to have been constructed of tinted glass. Across the street, a huge lumberyard sprawled along a railroad siding, thick with weeds. As Pearlie rumbled across the rusting tracks, I saw, to my left, the old train station, now vacant.

The road made an S-turn as it left downtown, climbed a hill, and widened, but I made a U-turn and headed for the newspaper office.

The *Pine Bluff Standard* is so small and nondescript my eyes almost missed it as I drove back through town. The newspaper office is shoe-horned between Johnson Realty and The Nook, a tiny craft shop in the row of buildings lining Pine Bluff's main street, cleverly named: Main Street.

Butterflies did loop-the-loops inside my stomach as I got out of Pearlie and slammed the door. I caught a glimpse of myself in the re-flection of the *Standard's* plate glass window: knit tam-o'-shanter cap, glasses, dark brown wavy hair below the shoulders, buckskin jacket, jeans, wool gloves, backpack slung over my shoulder. I felt as uncertain as a twelve-year-old at her first dance, but I was surprised to see I looked more confident than I felt. My stride was purposeful and my chin jutted forward almost aggressively as I scaled the two concrete steps and pushed open a dark green door of weathered wood. A bell tinkled as I stepped inside.

It took a minute for my eyes to become accustomed to the relatively dark room, which smelled faintly of stale coffee. From the far end, I heard the syncopated clacking of someone typing. A long wooden coun-ter stretched across the room in front of me.

As my sight became clearer, I saw the source of the typing sound: a white-haired man hunched over a computer keyboard at a desk at the rear of the office. His back was turned to me and he kept typing in spite of the jingle of the bell announcing my arrival.

A phone rang.

The man, wearing a starched, white shirt, continued typing.

"Muriel, will you get that?" the man hollered on the second ring.

Another ring.

"Muriel!" The typing faltered.

On the fourth ring, he swore, rose halfway out of his chair, and reached awkwardly for the phone on the desk next to him, muttering, "Where is that woman?" He fumbled with the receiver before getting it to his ear. "Pine Bluff Standard," he barked.

Pause.

"Hello?"

He swore again, slammed the phone into its cradle, and returned to his furious typing.

I thought about saying something, but decided to wait until he finished. The disheveled room contained three desks, strewn with paper. A computer terminal was on each desk. The computers looked out of place, modern, in an otherwise turn-of-the-last-century office, complete with a high, pressed-tin ceiling.

A light thump at the door behind me interrupted my room inspection. Turning, I saw a handsome, gray-haired woman in her fifties struggling to open the door. She carried a white paper bag in one hand and managed to balance two steaming Styrofoam cups in the other.

I opened the door for her.

"Thanks," she smiled. The woman's pretty face was flushed by the cold. She wore light brown corduroy slacks, a plum colored wool sweater and hiking boots. Carrying her cargo around the side of the counter, she walked briskly to Typing Man, her footsteps thudding on the floor's long wooden planks.

"Here you are, honey." She kissed him on the forehead and put one of the cups down on the desk next to him. "I brought you some fresh-brewed high-test and a bagel."

Typing Man grunted.

The woman took a bagel out of the bag and placed it neatly onto a napkin. Then she returned to me at the front counter.

"Now, what can I do for you?" she asked brightly, a wide, warm smile emanating from her face. In her youth, she must have been a beauty.

"Hi. I need to find a newspaper clipping about a car accident that happened twenty-five years ago."

The woman bit her lower lip, thoughtfully. "Hmm. Not sure the issues go back that far, but I suppose they do. We just took over the paper a few months ago, so we're still settling in," she explained. "Just a second."

She turned and went back to Typing Man. Bending toward his right ear, she whispered something. He paused just long enough to make an impatient wave toward a bookcase that took up the entire back wall.

"Over there," she said, pointing at the far end of the bookcase as she came toward me.

I thanked her and headed for the back of the office. As we brushed past each other, the woman said to me in a low, confidential tone, "Don't feed The Bear." She gestured toward Typing Man. "My husband can be a bit of an impatient grouch when he's writing his column on deadline," she said, flashing me a dazzling smile.

"Thanks. I'll be careful," I whispered. I liked her immediately. She'd just done a lot to make those butterflies in my stomach go away.

The staccato tapping continued as I tiptoed past him, shoving my gloves into my coat pockets on the way. The volume I needed was almost exactly where he'd pointed.

I took the book to the empty desk next to him. It faced the front of the office. I sat demurely, but before I could open the tome in my hands, a newspaper lying on the desk in front of me captured my attention. It was a July edition of the *Pine Bluff Standard*.

Displayed prominently beneath the banner was a black-and-white picture of the man sitting diagonally to my right, now scowling at his keyboard as he chewed a bite of bagel. The dignified man in the picture had an arrogant scowl, thinning white hair, and dark-rimmed glasses that made him look rather bookish. He wore a dark suit and a conservative, striped tie.

The headline read:

LIONEL STONE TO BECOME NEW *STANDARD* EDITOR

A sub-headline in much smaller type read:

Former *New York Times* Editor Returns to Boyhood Home

Quickly, I glanced at The Bear. His eyes fiercely scanned his computer screen.

I read the article written by Clifford Keller.

Pulitzer Prize-winning journalist Lionel Stone, 68, becomes the fifteenth Editor/Publisher of *The Pine Bluff Standard* August 1.

Stone, who recently retired as National Editor of *The New York Times*, purchased *The Standard* from outgoing editor Clifford Keller, who is retiring due to ill health. (See related story on page 2.)

Last week, Stone told *The Standard* he plans to return to his boyhood home of Pine Bluff to "keep tinkering" in his chosen craft.

In addition to working on the newspaper, Stone said he would lecture at the University of Wisconsin-Madison, attempt to mentor up-and-coming young journalists, and write his memoirs.

"It's time to come home," Stone said.

During a distinguished career spanning nearly fifty years, Stone had a front row seat as he covered several key events that have shaped US history, including the assassination of President John F. Kennedy, the Vietnam War, and Watergate.

He has written three books and reported on the presidencies of Kennedy, Lyndon Johnson, Richard Nixon, and Gerald Ford.

I snuck a peek at Lionel Stone, typing wildly one desk away from me. His name was only vaguely familiar. His mouth and nose twitched like a rabbit's as his fingers continued to make the keyboard click. It surprised me to see him only using his two index fingers to type, yet he somehow managed to make the keys clatter like a hailstorm.

And I marveled at his ability to concentrate as Muriel fielded the constantly ringing phone and dealt with the stream of people coming and going through the tinkling doorway.

Curious to know more about this apparent journalistic legend in my midst, I resumed my reading.

Stone was born here in Pine Bluff in 1937. He began his career in journalism as a paperboy, delivering weekly copies of *The Pine Bluff Standard*, later writing part-time for the paper as he worked his way through school.

He graduated with a BA in journalism from the University of Wisconsin-Madison in 1959 and covered the State Capitol for the Associated Press from 1959 to 1960.

In 1960, Stone was hired by *The New York Times* because of what the paper called his "insightful" coverage of the Wisconsin Presidential Primary that year.

On November 22, 1963, Stone was a White House Correspondent for the *Times*, riding in the press bus of President Kennedy's motorcade when the presidential limousine came under gunfire in Dallas, Texas.

For the next several days, virtually without sleep, Stone banged out his newspaper's coverage of the assassination. His book, *The Killing of Camelot,* became a national bestseller.

Quagmire, his first-person account of the year he spent as a Vietnam War correspondent, earned him the Pulitzer Prize in 1967. The book is credited—and blamed—for helping turn public opinion against the war.

Stone led a team of reporters in the *Times'* coverage of Watergate, the scandal that toppled the presidency of Richard Nixon, producing, in the

```
process, another bestseller, Obstruc-
tion of Justice, published in 1975.
```

"Wow," I breathed, putting down the paper. "Pretty impressive."

The typing stopped. "What?" Lionel Stone asked sharply.

"Huh?" I looked up, startled.

"Did you say something?" His eyebrows arched. He was irked.

"Oh, ah, nothing," I blushed. "I didn't mean to disturb you, Mr. Stone." Guiltily, I folded the paper and pushed it aside. "Sorry."

He let out a disgusted sigh, gulped some coffee, and resumed hammering the keyboard with increased intensity.

When I was certain The Bear was engrossed in his writing, I unfolded the paper and hurriedly finished the article.

```
    In 1974, Stone married the former
Muriel Johnson of Pine Bluff.
    Upon the election of Jimmy Carter as
president in 1976, Stone was named Na-
tional Editor of the Times, a position
in which he served until his retire-
ment this year.
    The Stones have one son, Paul, 24,
a journalist with the Associated Press
in Washington. A daughter, Holly, 22,
died last year in a mountain climbing
accident in Peru.
```

I sat thinking for a moment after I read the article. It occurred to me I had read *Quagmire* for a political science course during my freshman year. I remembered very little about it—the class or the book—even though I got an A. Political scandals had never interested me, so I was sure I hadn't read his book about Watergate.

Finally, I turned my attention to the bound back issues of the newspaper. I opened the book to the middle and quickly found what I was looking for. The front page contained a huge black-and-white picture of mangled metal. A policeman peered into the wreckage.

The caption read: "Bluff County Sheriff Roy Miller inspects the wrecked car in which George and Lila Chadwick were killed."

The headline above the picture read:

CAR/TRAIN CRASH KILLS LOCAL BANKER, WIFE

"A train?" I almost shouted.

"What?" Lionel Stone asked again, a scowl forming on his face. He reached for his bagel and took a big bite.

"Sorry, nothing." I returned my attention to the article.

The typing resumed.

"Miracle Baby Survives Crash," read the sub-headline at the top of the right-hand column.

Miracle Baby?

My eyes streaked along the lines of type spelling out the story of the crash that killed my parents.

```
    A Pine Bluff couple was killed in-
stantly Monday night when their Ford
Mustang convertible was struck broad-
side by a Southbound Amtrak train.
    Dead at the scene were the driver,
local banker George Chadwick, 26, and
his wife, Lila, 24.
    Mr. Chadwick is the son of Charles
and Francis Chadwick, Rt. 1, Pine
Bluff.
```

> The Chadwick's infant daughter, Lark, survived the accident unharmed. Bluff County Sheriff Roy Miller dubbed her "The Miracle Baby."

My heart pounded. My mouth was dry. I became aware it was hanging open in amazement. Gulping, I shook my head quickly as if trying to dislodge cobwebs. This news was overwhelming, stunning. *Why wasn't I told any of this?* my mind screamed. I had to fight to keep my eyes from skimming the story too rapidly to comprehend it.

> The accident happened at a grade crossing two miles West of Pine Bluff on Wisconsin 58. Amtrak officials said the signal lights at the crossing were operational when the crash occurred about 11:00 p.m. Monday.
>
> Officials were unable to explain what caused the Chadwick vehicle to stray onto the tracks in front of the train.
>
> The train's engineer, Vern Strozier, 52, and fireman Max Labelle, 53, both of Aurora, Illinois, were unavailable for comment.
>
> The weather was clear at the time of the crash and the convertible top of the Chadwick vehicle was down, according to investigators.
>
> Sheriff Miller said the little girl survived the crash because her car

seat apparently had not been strapped
to the back seat. Miller said the force
of the collision catapulted the baby's
car seat about fifty yards into a cornfield next to the tracks.

A passenger on the train, Jack Brad-
ford, 10, of La Crosse, found the baby
crying in the field shortly after the
collision. The baby is now in the care
of relatives.

"Amazing," I said, setting down the paper and sagging against the back of the chair.

"Okay, I'll bite. What's so amazing?" Lionel Stone asked, impatiently drumming his fingers on his desk.

"I'm sorry. I didn't mean to disturb your work, Mr. Stone."

"That's okay. I'm done with it now." He wadded his napkin and tossed it into the trash can next to his desk. "You look like you've just gotten some mighty powerful news, kid."

"Um…yeah. You might say that," I answered; then, more to myself: "This is really weird."

"What is?"

"Here, take a look." I spun the book around and slid it to the edge of the desk so he could read the story.

His chair creaked as he got up, came over and leaned on the desk with his hands resting on either side of the book. His blue and red striped tie dangled onto the yellowed page. Silently he scanned the article, his eyes swiftly sweeping back and forth.

He breathed noisily through his nose.

After a moment he asked gruffly, "Anybody you know?"

"Not exactly, but sort of." It sounded as ridiculous as I felt.

"I see…" Unconvinced, his eyebrows arched. He expected more.

"The people who were killed were my parents."

"Oh…I'm sorry to hear that." His voice softened and he lost his amused look.

"I never knew them," I said.

"Uh huh."

"And," I said, still disbelieving what I'd read, "I'm the so-called 'Miracle Baby.'"

He let out a long whistle. "No kidding?"

"Yeah," I said. "Isn't it amazing?"

"It is. And I get the impression all this is news to you, too." He was leaning against his desk now, arms crossed, sleeves rolled up past his elbows, his forearms a pelt of dark coiled hair.

"Yeah. I'd always been told my parents died in a car crash, but never that a train hit their car. And—and this really knocks me out—I'd never been told that I was there and survived."

"How come?"

"Good question. But I'm determined to find out," I said, looking again at the article.

"Hungry?" he asked, looking at his watch.

I nodded.

"C'mon. Let's grab a bite across the street." He pushed himself up, towering over me as he unrolled his sleeves and buttoned the cuffs.

"Well, ah…" I said, thinking of my virtually empty wallet.

"I'm payin'," he added, slipping on his suit coat. "Muriel," he called to his wife, "I'll be across the street."

Chapter Eight

It was almost eleven o'clock when we walked into The Korner Café, which was just beginning to fill with customers. A couple of people sat at the counter that paralleled the left wall. A few others sat at tables scattered throughout the long, narrow room. We chose a table for two at the window.

"Could you answer a question for me?" I asked as we took our seats.

"Shoot."

"How come they call this place the Korner Café if it's in the middle of the block?" I whispered.

"Oh, that's easy," he laughed.

Just then a waitress who looked to be about sixty was slinging two glasses of water in front of us.

"Hi, Millie."

"Howdy, Lionel."

"Lark Chadwick, meet Milicent Korner, owner of this honorable, but middle-of-the-block establishment."

I laughed and Millie smiled at Lionel Stone's teasing.

"Lark was wondering how The Korner Café got its name, Millie."

"My late husband thought it would be real funny," Millie explained, rolling her eyes. "When we bought it back in the sixties—" She turned to Lionel Stone. "That's the *nineteen* sixties, Lionel."

He held his hands out innocently. "I didn't say anything."

"Anyway," Millie said to me, "I told Archie the joke would get old awfully fast, but," she chuckled, "I'm constantly amazed when some-body new comes along and gets a charge out of it."

I laughed.

"Can I getcha anything to drink while you decide what to have?"

"Coffee. Black," he said, then looked at me.

"The same, with plenty of cream and sugar."

Millie hustled away.

Lionel glanced at the menu, but quickly tossed it aside. Obviously, he'd been here a lot and merely checked the menu out of habit, perhaps hoping he'd find something new this time.

I studied the menu more closely. There were about five or six "home cooking" plates that looked good, including pot roast, turkey, chicken, and steak, but I settled for my usual hamburger and fries.

As soon as I closed my menu, Millie was on us, pencil poised above pad. "What'll it be?"

We gave her our orders and Millie retreated behind the counter.

"So, kid," Lionel said, giving me a serious look. "How does it feel to be a miracle baby?"

"Weird. Very weird. I've never ever felt very miraculous. In fact, if anything, I've always felt like a horrible accident. Like, why am I here? It's become the question of my life, and now the drive to find the answer to that question is getting more intense."

"That's quite a story about you and your folks."

"Tell me about it," I said, glumly.

"You say you didn't know anything about this?"

"Not really. My grandparents and my aunt—my father's sister who raised me—all told me my parents were killed in an accident. But they apparently kept a lot of things from me, not the least of which is that I was in that horrible accident, but wasn't killed. Wasn't even hurt, for crying out loud."

"They probably wanted to protect you from the truth. There's a lot of that going around these days. Why don't you ask them about it, now that you know?"

"I wish I could, but I can't. They're all dead now. Annie—my aunt—killed herself just last week…or at least that's how it looks."

"Oh my goodness." He touched my arm. "I'm really sorry to hear that, Miss Chadwick."

"Lark. You can call me Lark."

"And I'm Lionel." He paused, uncomfortable. "I'm sorry if I was insensitive. It's an occupational hazard."

"That's okay. I'm fine. Well, I'm trying to be fine. The priest at my church encouraged me to look into my past as a way of getting a grip on my future."

"Sounds like good advice." He took off his dark gray suit jacket and draped it over the back of his chair. "So, how did you get such an unusual first name?"

"The story goes that my mom named me Lark because I was such a happy baby—you know, 'happy as a lark?'" *That's a laugh*, I thought to myself. *If she were to name me today, it'd probably be something like Basset Hound Chadwick.*

"What do you mean when you say Annie's death *looks* like suicide?"

I told him of my doubts and about the investigation currently being conducted by Dane County. Lionel listened intently, but only grunted noncommittally from time to time.

When I finished, Lionel asked, "Do you think she was murdered?"

The bluntness of his question stunned me for a moment. It was hard enough coming to grips with suicide; the possibility someone had actually killed Annie seemed too overwhelming to contemplate.

"I don't know what to think," I answered slowly. "I have so little to go on, I wouldn't know where to begin. Annie's death probably was a suicide, and I've simply been in denial about it. Right now I just feel this compelling need to find out about my past."

"Why's that so important?" he asked, rolling up the sleeves of his white shirt.

I told him about my feelings of drift, rejection, listlessness, of what it was like finding Annie's body, and of my renewed desire to somehow find purpose and direction in my life.

Lionel listened closely, interrupting only to ask brief clarifying questions. He sat with his elbow on the table, chin resting on his hand. When our food came, he ate while I talked. By the time I finished telling my tale of woe, he had demolished his tuna fish sandwich.

"You still in school?" he asked, wiping his mouth with a paper napkin after taking a sip of coffee.

"Not any more."

"When'd you graduate?"

My eyes dropped. "Um...I didn't."

"You didn't? he boomed. "Why not, girl? You seem smart."

Ashamed, I told him of dropping out to write the Great American Novel, and how the dream had gone haywire.

"Geez," he muttered. "Kids!" A pause. "Got a job?"

I shrugged self-consciously and slid a little lower in my chair. "I was a waitress, but I, um, quit."

"Maybe you're not so smart after all, kid." He shook his head in disgust, doing a masterful job of making me feel ashamed, and even a bit indignant. If he was going to keep calling me "kid," as in the Humphrey Bogart line, "Here's lookin' at you, kid," I might just start calling him "Bogie."

"I've got an idea," I said suddenly. "How about if I do an investigative piece and write a first person article for you about what I find?"

Lionel scowled.

I plunged on. "A lot of people probably remember the accident and would want to know what happened to that miracle baby."

"You just told me about how much of a failure you are as a writer."

"That's different. I aced the journalism class I took."

"Yeah? Who was the professor?"

"Um...um..."

"Just as I thought. C'mon, kid, you can't snow me."

"Hoyt!" I almost shouted, "Professor Hoyt."

His face relaxed. "Jim Hoyt?" Lionel nodded. "Good man."

Look," I said, pressing my advantage, "surviving a train crash is very compelling." The words tumbled from my mouth almost before I could think them. "Maybe I could find out what caused the crash and why I was never told about it. Plus, it's a much more engaging story if told in the first person by the Miracle Baby herself."

I smiled triumphantly.

He rubbed his chin, thinking.

"And you could sort of be my Sherpa guide," I added in a moment of inspiration.

That got him. He squirmed in his chair. "How much is this gonna cost me?"

"How does a hundred dollars sound?" My brazenness surprised me. *Maybe I'm more desperate for money than I thought.*

"Not as good as fifty."

"Seventy-five," I countered, "plus expenses."

More scowling.

I held his eyes.

"Agreed," he said, finally, "but only if it's good enough to publish."

I looked at him sternly over the top of my glasses.

"Don't worry, kid. You'll have a pro for an editor. Deal?" He held out his hand.

"On one condition," I smiled mischievously as I began reaching for his.

He winced. "Yeah…?"

"Every time you call me kid, I get to call you Bogie."

For an instant, he looked stunned, then burst out laughing. He smothered my hand with his, and shook it warmly. "It's a deal…kid."

"Thanks, Mister, um…Bogie."

Chapter Nine

The bell above the door of the Korner Café rang steadily as more and more customers crowded into the restaurant for lunch.

One of the arriving patrons brought Lionel to his feet. "Hey, Sheriff."

"Lionel!" The man greeted Lionel loudly as if they were long lost brothers. They stood shaking hands next to the table. The sheriff wore a brown uniform with gold trim. He had short-cropped, wiry, salt and pepper hair. I guessed him to be about fifty-five with the physique of a thirty-five year old. And he was huge. A giant. His hands, his arms, everything, seemed about two sizes larger than normal.

"Sheriff, let me introduce you to a colleague of mine. Roy Miller, meet Lark Chadwick."

He was an older version of the man whose picture I'd seen in the paper looking at the wreckage of Mom and Dad's Mustang.

"We met long ago," I smiled.

"Chadwick…Chadwick…" he repeated. "Not George Chadwick's daughter?" he asked in amazement.

"That's right," I blushed as he dwarfed my hand in both of his. "You called me the m—"

"The Miracle Baby, right, of course. How could I forget?"

"Lark is writing a follow-up article about the crash," Lionel explained.

"That's great," the sheriff said with enthusiasm. "It's a shame what happened to your folks, Lark, but it's so good to see you all grown up. Stop by and see me sometime for your article. It would be wonderful to talk with you for a while."

"I'd love to. Thanks, sheriff," I beamed. He was so warm and welcoming, I couldn't help but feel at ease around him, protected.

Lionel and the sheriff exchanged a few more pleasantries and shook hands before Lionel rejoined me. The sheriff went to a table in the middle of the room where three men—all ample-tummied farmers—rose as one when he approached.

"He's huge!" I whispered to Lionel when we sat down.

"His nickname is the Jovial Giant," Lionel explained.

Just then, the door opened, ringing in another person whose presence caused Lionel to spring to his feet once again.

"Good morning, Your Honor." Lionel was now shaking the hand of a diffident man in his late forties with greasy, slicked back dark hair, and wearing a three-piece suit.

"Good morning, Mr. Stone," said the man in what sounded like a British accent.

Lionel introduced me again as his "colleague" to Reginald Lange, the Mayor of Pine Bluff, Wisconsin.

"Lark Chadwick…" the man said. "Any relation to Charles Chadwick?"

"That's my grampa."

"Did you know Lark's father?" Lionel asked.

The mayor looked at me, his face darkening.

"George Chadwick," I prompted.

"I knew your father quite well," he said sadly. "A pity what happened." His accent wasn't exactly British, but he seemed to be affecting a dignified air.

"I'm writing a follow-up story for the paper about the accident," I told the mayor.

"Aren't you the little tyke who came through it all without a scratch? The little Miracle Girl, or some such name they called you?"

"Yes. The Miracle Baby," I corrected, feeling funny to be referring to myself that way. "Would you mind if I dropped by later and asked you a few questions about my father?"

"Do. By all means. I should love to sit and chat for a few minutes," he said, "but I'm not quite sure how long I can spare." He looked at the gold watch he pulled from his vest pocket. "I've been pretty busy these days," he said with a knowing wink at Lionel.

"The mayor is running for Congress," Lionel explained.

"Oh my," I said, surprised. "Well, good luck."

"Thank you, my dear. So good to meet you." He touched my hand gingerly as if it were a dead fish.

Lionel sat as the mayor shook hands with customers at a few more tables.

"He seems nice, but icky," I whispered to Lionel.

"See if you can have your article for me a week from today. It's the issue before the election," Lionel said, leaning across the table and speaking conspiratorially, then added, "And, since they both knew your folks, see if you can work both the mayor and the sheriff into the piece."

"How come?"

"Because the sheriff's running for Congress, too. They're running against each other. And," he added, looking back toward the center of the restaurant, "they hate each other's guts."

I followed his gaze. The sheriff and mayor were shaking hands and smiling fake smiles at each other.

"This should be great fun," Lionel said, mostly to himself.

Chapter Ten

Reginald Lange, Mayor of Pine Bluff, Wisconsin and Republican candidate for Congress for the 10th Congressional District, seemed to drag himself into the right rear seat of his dark blue Lincoln Continental. With a deep sigh, he slouched against the plush upholstery as Eugene, his chief aide and driver, closed the back door and took his seat behind the wheel.

I sat next to the mayor in the back seat, hoping I would now finally be able to get the interview he'd promised me. But my heart sank when I saw the haggard look in the mayor's eyes following a brutal afternoon of campaigning.

It had begun shortly after my luncheon with Lionel at the Korner Café. I'd gone to the mayor's office to see about scheduling an interview, but the mayor's secretary informed me he wasn't due for the rest of the day. She suggested I go, instead, to his campaign office—a dingy Main Street storefront next to Skoldvig's Bakery.

There I met Eugene, a clean-cut thirty-something, wolfing a sandwich while working the phones. His plain burgundy tie was askew and the sleeves of his button-down blue shirt were rolled back. He wore tan slacks and brown tasseled loafers. His navy blue sport coat was draped over the back of his metal folding chair. A handful of college kids stuffed envelopes and made phone calls.

When Eugene got off the phone, I explained to him my newspaper assignment and told him of my brief meeting with the mayor at The Korner Café. And, when I mentioned the mayor's willingness to talk with me about my folks, Eugene seemed genuinely thrilled.

"We need all the publicity we can get," Eugene said. "Why don't you tag along with us this afternoon?"

"Sounds great."

"Donut?" he asked, pointing to a Dunkin Donuts box on the edge of his desk.

"No thanks. I just ate." I looked around at all the commotion in the disheveled room. "You guys look busy. How's he doing in the polls?"

"Not good," Eugene said, shaking his head sadly. "We're almost twenty points behind Roy Miller."

"How come?"

"Roy's a natural campaigner. Loves to press the flesh. Reginald's just not that way, even though he'd make a much better Congressman."

"Does the mayor have a family?" I wondered.

"Nope. Lives alone. He's a fifty-year-old bachelor mayor, I guess you could say. He used to be in real estate. Went into politics about ten years ago when he ran for mayor. He's a real workaholic—no time for a wife and kids."

"Why's he running for Congress?"

"He got into the race after the sheriff declared his candidacy. Reginald just thinks he can do a better job than Roy Miller."

"I hear they hate each other's guts," I probed.

"Where'd you hear that?" Eugene asked warily.

"Oh…sources," I smiled coyly, warming up to my new role as an investigative reporter.

"You're not going to write about that in your story, are you?" Eugene asked, furrowing his brow.

"Too soon to tell," I said. "Is there anything to the rumor?"

"Not really. I mean, don't get me wrong: Reginald thinks he can do a better job than Roy, but I'd say it's more of a healthy rivalry than anything personal. The mayor wants to win on the issues, not by tearing down the sheriff. Going negative isn't Reginald Lange's style."

When the mayor arrived a few minutes later, he scowled when Eugene informed him I'd be traveling with them to Edgerton.

During the fifteen-minute drive, Mayor Lange was pleasant to me, but distant. "I apologize for not being able to give you my full attention yet, Miss Chadwick," the mayor said, "but I do need to go over the speech I'll be giving. I hope you understand."

"Of course," I told him.

I'd tried to carry on some small talk with the back of Eugene's head, but that went nowhere. After a few minutes, the mayor expelled an impatient burst of air and tightly suggested to Eugene that he and I talk once we're out of the car, "because I really do need to concentrate right now."

The rest of the trip was spent gazing out the window watching the scenery go by and wondering: A) what of value, if anything, was I going to get out of this guy for my article, and B) who'd ever want to vote for him for Mayor, much less Congress?

In Edgerton we made several stops: a speech at the local Lion's club, a walkthrough at a factory that made trailers for eighteen-wheelers, a shake-hands stroll through the downtown business district, and a speech at the local nursing home.

In each situation Lange was stiff and seemed unable to connect with people at a basic level. *No wonder he's getting clobbered*, I thought.

As Eugene pulled away from the front door of the nursing home, the last stop on the itinerary, Mayor Lange leaned toward his window and waved at the few people standing in front of the building. But it seemed ludicrous to me because the windows of his car were tinted and the gesture was probably not seen.

The mayor leaned against the back seat and rubbed his face with both hands. "Whew. That was terrible." He loosened his tie.

At last, I finally get my interview.

From my backpack, I whipped out a small tape recorder Lionel had given me to record interviews. "Mr. Mayor, do you mind if I tape our conversation?"

"What?" he asked, disoriented.

"You know…the interview you said you'd do with me about my parents?"

"Oh, yes…" he said, remembering. "Actually, Miss Chadwick, I'm awfully tired. Let's just talk informally without all that high technology," he said pointing at the machine I held between us.

I shrugged, disappointed. "Oh…okay." I put the recorder away, took out a notebook, and opened to a clean page. "How did you know my parents?"

"No notes, either."

"Excuse me?"

"I said I don't want you taking notes." He said it in a no nonsense I'm-used-to-getting-my-own-way tone.

"Why not?"

"Let's just talk."

"But—"

"Do you want to talk, or don't you?" He'd had a bad day and was taking it out on me.

"Fine." I slammed my notebook shut. *This guy is really ticking me off.* I fought my anger and tried for affability. "So, what can you tell me about my parents?"

"No. The question is: what can you tell me about your parents?"

"I'm sorry, Mayor Lange. I don't understand." *Who's interviewing whom?*

"It's a simple question, Miss Chadwick. Tell me what you know so I won't waste your time telling you what's old news, so to speak."

"I know very little, sir. I never knew them. That's why I'm here—to learn about them from the people who did know them."

"But surely, my dear girl, surely you were told something."

"Of course I was." I spit out a few facts to try to satisfy him, all the while thinking that in my journalism class they never told us some interview subjects could be real jerks. "Now you," I said finally, a slight edge in my voice. "What can you tell me?"

What little I told him must have been enough. He sat back. "I think I met your mother only once or twice. A very sweet and pretty lady, as I remember, but I barely knew her."

Great! Just frigging great.

"But you knew my father?" I asked hopefully.

"Yes. I knew him much better," he smiled, at ease now and happily in control.

"What was he like?"

"I was impressed with his integrity. I dealt with him quite regularly in connection with my real estate business, and I also knew him from Rotary. He was very cautious, attentive to detail, well organized, outgoing, friendly. I'm sure he would have become bank president, had he lived."

I was doing my best to memorize everything the mayor said so I could write it down later. "Do you have any idea what might have caused the accident that killed my parents?"

A cloud seemed to pass over his face. "I wish I knew, Miss Chadwick. I wish I knew. His death was a great loss to me—and to the entire community." The mayor turned to look at me. His face looked sad and drawn in the gathering twilight. "That's all I have to say," he said abruptly.

"But we just got started," I protested.

"I said 'that's all,' Miss Chadwick," his eyes drilled me.

"Yes, sir." I stuffed my notebook into the backpack. "Thank you for your time," I said through clenched teeth. It was a statement decidedly more civil than what I was thinking.

Chapter Eleven

It was nearing five o'clock when the mayor's stylish Lincoln stopped outside the newspaper office and deposited me next to Pearlie where I'd parked her that morning.

The sun had gone down, but the sky was still bright—almost white.

Disappointed and angry I hadn't learned more from the mayor, I hugged my coat around me as I watched them drive away, wondering why the mayor had so suddenly turned from Dr. Jekyll into Mr. Hyde.

Before returning to Madison, I decided to swing by the sheriff's office to see if I might be able to schedule something with him for the next day. When I arrived, I was pleasantly surprised to find Sheriff Miller in the reception area talking with his secretary.

She was about my size, but he towered over her. The office was cheerful, much like the sheriff's mood.

"Hi, Lark," he said, greeting me warmly.

My disposition improved immediately. His friendliness was in stark contrast to the rudeness I'd just experienced from the mayor.

"Hi, Sheriff," I said brightly. "I was just stopping by to see if I could schedule an interview with you for tomorrow. I didn't expect I'd actually find you here."

"Just got here, actually. I've been out most of the day campaigning. We could talk now, if you've got the time," he offered.

His eagerness to talk to me made all my exhaustion evaporate. "You're sure it's not a problem right now?"

"Not at all. Come on back to my office." He placed his arm on my shoulder. I expected to buckle under the weight, but his touch was gentle.

"You wouldn't believe the conversation I just had with the mayor," I said, as the sheriff steered me.

"Oh?"

I told Sheriff Miller how Mayor Lange's demeanor had changed so suddenly, ending our interview.

The sheriff laughed, but said nothing.

"I hear you two don't really like each other," I probed. "Any truth to that?"

Roy Miller laughed again, then lapsed into an impression of Dana Carvey doing an imitation of George H. W. Bush. "Not gonna go there. Wouldn't be pruuuudent at this junk-churr. Not gonna do it."

I laughed, and let the subject drop.

The sheriff's office was cluttered with piles of files and his desk was heaped with papers.

"Have a seat," he said, scooping a handful of manila folders from a small couch and dropping them haphazardly in a corner.

I sat at the end of the couch, closest to the door; the sheriff took a seat at the other end. His presence seemed to fill the room.

"Do you mind if I tape the interview?" I asked, placing the recorder precariously atop a small mountain of newspapers on the tiny coffee table in front of us.

"Not at all, Lark. Fire away." He sat leaning forward, elbows resting on knees, fingers entwined.

"First tell me what you can about my parents. Did you know them well?"

"I knew your dad better than your mom. I'd only met her once, and mainly just knew him to nod at when I was at the bank. Can't say he and I ever had a feet-up-on-the-desk get-to-know-you kind of conversation. I can tell you about the accident, though. That is," he paused, "if you're interested."

"Very much so."

He was silent for a moment, then he suddenly got to his feet. "I know! Showing is better than telling. Let me take you to the railroad crossing where it happened. The least I can do is help you get a better understanding of it." He stood tall, hands on his hips, ready for action.

"Great!" I switched off the tape recorder and put it away.

"Ride with me," he said, as we left the building through a rear door. He strode to an unmarked dark brown Crown Victoria parked in front of a green and white sign that read "Bluff County Sheriff." The inside of the car was as much a pigpen as his office.

Before I could sit down, I had to sweep aside a bunch of chewing gum wrappers and a roll of duct tape.

He screeched out of the parking lot and rocketed down Main Street. *He's probably breaking the speed limit, but what the heck—he's the sheriff!*

He slowed quickly, maneuvering the cruiser among the various downtown obstacles of pickup trucks, cars, and pedestrians. Within two minutes we'd passed through town and were careening west on Route 58. After about a mile, he suddenly turned right onto a crumbling-at-the-edges blacktop road.

"This back road used to be the main Route 58. It meandered all over the place."

He spoke loudly to be heard over the noise of gravel bouncing off the car's undercarriage.

"This road's sort of like a big horseshoe. It loops to the left, crosses the tracks, then loops left again before coming back to the main highway. Road's not used much anymore, except by the two farm families who live along here. The new highway we just turned off of was built about ten years ago. It's much straighter and a lot safer than this old thing. If we'd stayed on the new road, a bridge would have gotten us over the tracks, instead of that awful grade crossing we're coming to."

Old Route 58 curved to the left, passed a farm on the right, then ran between a grove of pine trees. Past the trees, Sheriff Miller pulled the cruiser onto the grassy shoulder. He stopped just short of the crossing in front of the silver signal lights.

The sun was below the horizon, but tossed a spectacular red glow onto the fleecy clouds.

I pulled the tape recorder out of my backpack and switched it on as we got out of the car and walked to the crossing. The wind had picked up.

"Now, Lark, here's how it happened as best as we can determine." He was in his just-the-facts mode. "The car your parents were in—"

"And me," I reminded him.

"Yes, of course. And you, too. The car was coming from that direction." He pointed toward the way we had come, then he pivoted to face the tracks. "And the train was coming from there." He pointed to his right.

"And the signal lights were working?"

"Yes, the lights were working." He seemed to be on a roll, so I decided to lay off with the questions and just let him go.

"Now then . . ." he paused, trying to remember where he was in his narrative, "the car and the train met right in the middle of the tracks, right here," he said, bounding to the center of the crossing. "The train was going about fifty miles an hour, maybe a little more. The impact killed your folks immediately and pulverized the car, sending it into that field over there."

I looked down the tracks to the left toward where he was pointing.

Sheriff Miller began walking along the railroad ties toward the Highway 58 bridge over the tracks. I had to trot to keep up with him. He gestured wildly as he continued to paint the picture of the accident for me.

"Now, the car—or what was left of it—came to rest here," he called, pointing to a ditch about sixty feet down the tracks from the crossing. "And apparently you and your car seat flew through the air," his right hand made an arc across the red sky, "landing in the field over there." He pointed off to the right toward the center of the barren field. "But we didn't know right away that you were there."

"Were you the first on the scene?"

"That's right. The train finally came to a stop down there, beyond where the overpass is now." He nodded toward the Highway 58 bridge about half-a-mile farther down the track. "It was a real mess, Lark. It took us awhile to tell how many people had been killed because there were body parts all along here." His hand swept the area between where we were standing and the crossing.

I winced. *I don't need to hear this.*

"We must have been on the scene at least half-an-hour before some kid who'd been on the train hollered from out there," he motioned again toward the center of the field. "The kid said that he'd found a baby crying. We all raced over, amazed and overjoyed that someone—you—had survived. The field was full of tall corn and it cushioned your fall perfectly. You were snug in your car seat, not a scratch on you.

"Apparently your folks had forgotten to strap you to the back seat. No one should have lived through that crash, Lark, but by some miracle, you did, and, I might add, I don't usually use the word miracle."

I was silent, taking in all that he had said. In my mind's eye I could see the powerful collision. "But how could it have happened? Why?"

"We'll probably never know for sure. All I can offer you are a couple of theories."

We began walking slowly along the tracks toward the crossing. "I have two theories. One is that your dad never knew the train was coming. It was a nice night—beautiful, in fact—maybe they were distracted by the moon and stars, were looking at them rather than paying attention to the road and the railroad crossing. If the radio was blasting, too, they might not have heard the signal bells or the train whistle until it was too late. The other theory is that he came to the crossing, saw the train coming, but thought he could beat it."

"Which theory do you accept?"

"Either theory could be valid. My personal choice is that he tried to beat the train—that's how most of these things happen. But, as I say, we'll probably never know."

When we were back at Sheriff Miller's Crown Vic, I surveyed the scene once more. Something caught my eye on the other side of the tracks about a hundred yards down the road. It was a dark sedan, parked, facing us, lights off, but because of the bright colors of the sunset behind it, I couldn't make out any details. Suddenly, the car made a sudden U-turn in the middle of the road and bolted toward Madison.

"That was weird," I said, looking at Sheriff Miller.

He shrugged and smiled, "Maybe he doesn't want to tangle with the Jovial Giant."

I turned my attention to the spot where the road crossed the rails. "What could have possessed my dad to race a train, with his wife and infant daughter sitting trustingly in the car with him?" I turned my face toward the deep crimson sunset…and sighed.

"We'll probably never know…" the sheriff repeated.

Chapter Twelve

It was almost eight by the time I pulled Pearlie into the driveway on Dale Drive.

I'd stopped at a McDonald's on the outskirts of Pine Bluff and eaten a small cheeseburger and fries on the drive back to Madison. I drove slowly with the radio and my cell turned off, letting the events of the day marinate.

The house was dark, cold, and achingly empty. For one stimulating day, at least, I'd been able to put Annie's death behind me, but now the pain of her absence was more acute than ever. I switched on as many lights as I could, trying to bring some cheer to the gloom.

"Annie, I'm home," I called.

The sound of my voice echoed through the house. I knew she wouldn't answer. Would never answer, but just the same, I needed to reach out. Needed to bring life back to the empty rooms.

"Annie, I wish I could tell you about today," I sighed.

As I sorted through the mail, I turned my phone back on and saw I'd missed a call and had a voice message. I teed it up and pushed *play*.

"Hi, Lark. It's Father Dan. Just calling to see how your day went. Gimme a call when you get in. Any time."

Thankful for a friendly voice, I called him back without even taking off my coat. He picked up on the second ring.

"Hi, Father Dan. It's Lark."

"So, how was your day?"

"Wow." My enthusiasm was back.

"Tell me." He sounded eager to hear.

"There's so much to tell, I don't even know where to begin."

"Have you had supper?"

"Yeah. I caught a quick bite on the way home."

"Oh." He sounded disappointed. "Um…" he hesitated. "I know! It's a beautiful night, almost Indian summer. I'm on State Street right now. We could meet at the foot of Bascom Hill and stroll toward the capitol."

"There aren't any funeral parlors along the way, are there?"

He laughed. "Only the Cave, but that's on University Avenue and it became a blues joint years ago."

He must have sensed that I was debating whether to go out, because he added, "C'mon, Lark. You don't want to spend a lonely night at home, do you? You could be telling me all about your day."

"Okay. I'll meet you there in fifteen minutes."

As soon as I hung up, I suddenly—irrationally—began fretting about my hair and what I would wear. My hair was the least of my worries, only because I can never do anything with it, so why bother? It's naturally thick, and that drives me nuts because it's so heavy. Yet it always amazes me when people compliment me on it.

Once a girl who sat behind me in class remarked, "I think it's marvelous that you never seem to have a bad hair day."

And one frat boy who'd drunkenly tried to get into my pants (unsuccessfully) had, as part of his supposed foreplay, praised my "luxshurioushly shenshual" hair.

After wasting nearly ten minutes brushing and futzing in front of the mirror, I gave up. Clothes, however, were another challenge. I thought about changing into something fancy, but I absolutely hate dressing up, so I decided to stay with the current ensemble—a burgundy sweater and jeans. I love wearing jeans. They're for my butt what comfort food is for my tummy.

I was a fashionable ten minutes late, but Dan seemed unperturbed. He was sitting on the low concrete retaining wall at the foot of Bascom Hill where the State Street pedestrian mall begins. When Dan saw me walking toward him from the Park Street ramp, he waved and stood to greet me, smiling broadly. He wore a dark blue polar fleece sweater, jeans—and no white collar. *Does this mean he's off duty?* I wondered. (Hoped?)

When I got to him, he bowed gallantly. I'm not used to that kind of chivalrous treatment. Part of me wondered if I was getting the treatment, but I decided that, for once, I wasn't going to be suspicious. I know. I have "trust issues" with men, but I really wanted to be able to put those aside. At least for tonight.

As we slowly walked toward the gleaming alabaster dome of the capitol, I jabbered on and on about all the discoveries I'd made that day. Dan listened, seemingly enthralled, as I told him about the "Miracle Baby" newspaper clipping, meeting Lionel Stone, Sheriff Roy Miller and Mayor Reginald Lange, and convincing Lionel to let me write a follow-up story. The more I talked, the more enthusiastic I became.

We passed Brown's Book Store, Yost's Sportswear, a jewelry shop, and a bar every twenty yards or so. One of them seemed to pulsate with loud, throbbing music. A boisterous crowd of boys had congealed at the front door, waiting impatiently to get inside where it would be even noisier. Someone had vomited recently in the gutter outside another State Street nightspot. Dan and I quickened our pace to get away from the overpowering stench.

In what seemed like no time we had walked the mile to the capitol, circled it, and headed back toward campus—this time the Abe Lincoln statue in front of Bascom Hall was in our sights. We walked, and I talked, until almost ten.

"I'm glad things went so well for you today, Lark," Dan said when we got to my car.

"Me too."

"Will you promise to keep me up to date?"

"It's a promise," I beamed.

"Great." Then, he took me by surprise when he leaned in and kissed me lightly on the cheek.

It was still tingling as I drove away.

Chapter Thirteen

THURSDAY, OCTOBER 24TH
DAY 6

My first waking thoughts the next morning were of Dan. I snuggled deeper into my warm bed, pulling the blankets up to my neck. What did his chaste peck on the cheek mean? I'd never been treated that tenderly before. The few dates I went on in high school were dismal affairs—hours wasted with immature, bumbling, jerks. After every disappointing date, I'd vow never to go out again, only to repeat the mistake a few weeks later. Apparently guys found me attractive, because I kept being asked out, only to find myself, once again, either having to carry the entire conversation, or having to fend off oafish attempts to grope me. It wasn't long before word spread among the boys who fancied themselves studs that Lark Chadwick was a dedicated, virginal, goody-two-shoes.

In college I met some guys I liked in a few of my classes, but living at home with Annie on Dale Drive complicated things a little. Most guys didn't have cars and stayed on campus within walking distance of everything. Sometimes I'd drive to campus and meet them at the movies or something, and I also went to a few parties, but they were noisy, smoky, crowded, and superficial. Most of the guys I met at parties were stuck on themselves, drunk—or both.

There had been one boy I liked—Ned. I met him my sophomore year in English class. We spent a lot of time talking about the books we were reading. It became a habit for us to go to Babcock Hall for freshly made ice cream. We'd sit on the grass eating and talking. In the winter, we'd do our talking in the student union while drinking coffee or hot chocolate in the Rathskeller. In the fall and spring, we'd walk along the path by the lake or sit on the union terrace and "people watch."

Ned was shy, though, and if he'd ever been interested in me romantically, he never quite got around to telling or showing me. Ned was from somewhere in Massachusetts and didn't return to school our junior year. I didn't have his address—snail or e-mail—so I wasn't able to track him down to find out why he didn't come back.

When it came to Annie, she wasn't much of a role model. She teased me about "your cute little friend Ned," and called our friendship "quaint." Yet all the while, she frequented bars with girlfriends from work and seemed to constantly throw herself at one man after another. It seemed each relationship ended after only one or two wild nights.

Routinely, the day after yet another relationship ended, she would take me aside and, while nursing a drink, recite her credo: "Men are no good, Lark. Take your time."

As I got older, and could see the contrast between her advice and her life, I'd ask, "So why don't you practice what you preach?"

She'd sigh, shake her head and say, "I can't. It's too late for me. But you still have a chance. Don't make the mistakes I've made."

I saw her misery up close. It's probably why I always intended to remain a virgin before marriage.

And then I met Professor Ross Christopher.

I took Ross's "Twentieth Century American Writers" class the first semester of my senior year. On the first day of class something leaped inside me. He was unlike anyone I'd ever met before: he was grown up (ten years older than I), sophisticated, mature, yet in touch with people my age. His rugged good looks made him the kind of man to fantasize about.

And I did.

I dreamt about him one night during the first week of classes. The details of it are hazy to me now, but I remember waking up in a sweat, wanting him so badly. I tried to get back to sleep that night, but the attempt to pick up the dream where it left off was futile—and very frustrating.

For weeks, I carried on a torrid romance with him—at least in my mind. I knew that in real life he was totally unaware of me, so entertaining these fantasies seemed safe enough. I imagined him complimenting me effusively on my writing, or nodding in admiration at a particularly thoughtful and provocative question I would ask in lecture.

Of course, back in those days I wouldn't dare raise my hand in front of hundreds of other people and risk blurting out something dumb. So, instead, I began writing a stupid romance story with Ross and me as the main characters. It quickly became pornographic and I furtively tore it up and threw it away for fear someone might discover it.

But apparently he had noticed me. When he tapped me on the shoulder late one Friday night as I studied at the library, I was more than ready to join him for a beer, and then go with him to his apartment. I remember being surprised at how clean a bachelor pad could be.

During the entire evening, Ross was a prince, hanging on my every word. We sat at opposite ends of a wheat-colored sofa draining a bottle of wine. Ross had created an intimate mood of candlelight, shadows, smooth wine, and even smoother jazz.

I love jazz. The soft sounds flowed into the room from a CD player, its turquoise digits gleaming coolly from the entertainment center in front of us. The only other light came from a candle stuck into a tall wine bottle. A Technicolor lava flow of dried wax caked the neck of the bottle, lining the side all the way down to the coffee table.

Ross sat casually at the far end of the sofa, left arm draped across the back, left leg hooked beneath him so he could look directly at me. He wore a dark blue turtleneck and jeans.

"So, who's your absolute favorite author?" he'd asked, taking a nonchalant sip of wine. His voice was smooth, sexy; it made me squirm.

Mellowed by the alcohol, I yammered on and on about the merits of Steinbeck and Hemingway, confessed that my "secret vice" is John Grisham, and disdained Faulkner as "the king of the run-on sentence."

I was so in love with the sound of my own voice I failed to notice that he'd moved closer. His hand rested lightly around the back of my neck. Gently, almost absent-mindedly, he stroked my hair.

I felt light-headed, dreamy, yummy. My alcohol-numbed mind spun. I felt very close to Ross and ached to be even closer. Then, I felt his lips on mine. My eyes flew open in surprise and I stiffened, but just as quickly I relaxed and kissed him as eagerly as he was kissing me.

The soulful notes of a lush saxophone arpeggio seemed to lift me. I pressed myself against Ross and hugged him close.

He shifted positions and gently maneuvered me onto my back.

I squirmed and whimpered with delight, even as I began to feel uneasy. I liked Ross. Wanted to be close to him. Things had been going so well this evening because Ross had been casual, relaxed, careful not to rush or pressure me.

Now that was changing.

Fast.

I needed time to think, to savor our time together. The side of me that was uncomfortable in this situation—the part of me I was used to listening to—said, *time to leave*.

"Ross, no. I have to get going." I tried to extricate myself from beneath him, but he was too heavy.

He ignored me. The expression on his face was not sensuous or dreamy anymore; it was stern.

Something inside me switched off—this was no longer romantic. Alarmed, I realized I had lost control of my body. Ross was in charge. He was trying to undo my belt.

"No...stop," I croaked.

I tried fiercely to kick him, but in an instant he was back on top of me, pinning me roughly to the sofa. I tried to hit him, but I could barely move. He was too strong for me and my wriggling only seemed to excite him.

Once more he released me and fumbled with my belt buckle, trying to get into my jeans.

I managed to wrest a leg free. Swiftly, I raised my knee until it almost touched my chin, then, with all my might, I kicked Ross in the chest with the heel of my hiking boot.

"Get off me!" I yelled.

The kick sent him sprawling backward into a bookcase and to the floor. Several big books fell onto his head and shoulders.

I sprang to my feet and backpedaled toward the door.

Ross struggled to get to his feet.

"You stay away from me," I shouted, stabbing a warning finger at him. I was having trouble catching my breath.

"What's your problem?" His voice was raspy.

"What's *my* problem?" I shrieked. "What's *your* problem?"

I stumbled onto the front porch, and slammed the door, shattering the storm window. Through the broken shards I could still hear the music oozing from Ross's apartment. But the music was no longer sensual. It had become frenzied, cacophonous.

That was three years ago.

Father Dan seemed different. He was patient, caring, sensitive. I'd been admiring him from afar for almost a year, but because Annie was the one who had his attention, I just figured he was out of reach.

I touched my cheek where he'd kissed me.

Is he falling, too? (Too? Am I falling?)

Chapter Fourteen

Lionel and Muriel were in the office when I arrived somewhere between nine-fifteen and nine-thirty. Lionel sat perched atop a desk facing the door, reading the paper.

He wore a clean white shirt, sleeves rolled up past the elbow.

"It's almost nine-thirty," he announced, looking at his watch. He seemed annoyed.

I didn't know what to say, so I avoided his eyes as I shed my coat. I felt myself beginning to cower in much the same way I did so automatically when Mr. Green would launch into a critical tirade.

"What do you have to say for yourself?" Lionel prodded.

"Lionel—" Muriel said.

"Not now, Muriel. I want to know why the girl didn't get here at least by seven-thirty."

"Um, you never told me to?" It was a question, as if I wasn't sure of the right answer. It should have been a bold statement—he really hadn't told me when to be in.

Because my body clock was still set to working a night shift, nine-thirty really felt like seven-thirty.

"Not good enough," he countered. "You should have known that in journalism, the day begins before everyone is up, and ends after everyone's in bed."

"Lionel—" It was Muriel, trying again to soften Lionel's attack.

"I said 'not now,' Muriel."

She sighed in resignation.

"I'm sorry, Mr. Stone. I didn't realize that's when you wanted me in. It won't happen again."

Okay. So I caved. I was trying to tame the hotheadedness that had already lost me one job. I couldn't afford to let it happen again, especially since I was embarked on such an exciting quest, with the added lure of getting paid to solve the vexing mystery about my past.

Muriel broke the tension in the room. "Can I get you some coffee, Lark?" She leaned against the counter, with the newspaper spread out in front of her, and a steaming mug in her hand.

"No. Thanks. I got some on the way in. I'm really anxious to get working. I want to make some phone calls today to try to find the witnesses to the crash who are named in that old clipping."

"How did it go yesterday?" Lionel asked.

"Pretty good." I told them about campaigning with the mayor, and the twilight trip to the railroad crossing with the sheriff.

"Does Miller know how the accident happened?" Lionel asked.

"He thinks my dad was distracted by the stars or, more likely, was trying to beat the train."

Lionel grunted. "What do you think?"

"I don't know. Both theories seem pretty far-fetched."

"Why?"

"First, the top was down. It's hard to believe they would be oblivious to the approach of a train shining its light and blasting its whistle at them."

Lionel nodded.

"Second, trying to beat the train doesn't seem to be in character for my dad," I continued. "From everything I've ever heard about him, he wasn't a reckless man."

"Uh huh."

"And third, it's even less likely he would take the risk of trying to beat a speeding train if his wife and infant daughter were in the car with him."

"Good analysis," Lionel said, almost grudgingly.

"Thanks," I blushed, surprised. Praise had never been in my former boss's repertoire. I suddenly realized I craved it like a drug. "Maybe, if I can track down the witnesses, I'll get a better idea of what happened. Right now it's all speculation."

"Good luck." Lionel took a sip of coffee and resumed reading the paper.

Riding high on Lionel's unexpected encouragement, I glided to the archive in the back of the office and quickly found the old newspaper clipping of the accident, made a copy of it, and placed it in a new manila file folder. On a hunch, I checked to see if any follow-up stories had been done on the crash. I only found a brief account of my parents' funeral in the following week's paper.

> Funeral services were held on Friday for Pine Bluff banker George Chadwick and his wife, Lila.
>
> The couple died Monday night, July 25, when an Amtrak train struck their car at a grade crossing on Highway 58, two miles west of town.
>
> Their infant daughter, Lark, survived the crash uninjured.
>
> The service was held at the Episcopal Church of the Redeemer, The Rev. Harlan Bell officiating.
>
> The couple was buried in Oak Grove Cemetery.

While I made a copy of the article for my file and another copy for my journal, I asked Lionel how I could get in touch with Clifford Keller, the former publisher of the paper who'd written the article about the accident. Lionel told me that Keller, a widower, had died of cancer a month after selling Lionel the paper.

"Too bad he didn't write many follow-up stories about the accident," I remarked.

"Yeah," Lionel said, turning a page of the paper in disgust. "Keller let a lot of stuff fall through the cracks. I'm trying to overcome that problem, so that less is left to word of mouth and gossip. It's always a problem in a small town."

Keller's original article about the crash mentioned Max Labelle and Vern Strozier, the fireman and engineer respectively, and listed them both as residents of Aurora, Illinois. I dialed directory assistance, but could only find Labelle's number. The operator told me the Strozier number was unlisted.

After dialing Labelle's number, I held my breath as it rang, excited I might be closing in on getting some answers about my murky past.

"Hello?" The voice belonged to an older woman, very sweet and lilting.

"Hello. Is this Mrs. Labelle?" I asked.

"Yes it is. Who's calling, please?" She was pleasant, but suspicious. Probably thought I was some telemarketer.

Better talk fast to keep her from hanging up.

"Mrs. Labelle, my name is Lark Chadwick. I'm calling from Pine Bluff, Wisconsin about a collision your husband's train had with a car about twenty-five years ago. May I speak with your husband?"

"Oh dear, ah—" She sounded a little flustered and disoriented. "Well, Miss, ah, Chad..."

"Chadwick."

"Yes. Chadwick. My husband died about two years ago."

"Oh. I'm terribly sorry to hear that."

Great. This is going nowhere fast.

"Why were you interested in talking with him?"

"The two people who died in the accident were my parents."

"Oh, my. How terrible."

"I was only a baby at the time. Somehow, I survived the crash. I'm interested in learning more about what happened. I guess it's sort of a way to get reconnected with my past."

"Well, um…" She seemed uncomfortable. "Now that you mention it, I do remember him saying something about a baby being rescued. I'm so glad for you," she said warmly.

"Actually, I only learned about it a few days ago."

"Really?"

"Yes. I was raised by my father's younger sister."

I sat back and told her my story. As I did, I looked sadly at my almost blank sheet of notebook paper—a metaphor of my empty life? This was supposed to be an interview, but I was the one imparting almost all the information. I doodled as I talked.

"Max used to talk about the accident all the time," she said when I'd run out of things to say. "He had terrible dreams about it."

"Did he ever give you any indication as to how the accident happened?" My pen was ready.

"Not that I can remember, Miss Chadwick. He just said the car had suddenly appeared in front of them. When your train is going fifty or sixty miles-an-hour, there's nothing you can do to avoid a crash. It upset him terribly. I don't think he ever got over it. He had to take a month-long leave of absence—medical leave—before he was able to go back to work."

"You say he talked about the accident all the time?"

"Yes. That's right."

"Do you remember any of the specifics?"

"He and Vern—Vern Strozier was the engineer—he and Vern were on a routine run when the car suddenly appeared on the tracks ahead of them. There was nothing they could do. It took a mile to stop the train. That's about it. I'm sorry I can't be more helpful."

The lack of progress was frustrating. Sure, she'd told me a few things, but not enough. She wasn't an eyewitness.

"Oh!" I said, suddenly remembering, "I'm also trying to get in touch with Vern Strozier, the engineer. Do you have his phone number?" I sat up straight again, eager to hear her answer.

"Why, yes, I do. Just a minute."

There was a clunk as she set down the receiver. I heard her rummaging around before she picked up the phone again and dictated the number to me.

As I wrote it down, I asked, "And he's in Aurora, too?"

"Yes. That's right."

I thanked her and expressed my sympathy for her loss. As I hung up the phone, I noticed Lionel had moved to the desk next to mine. He sat with his feet up watching me work.

"Lemme tell you something." He twiddled his thumbs on his modest paunch.

"Sure." I wondered what I'd done wrong and worried Lionel had second thoughts about having me do the article.

"Two things about interviews: First, They talk, you listen."

"But—"

"An interview isn't about you."

"Well, actually—"

He held up his hand like a traffic cop. "Second, if you're interviewing someone for a newspaper story, you need to let them know you're writing for publication. This way you're being fair with them and letting them know they're speaking on the record." He took his feet off the desk and leaned toward me for emphasis. "It's the ethical thing to do. Sometimes people gab and gab, and then they're stunned when they see in print what they thought was a private conversation. They can get very irate and nasty. If they're not a public figure, they might sue. Or, you might lose them as a source the next time you need them. My policy has always been to make it clear that I'm a reporter and they're on the record."

"Okay. First—" I put down my pen and faced him squarely. "She was uncomfortable being interviewed." I used my fingers to bracket the word "interviewed" in quotation marks. "I was trying to loosen her up." I leaned toward him to make my point. Our faces were only a few feet apart. "And it worked, I might add." I looked him straight in the eye.

He grunted. And leaned back.

"Second, doesn't making a big deal about this being a formal interview tempt the person to be less than honest?"

He scowled in annoyance, but answered the question anyway. "That's a risk you have to take. Most people usually do choose their words more carefully when they know they're speaking for the record. It just means you've got to work harder to draw them out and be very alert for a snow job. I have no patience with people who get stories through false pretenses."

"I wasn't trying to be misleading."

"I didn't say you were." He got to his feet and returned to his perch on his desk.

Winning Lionel's approval is going to be tough.

I picked up the phone and dialed Vern Strozier's number.

A man with a high-pitched, wheezy voice answered.

"Hal-lo." It was more a greeting than a question.

"Is this Mr. Strozier?" I asked.

"What?" the man hollered.

I raised my voice. "Mr. Strozier?"

"That's me. You'll have to speak up. I don't hear too good these days. Too many years spent in the cab of a noisy locomotive," he chuckled.

"Mr. Strozier," I said loudly. "I'm Lark Chadwick, calling from Pine Bluff, Wisconsin. How are you today?"

"Still breathing," he coughed. "What can I do fer ya?"

"Sir, I'm writing a news story for a weekly newspaper here in Pine Bluff about a car-train crash twenty-five years ago that killed my parents." I talked slowly, straining to emphasize every word.

"Oooo-eeee," he said.

"I understand you were the engineer on the train?"

"That's right. You're a reporter, huh?"

"Not exactly. I was an infant at the time of the crash and survived the accident. I'm now trying to reconnect with my past, so I'm writing a story about it for the newspaper."

"I see."

Silence.

"Do you mind if I ask you a few questions about the accident?"

More silence, then: "I wish I could forget about that," he said quietly. "It was a real mess." His voice trailed off.

I remembered the sheriff telling me about the body parts strewn along the tracks.

"I can imagine how you feel." It felt weird shouting my empathy.

Mr. Strozier said nothing, but I could hear him wheezing in my ear.

"It would mean a lot to me if we could talk," I coaxed.

"You're in Pine Bluff, you say?"

"That's right."

"Well, I spoze we could..."

"Great. My main ques—"

"But I want to meet you face to face, first."

"Pardon me?"

"I said I'd like to meet you face to face."

"Oh! That would be wonderful."

Vern Strozier gave me directions to his home. We agreed to meet about one o'clock.

"Haven't seen you since you was a baby." He chuckled. And then, as he was about to hang up, he said a curious thing: "Yep. I've always wondered why that guy drove onto the tracks when he knew we were coming."

"You mean you don't think it was an accident?" I asked, surprised.

"Nope. Never did. Seemed deliberate to me."

"What do you mean?"

"Come. We'll talk."

Slowly, I put the phone back on the hook.

Lionel, reading at the desk next to me, did a double take when he looked at me.

"What's wrong?" he asked.

"Theory number three—" I said. "The accident wasn't an accident at all. The engineer says it was...deliberate."

Lionel closed his newspaper and let out a long, slow whistle.

Chapter Fifteen

"I'm gonna tag along on your interview," Lionel announced suddenly. "I'll drive."

I had mixed feelings about that. First, I was grateful I wouldn't have to shell out fifteen bucks at the gas pump, but I worried Lionel would be critical of me all the way to Aurora and back. Yet, I also held out hope I might be able to get to know him better, learn from him, and maybe soften that gruff exterior.

"Muriel?" Lionel called over his shoulder. "Want to go with Lark and me to Aurora?" He went over to her by the counter, hitching his tie and buttoning his cuffs as he walked. "She's going to interview the engineer of the train that killed her folks. He says the accident was, quoting here: 'deliberate.'"

He slid on his navy blue suit coat, shrugged into a dark gray overcoat, and tapped a homburg onto his white head.

"Sounds intriguing," she said, "but no thanks. You two run along. I've got plenty to do around here."

Before we were even out of town, as he steered his burgundy Volvo east on Route 58 toward the interstate, I asked him why he wanted to go with me to Aurora.

"It's been a busy week, the paper came out today, so the pressure's off, and, to be honest, I want to see how you work," he explained. "It's your story, but it's my paper and my reputation on the line."

"But your reputation is well established."

"Maybe so, but credibility is the coin of the realm." He wagged an index finger. "If people don't trust you're telling them the truth, if they think you're grinding someone else's axe, then they're less likely to believe you. And if your information is unreliable, you become irrelevant."

"So, once a reputation is established, it has to be maintained?"

"Bingo. You're only as good as your last article, or in my case, issue. You keep having to prove yourself."

We rode in silence awhile before I ventured another question. "What's it been like returning to Pine Bluff after having been away for so long?"

"Great," he said, taking in the scenery. "Wisconsin's a beautiful state."

"I thought you're supposed to be retired, but from the looks of things, it doesn't seem as if you've slowed down much," I observed.

"I know. I know. You sound like Muriel. I've got ink in my veins, Lark. Journalism is an addicting craft."

"But why do you work so hard?"

"Because it doesn't really seem like work. But there's an added benefit."

"What's that?"

"Lecturing at the university."

"Why do you do that?"

"I owe a great debt to this profession, so I figure the best way to pay it off is to do as much as I can to help the next generation of journalists get off to a good start."

"Are you optimistic?"

"Frankly, no." He adjusted the heater, inching the temperature down a tad.

"Why not?"

"Thirty years ago, everybody wanted to be the next Woodward or Bernstein. Investigative journalism was in vogue. But then things began to change. Journalism turned increasingly into show biz. Newspapers began to fold, edged out of existence by television. People don't read anymore."

"But TV news is good because you can actually see important events as they happen, like on CNN."

"Oh, that's true. But a lot of important stories—stories about land use or tax policy—don't make for good television. Television thrives on sensational crimes and celebrities. And if you've got a celebrity accused of committing a sensational crime—then that's the ultimate. No, I take that back—it's only the ultimate if sex is involved."

I laughed.

"Whatever happened to holding local elected officials accountable to the public?" he asked, waving his right hand for emphasis. "Whatever happened to—" He paused, then coughed self-consciously. "Sorry. You're a captive audience. I shouldn't carry on so."

"No. What you're saying is fascinating. I've never thought seriously about any of this stuff before."

"That's cuz you dropped out of school," he said. For a change, his tone was gentle, but I still felt the sting—and knew he was right.

We drove in silence for a few miles. Highway 58 was winding, narrow, and hilly, not nearly as straight and spacious as on the west side of Pine Bluff, the stretch toward Madison. When we came to Interstate 90, Lionel made a right turn onto the entrance ramp and eased the car into one of the southbound lanes toward Chicago.

"Let me know if you get hungry or need to use the john," he said after awhile.

"Okay. I'm fine right now, but thanks."

"Got your tape recorder?"

"Oh no…" I whined. "I forgot it." I looked at him, fearfully.

He jerked his thumb toward his briefcase lying on the back seat. "You're in luck. I brought one."

"Whew. I feel like such a dope. Thanks for being patient with me."

"It's okay. Even some of the best ones mess up."

"Did that ever happen to you?"

"Oh sure…of course."

"What's the stupidest thing you ever did as a reporter?" I asked.

"Let's see…" He rubbed his chin. "I've tried to forget all that."

"Come on. No ducking the question."

"Okay. Okay. The absolute stupidest was getting drunk while covering the McGovern campaign in seventy-two. I was White House Correspondent for the *Times*, but broke away for a week to get a feel for McGovern. It was a coast-to-coast whirlwind. We'd hear the same speech about twenty times a day. The most dreadful part was when he'd begin quoting the Old Testament prophets. It was like being back in Sunday school. We'd close our notebooks and squirm.

"Anyway, near the end of the trip, at the end of a very long, draining day, a bunch of us hunkered down at a hotel bar somewhere and I got big-time blasted. I was so drunk, I passed out at the bar and wasn't able to file my story. The guys I was with had to pour me into my room."

"What happened? Did you get fired? Or punished?"

He looked at me and grinned. "My editors never found out."

"Why not?"

"A buddy of mine with *The St. Louis Post-Dispatch* wrote and filed my story for me. The national desk in New York never knew the difference."

"So…forgetting a tape recorder isn't that big of a deal, right?"

"Relatively speaking," he chuckled.

We drove another mile or two. Traffic on the interstate was light, but Lionel stuck to the speed limit. The gently rolling hills of southern Wisconsin gave way to flat farmland.

"So, tell me more about this guy we're going to see," Lionel said, as he checked his mirrors and pulled out to pass an eighteen-wheeler.

"Strozier?"

"Right. The engineer."

"He didn't have much to say on the phone."

"What do you make about the accident being deliberate?" Lionel asked, glancing at me.

"That certainly does sound intriguing. Makes it seem like it might have been a suicide, doesn't it?"

Lionel nodded. "A murder-suicide." He turned his head to gauge my reaction. "Or maybe a suicide pact."

The weight of his words pinned me against the seat. I focused first on the word murder. If the crash had, indeed, been a murder-suicide, it would mean my dad had done a horrid thing. People can argue about the right of a terminally ill person to end his or her own life, but my mother may not have had a choice in the matter. If Dad really did kill himself, then he meant to kill Mom, too—and me. And a suicide pact meant they both tried to kill me.

I shuddered.

"You really want to go through with this whole thing?" Lionel asked gently, continuing to throw worried glances at me. "It's not too late to call the whole thing off if this is getting too heavy for you." He cut back on the accelerator to emphasize his concern.

I thought for a moment. The car slowed and Lionel waited. My Quest was certainly taking me in an unexpected direction, but my curiosity wouldn't let me abandon it just because I didn't like where it was going.

Curiosity. An interesting word. I'd always thought of it as purely cerebral, intellectual, dry. But now there was an emotional dimension to it—an almost irresistible urge to find out. It's the thrill of what it must be like to venture down a long corridor of an opulent mansion, carefully opening each massive door along the way to see what's on the other side.

And, if I do find out the truth, then what? I couldn't see myself not writing about it—whatever it might be. Even if the facts turn out to be as bad as they seem, something inside told me maybe somebody else would be helped by whatever My Quest uncovered.

"It's not easy," I said finally, "but I feel compelled to go through with it. I have to find out what happened, Mr. Stone, no matter what the truth might be."

"That's my girl." He returned his attention to the road and resumed his sensible speed. "And I told you before: call me Lionel. I'm old, but I'm not that old."

We were running ahead of schedule, so we pulled into the Belvedere, Illinois Oasis—a rest stop straddling the interstate. While Lionel got gas, I went to the bathroom. Then we went into the over-the-road cafeteria for lunch. Lionel picked up the tab.

"Thanks for lunch, Lionel," I said, as we carried our trays to a place to sit by a window overlooking the southbound lanes.

"You said it yourself: 'Plus expenses,'" he smiled. "It's in your contract."

I was quiet through most of our lunch, sobered by what I might learn in my upcoming interview, and grateful Lionel didn't seem uncomfortable with my silence. But when I felt my emotions slide from sober to sullen, I thought it best to take things in a more positive direction.

"Tell me more about Muriel. How did you two meet?"

He wiped his mouth with a napkin as he swallowed. "She's a peach, isn't she?"

"She's great, but I really don't feel as if I've gotten to know her, yet." I speared a piece of tomato from the center of my lettuce salad.

"She's a lot younger than I am. Met her in Pine Bluff when I came home for a book signing when *Quagmire* came out in sixty-seven. She was still in college. Gorgeous and smart—wise beyond her years. We had an intense letter writing relationship for several years, which accelerated during her senior year when her parents were divorcing. She was devastated. That's when I realized how much I cared for her."

"But you didn't get married for a long time after that. How come?"

"We cared a lot for each other, but I wasn't ready to settle down. Had a lot of wild oats to sow. She became a teacher. Taught history at Pine Bluff High School. In fact, maybe she had your mom and dad in school. We should ask her."

"What caused you to change your mind about marriage?"

"It was in seventy-four—the summer Nixon resigned. That was sort of a pivotal year for me. I'd covered the Kennedy assassination and Vietnam, and had become very cynical, but that cynicism was beginning to be corrosive. I didn't like what was happening to me. I'd become bitter.

"During that time I wrote her letter after letter pouring out my frustrations about life and my despair about where the country was going. It was very cathartic to put my deepest feelings on paper. Liberating, too, because it was not a luxury I had in my newspaper stories. It was like I'd been forced by my profession to put a lid on my emotions, yet they continued to build, like fizz in a pop bottle. The pressure needed somewhere to go—it had to come out. Thank God Muriel was there to listen."

"What happened?"

"She proposed."

"By mail?"

"By mail. Her letters were always very supportive and encouraging. She didn't puke and run away when I shared with her my deepest feelings. She simply wrote she wanted to be with me for the rest of our lives and would I consider marrying her."

"What was your reaction?"

"I was floored. I'd never thought of her that way. She was a friend."

"And then, when you needed a friend, she was there for you."

"Exactly. And the timing was right. I'd sowed all those oats and it had gotten old and unfulfilling. She accepted my invitation to come to Washington for a visit. We became tourists. I'd never done touristy things like go to the Smithsonian, or the Washington Monument. And we talked and talked. By the end of the week, we'd gotten married."

"Did she mind leaving Pine Bluff?"

"Not at all. She was ready for a change. She taught school near where we lived in Maryland. And she was a consummate entertainer. She loved to have dinner parties."

"So why did you come back to Pine Bluff?"

"Several reasons, all converging at once. I had a couple of heart attacks. Workaholism was catching up with me."

"Was the other reason your daughter?" I asked timidly, remembering the newspaper article reporting her death while mountain climbing in Peru.

He nodded curtly, lips pursed.

"I'm sorry, Lionel. I shouldn't have brought it up."

"It's okay." He raised his head, jutting out his chin. "It happened. It's a fact. I've learned to face reality." He paused, then added softly, "But Holly's death was—is—the toughest thing Muriel and I have ever had to face."

"So, you came back to more familiar surroundings?" I tried to steer the conversation out of the emotional minefield.

"Right. Washington can be a very unreal place."

"Was it hard for you to come back?"

"Not really. I needed to slow down."

"Yeah. It really seems like you have," I teased.

"I know, I know. But that'll change once I can hire a couple reporters. That shouldn't be too hard. There's quite a pool of eager beavers at the UW J-school."

After finishing our meals, we got back on the interstate and soon arrived at the Aurora exit. Lionel followed my directions as I navigated him past flat farmland, an enormous golf-ball-on-a-tee water tower, and a string of shopping centers. Finally, we turned onto a four-lane road with a grassy safety island that led to the Strozier townhouse.

As I rang the doorbell, I took a deep breath. I was about to discover Vern Strozier's definition of the word "deliberate."

Chapter Sixteen

A haggard woman in a drab house dress answered the door. Her stringy, dishwater hair was brushed haphazardly.

"Come on in. He's expecting you," she said in a tired voice.

Stale air billowed from the house as she opened the door to let us in. She took our coats and Lionel's hat and put them in the closet. The heels of her slippers slapped the tile floor as she led us into a sweltering room at the back of the house. A large-screen TV, tuned to a golf tournament, dominated the far wall.

"Here are your visitors, Vern," the woman said in a loud voice as she led us behind and to the left side of a huge recliner chair. "You'll need to speak up," she advised us, "he doesn't hear so good any more."

We looked down on a frail old man, dwarfed by the chair, with his feet elevated. Mr. Strozier cocked his head uncomfortably, straining to look up at us.

"Hi, Mr. Strozier," I nearly shouted, holding out my hand. "I'm Lark Chadwick."

His hand was brittle and bony, the skin felt dry as parchment.

"How do?" he rasped. A clear plastic tube led from his nose to a large oxygen canister standing upright next to his chair.

"And this is Lionel Stone, the editor of the paper I'm writing the article for," I said in my best stentorian voice as I moved farther into the room, making way for Lionel to shake hands with Vern Strozier.

"Hello, Mr. Strozier," Lionel said.

"Pleased ta meetcha," the ex-engineer shouted. "Pardon me for not gettin' up. This emphysema's killin' me."

Lionel and I stood awkwardly, looking down on the shriveled man who wore a red and black plaid flannel shirt that seemed two sizes too large for him. Stains of spilled food blotched its front.

"Have a seat." He waved a delicate hand at a gigantic couch to his right. "Sadie, fetch something to drink for these two," he ordered.

"No, that's okay, Mr. Strozier," I said, taking a seat closest to him at the end of the couch. Lionel sat in a chair across from me, to Mr. Strozier's left. "We stopped for something just before we got here."

"You say you want a beer?" He turned to his wife. "Sadie—"

"No, Mr. Strozier," I said, touching his sleeve.

He turned and looked at me, startled.

I leaned closer to his face. "No thank you," I said, enunciating every word. "We had something before we got here."

"Oh."

Mrs. Strozier sighed and drifted from the room, no doubt relieved her services wouldn't be needed. She'd probably heard his story a million times and needed a break from being on call.

Mr. Strozier took a long, hard look at me. He had large, rheumy blue eyes that seemed to bulge out of their sunken sockets. I felt a little uncomfortable, but I smiled at him. A beer commercial came on the tube, its jingle blaring into the room.

"So you're the Miracle Baby," he said, rubbing the gray stubble on his chin.

"Yes, sir." I nodded and smiled, but I was beginning to hate that term. It's hard to believe your life is a miracle when the deaths of the people closest to you make you feel so alone.

He winked at me. "I've always wondered what happened to you…"

"I'm still wondering," I laughed.

Either he didn't get my irony, or didn't hear me because he plunged on. "It really is amazing you lived through that, you know."

He took a swig of beer from a can of Old Style he'd been holding in his left hand. He put the brew on a table to his right. "That car was so crumpled up it was impossible to tell what kind it had been. No one should have been able to live through that. But you were probably so relaxed in your car seat that you just flew gracefully through the air, landing soft as you please in that corn field." His fragile hand undulated to the right in a gesture tracing my trajectory.

I wondered how many beers he'd had before we arrived, as I switched on Lionel's tape recorder and got out my notebook. "Do you mind if I tape record the conversation?" I asked, holding up the machine for his inspection. "It makes for more accurate note taking."

"No, that's fine," he said dismissively.

I put the tape recorder on the coffee table in front of me. "So, tell me what happened that night, Mr. Strozier."

"Well, me and Max—"

"Max Labelle?" I interrupted.

"Right."

"And do you know how to spell his last name?" I asked.

"L-E...or is it L-A? Sadie!" he hollered.

Sadie appeared in an instant, expressionless.

"Get me the phone book. She wants to know how to spell Max's last name."

Sadie turned to leave.

My heart went out to her. "That's okay, Mrs. Strozier. I can look it up myself later." *Note to self: Quit interrupting an interviewee with every little question that pops into your head. Listen! Be patient!!*

Sadie stopped and looked questioningly at Mr. Strozier.

"Suit yourself," he said to me.

She shrugged and shuffled from the room.

"And you're how old, sir?"

"Seventy-eight years young," he chortled.

"Great. Thanks," I said, backing away from the blast of his beer breath. "Thought we'd get all the bureaucratic stuff out of the way first." I smiled, trying to loosen things up. "Now then…the night of the accident you and Max were on your way to Chicago?"

"Right. It was our usual run between Chicago and Minneapolis. We'd go to Minneapolis, spend the night, then the next day we'd run a train back to Chicago. We did that two, maybe three times a week. It was pretty routine work." He talked rapidly, gesturing with a left hand that looked like a white flag on a stick.

"Had you and Max worked together a long time?"

"Oh, yeah. Max and me was good buddies. We probably made that same run hundreds and hundreds of times over a period of about fifteen years."

"What was Max like?"

"He was a fine man, a fine man…" Mr. Strozier paused, a faraway look on his face.

At first I thought he was thinking of his old friend, but then I realized that Vern Strozier was watching Tiger Woods sink an eighteen-foot putt on TV.

"Um, Mr. Strozier?"

"Huh?" He looked at me, surprised.

"Do you mind if we turn off the TV? I'm afraid the sound might drown out what you're saying," I said with as much tact as I could muster to mask the frustration I was beginning to feel.

"Oh sure! No problem." He fumbled for the remote next to his beer can and zapped the tube. "There. Better?"

"Much better. Thanks."

The room was silent except for the hum of an electric space heater in the far corner and the wheeze of his oxygen machine.

"Now, where was I?" he asked.

"You were telling me about Max."

"Oh, right. He was a great guy." Now that the TV was off, Mr. Strozier turned his full attention to me. "I remember one night," he began to chuckle, "we was just north of La Crosse, going along the Mississippi River towards Minneapolis. We got this urgent message from the dispatcher about a pickup truck heading straight for us."

"Oh, my gosh..." I said.

"Yeah," he laughed, "that's sort of what I said. Turns out some drunk left a bar and turned onto our right-of-way instead of the highway. Luckily, a cop saw it happen, so he quick radios in the problem. It only took a few minutes for his dispatcher to contact ours, who contacted us, so I began slowing way down. Pretty soon, sure enough, way off in the distance, there's the two headlights from the pickup heading down the tracks right at us."

"What did you do?"

"There's not much you can do: hit the horn, apply the brakes, and hold on."

"What happened?" I couldn't help myself. As much as I wanted to learn about the accident that killed my parents, I had to hear how this story ended.

"We hit the drunk, of course," he cackled.

"Did he get killed?"

"Heck no. He was so schnockered he never felt a thing. We was only going about ten miles an hour by the time we hit. Totaled his truck, though."

"That's very interest—"

"But that's not the end of the story," Mr. Strozier laughed. "The guy hauled Max and me into court!"

"Why?" I couldn't believe it.

"For wrecking his truck!" he giggled.

Lionel and I were laughing, now, too.

"That's outrageous!" I guffawed. "Are you serious?"

"I swear…" He crossed his heart and held up a feeble hand as if taking an oath.

"I'm afraid to ask—did he get any damages?"

"Almost. Took the jury four hours to decide the guy shouldn't have been driving down the railroad tracks three sheets to the wind. Seems to me the case never shoulda gone to trial. A smart judge woulda thrown it outta court and ordered the guy to get help. Me and Max laughed about that one for years."

I smiled and shook my head. "So, anyway," I said, moving on to the reason for my visit, "you and Max were riding together the night of the accident that killed my parents?"

"Yeah. Max was never the same after the accident. He'd always been the careful one. Very careful. Safety conscious, y'know? I think he was always afraid we'd have a wreck, so he was Mr. Eagle Eyes. Eagle Eyes. That's what I called him," he laughed.

I smiled. "Was Max the first to see the car?"

"Yep."

"What happened?"

"We were going about fifty miles-an-hour on our way toward Chicago. Amtrak was still pretty young back then. The roadbeds in a lot of places still needed work in Amtrak's early years, so instead of the eighty mile-an-hour cruising speeds we hit later on, we were only able to go about fifty in that stretch near Pine Bluff. Come to think of it," he poked my knee with a scrawny finger, "if we'd been goin' eighty, you mighta been killed too, Short Cake."

I smiled gamely.

"Anyhow, Max suddenly hollers out that there's a car ahead, its lights out, just creeping toward the crossing."

"Its lights were out?" I leaned forward.

"That's right. That's what had caught Max's eye. The car's lights were out, but it was moving real slow-like toward the crossing."

"Did you see it?"

"Not right away. I took a closer look and sure enough. There it was. I hollered back at Max that I saw it too and I throttled back a little bit."

"Can you describe what the car looked like to you at that moment?"

"It was a convertible. The top was down so you could see right into the car as we got closer. A man was driving. A woman was sitting with her back to the door—her back was to us. Her left arm was slung over the seat and she was looking at something in the back seat. Prob'ly you." He looked at me and smiled. A lot of his teeth were missing. The remaining ones were yellowed.

I realized I was breathing a little faster and had moved to the edge of my seat.

Mr. Strozier picked up on the change in my body language right away. "You okay?" He pressed his bony finger against my knee, gently this time.

"I'm fine, sir. I can't tell you how much I appreciate finally learning what their last moments were like. You're helping me get to know my mom and dad."

That seemed to satisfy him. He turned to look at Lionel and continued his narrative.

"Anyway, the driver had a crew cut, it looked like. He was looking past the woman and right at the train. The car kept inching closer and closer to the crossing."

"Did it look like he was coming to a stop?" I could barely get the question out, the lump in my throat made it almost impossible to talk.

"Heck no. In fact Max said that when he'd first seen them, the car was parked a ways back from the crossing. As we got closer, the car began rolling slowly toward the tracks. That, and the fact that the car's lights were out, were enough out-of-the-ordinary to raise Max's concerns. And mine."

Mr. Strozier stopped for a minute and had a horrific coughing fit. He grabbed a Kleenex tissue from a box on the end table and coughed up a wad of phlegm.

"Sorry," he said, wiping his mouth.

"That's okay," I said, trying to be patient. I felt sorry for him, and helpless there wasn't anything I could do.

"The doctor says this stuff is going to drown me someday, so I do my best to get it out. I should never have taken up smoking," he muttered. He wadded the tissue and dropped it onto a pile of spent ones filling half the rubber waste basket on the left side of his chair. He coughed some more. The congestion in his lungs sounded as if he had a bad, full bloom chest cold.

I felt myself wanting to help him by coughing, too.

"There!" he announced finally. He took a big gulp of beer, draining the rest of the can. "Anyway," he said, licking his lips, "me and Max both watched as the car kept rolling toward the crossing."

"How close were you to the crossing?"

"At that instant, geez that's hard to say. We were getting close and closing fast. I'd say we were maybe a quarter mile away when we first saw 'em—maybe less."

"What did you do?"

"I laid on the horn pretty good and there was our bells, too. They come on automatically when you hit the horn, but none of it seemed to make any difference. The driver was lookin' right at me. I knew he saw us, but he kept right on comin'. When we were about a hundred yards away I really became concerned we were gonna hit him. I began pumping the horn handle with all my might." He worked his right arm up and down furiously. "Then, with my left hand, I applied the emergency brake." His arms moved with amazing agility. "There was a tremendous burst of air from the brakes and the release of sand—"

"Sand?" I asked, confused.

"Right. The sand coats the track to give us more friction to stop."

"Oh..."

"Anyway, the train was makin' a heck of a racket—groanin' and screechin'. The brake shoes were scrapin' against the wheels and the wheels were grindin' against the sand on the rails. It was loud."

He was sitting forward in his recliner now and I was leaning toward him, straining to catch every word.

"I was tryin' with all my might to stop a five thousand-ton train. I knew there was no way we could stop in time," he bellowed, "but if I could slow down even just a little bit, maybe it would give the guy time to gun it and get out of the way, or come to his senses and stop, or maybe we wouldn't hit them as hard and somebody might survive."

"Were the crossing signal lights working?"

"Oh, yeah. They were flashin' fine. I could see the light from 'em reflecting off the hood of the car."

"How clearly could you see?"

"It was like high noon. Those headlights are bright. They throw light a quarter mile down the tracks, plus they rotate back and forth in a sort of horizontal figure-eight pattern. Nowadays, the newer engines have ditch lights low near the rails that blink on and off alternately on each side of the roadbed."

"Why do the lights blink and rotate?"

"It's a safety feature. Amtrak engines have strobe lights, too. Lotsa times people or animals stray onto the tracks cuz they're not payin' attention. You'd be surprised at how quiet-like a train can sneak up on you. By the time you realize it's comin', you don't have much time to get out of the way. Those rotating lights and strobes sometimes catch a body's attention and they get out of the way in time."

"But not this time."

"Not this time, that's for sure. I was doin' everything I could to get that guy out of the way. Max was screamin' at him, even. I knew the guy saw us. It was as if he was timing it so's he'd get to the crossing just ahead of us."

"Didn't my mom realize what was wrong?" My heart beat faster.

"Not at first. The car was moving slowly, just inching along, and she was preoccupied with the baby in the back seat. It looked like the driver was trying to sneak up on the tracks without her realizing it."

"Could you see the baby in the back seat?"

"No. I just knew the woman was looking back there. It was only a lot later that we realized the baby—you—had survived. Then we put two and two together and figured she was looking at you as the car approached the crossing. But yeah, my honking must of got her attention because all of a sudden she swung around and saw us."

In my mind's eye, I could see Lila turn, her wavy shoulder-length hair flinging out to the side. I felt the terror bolt through her.

Mr. Strozier stopped and bit his lip. "I'll never, ever get that look out of my mind," he said softly. "We were almost on top of 'em by this time, maybe ten seconds away. When she—" he stopped again, then continued, "she began screaming."

Mother! My mother! Tears streamed down my face.

His narrative went on, relentlessly, "I couldn't hear her, obviously, but her eyes got real big and her mouth was wide open. In those last few seconds of her life, God bless her, she really tried to get out."

Tears flooded into his eyes and overflowed down his cheeks. He shook his head helplessly as his body shuddered. Then he bowed his head into his hands and sobbed.

I cried little involuntary yelps, too. I reached out and gently stroked his right sleeve. After a moment, he grabbed another tissue and blew his nose. When he saw the tears coursing down my cheeks, he got another tissue and handed it to me.

"Thanks," I managed to blubber.

I glanced at Lionel. He was sitting on the edge of his seat, his chin resting in the palm of his left hand. He was dry-eyed, intently studying Mr. Strozier.

Slowly, Mr. Strozier regained his composure. He sighed deeply and looked at me.

"You sure you want to hear all this stuff?"

"Yes, sir." My voice quavered. "I insist that you tell me. I've been kept in the dark about my past way too long. I can take it. I have to."

"Okay…" he said in a suit-yourself tone. "Anyway, your mama tried to get out of the car. I could see her struggling and scrambling to pull herself up so she could jump out. I actually thought she might have been able to jump free. I hoped so, anyway, but we lost sight of them in that fraction of a second before impact when the nose of the train gets in the way of what's immediately in front and below. Max and I both had dreams for years about that instant. In my dream I keep struggling to try to help the woman jump free, but I wake up before I find out if this time she gets out in time."

He slumped back in his chair, exhausted. I was about to reach for the tape recorder when he continued.

"The last thing I saw before we hit, and this has haunted me, too, over the years. The last thing I saw was the look on the guy's face. He was—I swear—he was…grinning."

Chapter Seventeen

Lionel and I left the Strozier townhouse about ninety minutes after arriving. Neither of us said anything for what seemed like a long time, but I think Lionel purposely stayed quiet until I said something first. When I let out a very deep sigh, it was enough of a pretext for Lionel to go wading in after it.

"You okay?" he asked quietly.

"What?"

"Are you all right? He dropped a lot of stuff on you."

"Yeah…" I said, trying to convince myself I really was all right. "How could he do something like that?"

"Who? Strozier?"

"No. My dad. How could he deliberately go on the tracks, directly in front of a train, with Mom and me in the car with him? How could he do it? Why did he do it? It's so monstrous. Mom trusted him." I was breathing hard.

"Happens a lot more than you might think," Lionel said.

"You think so?"

"I know so. Covered a bunch of 'em over the years."

"But why? Why would someone do such a sick thing?"

"You just answered your own question—they're sick. Mentally ill. Maybe she was gonna leave him and he flipped. Who knows? Might be worth looking into, though. Probably a lot of folks suffer in their own private hells thinking that killing themselves and the ones they supposedly love makes perfect sense. Maybe your piece will help a lot of people, Lark."

"Yeah, maybe you're right." I looked out the window. Light from the late afternoon sun deepened the golds and browns of the fields and trees. Normally, this was my favorite time of day because of the richness of the colors, but at that moment the landscape's coloration seemed gaudy.

"God, I feel so alone," I said, mostly to myself.

I missed Annie. Wished I could talk with her about the parents I never knew, but she did.

As we drove, Lionel pulled a cell phone from his coat pocket and punched some numbers. "Gonna check in with the boss," he explained. "It's me," he said, when Muriel picked up. "What's new?" He listened, then said "rough," as he glanced at me. After more listening, he put the phone to his chest. "She wants to know if you'll have dinner with us tonight."

"Oh, I couldn't do that to Muriel. She probably doesn't have a thing on hand."

"You obviously don't know Muriel," he said.

"Sure. Thanks, Lionel." I felt a surge of well being as if engulfed by a warm, loving embrace.

"She says that'll be okay," Lionel said into the phone. "We'll be there in about an hour." He paused. "Okay, no problem. See ya." He hung up and returned the phone to his pocket. "She only asks that we stop and pick up a bottle of wine on the way. I hope you like spaghetti."

"Are you kidding? Spaghetti is ambrosia. Thanks, Lionel." My spirits were improving.

Lionel pulled off the interstate at the very next exit and found a grocery store at a mall near the highway. While he went in search of wine, I went inside and found a bathroom. A contorted, tear-streaked mess stared back at me from the mirror. Taking off my glasses, I splashed water on my face, then tried to run a brush through the thicket that is my hair.

"A word to the wise," he said once we were back in the car and on our way again.

"What's that?"

"You should take the time right after an interview to go through the tape and note the key facts and quotes. Maybe even transcribe it. Then write a rough draft. If you do it while it's fresh in your mind, you won't be spinning your wheels trying to remember stuff if suddenly you have to write your story on deadline. I learned about constantly updating a story when I was a wire service reporter."

"That's good advice, but I really don't feel like doing it right now." The Strozier interview was so troubling I preferred to navel-gaze.

"Y'know, kid, as tough as it is, ya just gotta suck it up and shove those emotions aside."

So, without comment, and with absolutely no enthusiasm, I dug out my notebook.

Writing quickly, I put down what I thought were the most important things Strozier said.

Amazingly, the act of enumerating the main points helped me distance myself from my feelings—feelings so intense that even now, it's hard to explain what I mean.

The images Strozier painted of my screaming mother and my grinning father had an intense, visceral effect on me. I was sickened, confused. Yet even those words, though accurate enough, made it hard to convey the stricken introspection they ignited. But, when I started to write, I began to see things more clearly, in a detached and less emotion-charged way.

I warmed to the work and soon had combed through the tape of the Strozier interview, extracting exact quotes and details essential to the story. I also jotted down the key points I remembered from my conversations with Sheriff Miller and Mayor Lange.

Later, I would transcribe the sheriff's interview and write a first draft of my article. I also wrote down questions to myself that I would try to answer during the course of my investigation. Topping the list: Was Mom having an affair? Had she told Dad she wanted a divorce? More than ever, curiosity powered my research. Why did Dad do this?

I had to find out.

The harder I concentrated on my work, the faster the return drive to Pine Bluff seemed to go. As we approached the town, I prevailed on Lionel to drop me off at Pearlie so he wouldn't have to drive me to my car after dinner.

After making a U-turn in the middle of Main St. to follow Lionel home, I checked my rearview and was surprised to see the headlights of another car also making a quick U and falling in behind me. Even though the car followed at a discrete distance, it still gave me the creeps. I breathed easier when, a few blocks later, the car went straight after I followed Lionel's left turn down his street.

Lionel and Muriel live in a modest, two-story red brick house on Pine Bluff's East side—the good side of the tracks. Muriel, wearing a blue and white ski sweater and brown corduroys, greeted us warmly and led me into the living room where a fire crackled in the fireplace. Light from the flames reflected off the portions of the shiny wooden floor not covered by a large Oriental rug. We sat and had wine by the fire in a cozy arrangement of easy chairs and a Chesterfield sofa.

"Thank you, Muriel, for letting me invade," I said as I plopped into the chair closest to the fire.

Muriel and Lionel took seats at opposite ends of the sofa.

"It's no trouble at all, dear," Muriel said. "We miss having young people around. We don't see Paul nearly enough now that we're here. He's something of a workaholic like his dad," she said, glancing at Lionel, who smiled sheepishly.

Muriel didn't mention Holly, but family pictures of her were all around the room. Holly had been a beauty with long, straight, blonde hair, a clear complexion and straight, beautiful teeth. She could easily have been a model.

"How was your trip to Aurora?" Muriel asked.

"Grueling," I said. "I learned more than I really wanted to know." I took a sip of wine and swished it luxuriously around in my mouth, savoring the fruity taste.

"I see…" Muriel paused. Apparently deciding to hold her curiosity and her tongue, she quickly steered the conversation to safer ground. "Lionel tells me you were an English major at the university."

"That's right. I dropped out to write, but that didn't work out very well."

"What are your plans now?" she asked.

"I'm not sure."

"School?" she asked hopefully.

I shrugged. "School doesn't really interest me. What's the point?" I sighed. What I didn't say is that even though the guy who attacked me has long since been put behind bars, school still holds too many bad memories of professors who abuse their power by taking advantage of their female students.

"The point is to get your degree." Her brow furrowed and she turned serious. "You're much more marketable if you've got a college degree."

"But I'm not sure I want to make a career out of English."

"Who says it has to be English? Once you have the degree, you can swerve in any direction you want," she said.

"But I can do that right now without having to go through the hassle of graduating, can't I?"

"Of course you can," Muriel leaned forward to make her point, "but what signal will that send to a future employer?" She plunged ahead without waiting for an answer. "It will say you don't finish what you start."

As direct as she was, I didn't feel threatened or offended by Muriel. She seemed like the kind of person who could goad you into doing better, even while being unconditionally accepting.

"You're right," I said, sloshing the wine in my glass and studying the light from the fire as it deepened the wine's golden glow. "Father Dan says I tend to make choices based on the way I feel," I scowled.

"Father Dan?" Muriel asked.

"He's the priest at our church. He's been helping me a lot since my Aunt Annie died. He says making decisions based on emotion alone is like building a house on shifting sand—the emotions come and go with incredible intensity, but don't always resemble reality."

"Sounds like the guy would make an excellent journalist," Lionel said. "I'd like to meet him someday. Sounds like a man after my own heart."

"Lionel?" Muriel turned to her husband at the other end of the sofa.

"Yes, dear?"

"Honey, would you please make a salad? Everything else is under control."

"Okay. Sure." Lionel dutifully got up and strode into the kitchen carrying his wine glass.

"He's a sweetie," she said to me after he left the room.

I smiled.

"He thinks the world of you, Lark. I don't think I've seen him this alive since…since Holly died."

I took another sip of wine, unsure, at first, what to say. We both sat mesmerized by the orange flames snapping in the fireplace. For an instant I considered asking about the mountain climbing accident, but then thought better of it. Instead, I broke the silence by asking, "Were they close?"

"Hard to say. They had a complex relationship. She was the apple of his eye, but he had trouble showing affection. He was autocratic and didactic." Muriel tore her eyes from the fire and turned back to me. "He'd always wanted her to go into journalism, but she resisted, choosing archaeology, instead."

"Did that bother him?"

"Big time. He really put the pressure on her. But she was feisty and stood up to him." Muriel's eyes glistened, but her voice remained strong. "They clashed a lot over it until I finally got him to see that she should be free to choose her career without pressure from Mom or Dad. He was just coming to accept that when..." Muriel paused, "when we lost her."

Talking with Muriel was making me see that my grief, though intense and personal, wasn't unique. Others had their own sorrows to bear. Had I not read about Holly's death in the newspaper article about Lionel, I never would have been able tell that Lionel and Muriel had lost a child. They both seemed so strong and purposeful, yet so willing to publicly acknowledge their loss, rather than pretend Holly had never existed.

"How did he handle her death?" I asked Muriel.

"It was hard on both of us, as you can imagine. Still is. But he and I are blessed with a very close friendship. We're able to communicate even nonverbally, we know each other so well." She gazed into the fire again. "When Holly died, he went into a deep depression. He drank more than he should. He was really hurting. Kept it all inside. I think that was the main reason for his second heart attack. It was then I suggested a return to Pine Bluff." She clasped her long, elegant hands in front of her.

"How eager was he to make the transition?" I asked.

"He resisted it at first, but the more we discussed it, the more he saw it made sense to establish a vehicle where future journalists can get their start—and we could work together."

"Has that helped him deal with Holly's death?"

"I think so, but he still works way too hard. That's why I think you're such a good influence." She smiled warmly at me. "You have a personality similar to Holly's. That's why I was glad when he offered to go with you on your outing today. I know he's been hard on you sometimes, but just be patient with him, Lark." She touched my knee. "In his own way, he's groping to find a way to reach out to you. I'm sure of it."

"He also told me the story of how you proposed to him by mail," I teased.

Muriel giggled. "Ah, yes...mighty cheeky of me, wasn't it?"

"Before I forget, Lionel says you used to teach school here."

"Yes. History at the high school."

"When would that have been?"

"Well, let's see..." She thought a moment. "Probably from about 1968 until 1974, when we got married."

"So you might have had my dad in class? George Chadwick?"

"George Chadwick...let me think..." She got up. "Let me check my yearbooks. What year did he graduate?"

"He was twenty-six when he died in '77, so ten years earlier he would have been sixteen and in high school."

"Okay. Let me check." She left the room, but was gone only a minute before returning with an armful of yearbooks. She placed them on the coffee table between us, then picked up the '70 yearbook and riffled the pages. "Let's see...Chadwick, Chadwick...Here he is. George Chadwick, pages 23, 31, and 40." She turned more pages. "Handsome man. I wish I could place him."

I came over to her side of the coffee table and sat next to her, studying my father's senior picture. I'd never seen it before. He had a crew cut, black horn-rim glasses, and a warm, friendly smile.

"Maybe he had the other history teacher, Miss Brown," Muriel continued. She pointed to a line of text beneath his picture. "Says here he was in the band and economics club. I'm sorry, Lark, I can't place him."

"And you were already in DC by the time his younger sister Annie went there. She's the one who died last weekend."

"I'm sorry for your loss, Lark," Muriel said, putting a firm hand on my shoulder. "This must be a tough time for you."

"It is," I admitted, "but this research project has been keeping me going." I smiled at her with genuine enthusiasm.

Lionel ambled back into the living room. "Soup's on," he announced.

We ate by candlelight. It was a marvelous evening. I came away feeling as if I knew Muriel much better—and liked who I was getting to know.

On the long drive back to Madison, I kept glancing in my rearview mirror. A pair of headlights seemed to shadow me the entire way, but when I turned off Midvale and onto Dale Drive, the lights behind me were gone.

***

I awoke during the night with a mild stomachache. When I couldn't get back to sleep, I decided to write in my journal again, which in the past had helped calm me and focus my thinking.

So many questions.

Why did my father kill himself, my mother, and almost me?

Was Lila having an affair?

Did Dad find out?

Was she planning to divorce him?

Why wasn't I ever told the truth about the accident?

What did Gramma and Grampa know?

What did Annie know?

Why did Annie kill herself?

Did Annie kill herself?

Has the coroner found any evidence pointing toward, or away, from suicide?

What does Dan know about Annie's death that he's not telling me?

I'm adept at asking questions, but clumsy at finding answers.

I sighed as I closed my journal and put the cap back on the pen. Questions…questions…always more questions. Amazingly, I was actually able to get back to sleep. Was it because of exhaustion…or depression?

Chapter Eighteen

At eight-thirty Friday morning, I showed up unannounced in the office of Dane County Coroner Ed Sculley. The walls, chairs, and desks were all various shades of gray.

"Hi, I'm here to see Mr. Sculley," I smiled at the receptionist.

The receptionist, a scowling middle-aged woman with gray hair (of course) greeted me with suspicion. "Do you have an appointment?"

"No, but I want to get an update from him on the status of his investigation into my aunt's death."

"Your name?"

"Chadwick. Lark Chadwick."

"Just a moment." She picked up a phone. "There's a Lark Chadwick to see you, sir." After a moment, the receptionist hung up. "You're in luck. He says for you to go on back." She pointed to an office door behind her at the far end of the room.

I passed the desks of various stenographers wearing earphones, their fingers clacking away at word processors.

Sculley met me at his office door. "Morning, Mizz Chadwick. Come on in and have a seat."

He didn't shake my hand, merely motioned to a chair in front of his gray metal desk, which faced the door.

"Can I get you some coffee?" He ambled behind his desk and sat down.

"No, thanks." I took a seat in a metal folding chair. It, too, was gray.

His office made me feel claustrophobic, all the more so because of a pronounced odor of flatulence. The only color in the room came from Sculley's light green, short-sleeve shirt and brown striped tie. The tie only came down to the top of the enormous paunch protruding well beyond his belt.

"Here it is," he said, straining to push a manila folder at me between two thick stacks of similar-looking files perched on either end of his desk.

I reached for the file. It wasn't very thick. "You're all done?"

"Yup. Wrapped it up yesterday. I just went over it this morning and was going to put it in today's mail. Your visit just saved Dane County taxpayers exactly ninety-two cents in postage."

"Always glad to help out," I said, thumbing through the pages.

"It's all there," he said, impatiently. "Autopsy. Detective Silver's report. Everything."

"Bottom line?"

"Suicide. Granted, there was no note, but it's a suicide, just as we thought." He crossed his arms.

I shook my head in disbelief. "But what about the ransacked room? What about Annie's comments to me and to Reverend Houseman? Don't those suggest something other than suicide?"

"They suggest paranoia and instability," Sculley said bluntly.

"But the ransacking?" I protested.

"I'd hardly call it 'ransacking,' Mizz Chadwick. It was just the contents of a few desk drawers dumped onto her bed. The rest of the room looked nice and tidy. Maybe she'd lost something and it was making her crazy."

"She was a neat freak. The rest of her life may have been out of control, but she was obsessive about keeping her room orderly."

"She was wigging out, Mizz Chadwick. For whatever reason, she'd come to the end of her rope. She was simply coming unglued. We see this all the time. In one case we had, the chick…excuse me," he bowed slightly, "the young woman stuffed her husband's socks in a kitchen drawer with all the silverware before she did herself in."

"What about Annie's references to a crime she had to check out?"

"What 'crime' was she referring to? We went through all of her stuff and found nothing that shed any light on her alleged statements. No documents. No fingerprints. Nothing."

I didn't like the way he stressed the word alleged when referring to what Annie had said to Father Dan and me. "What if I told you that my father and mother died twenty-five years ago in a car-train collision in Pine Bluff?"

"That's not a crime. Besides, Pine Bluff's in Bluff County. It's out of my jurisdiction."

His folded forearms rested comfortably atop his paunch.

"According to the engineer of the train, it was a murder-suicide." My voice was beginning to rise. "What does that say to you?"

Sculley scowled, but only for an instant. When he spoke, his voice was slow and emphatic. "Here's what it says to me: Obviously, Mizz Chadwick, suicide runs in your family."

Chapter Nineteen

I was still seething later that evening as I sat discussing the coroner's report with Father Dan in his basement office at St. Stephen's Episcopal Church, a charming stone building on Regent Street, a block away from Camp Randall Stadium. He'd called me early in the morning, before I'd left for Sculley's office, and invited me to stop by the church for a chat, and then go with him to Evening Prayer.

Naturally, I was thrilled to accept. I was looking forward to being with him again, plus I'd never been to Evening Prayer before and was curious. Besides, Lord knows, I needed plenty of time to reflect.

Dan wore a navy blue rugby shirt and jeans as he tilted back in a swivel chair, his white priest's collar tossed casually on his antique roll-top desk.

"I read the whole coroner's report today and I just don't know what to think," I told Dan. "The coroner ruled Annie's death a suicide."

"Do you agree?"

"Not really. Oh, I don't know…"

Dan's chair creaked as he leaned forward. "But you can see why suicide's the logical conclusion, can't you?"

"Sure. Who knows? Maybe I'm just unwilling to accept it. The report said Annie had a blood-alcohol level of point-oh-eight. That's not drunk, but it's certainly impaired."

Father Dan glanced at his watch. "Oh my gosh. It's almost time for Evening Prayer." He scrambled to his feet. "Still wanna come?"

"Absolutely!"

The chapel, a dim, drafty, austere room with thick stone walls, was located just off the chancel where about a hundred people regularly attend Sunday services. The tiny room was ideal for small gatherings. And this one was small, indeed: me—sitting alone and aloof against the far right wall about three quarters of the way back—and three others.

A slender, well-dressed man of about forty, wearing glasses and an obvious toupee, sat two rows in front of me. I'd only seen him on rare occasions. On the other side of the aisle, two women sat together in the front row. One was Miss McLaine, a humorless spinster in her early sixties who had been my Sunday School teacher in third grade. Sitting next to her was a woman, perhaps five years younger, whom I knew by sight, but not by name. She wore a pink cardigan sweater and distinctive half-moon glasses.

We stood when Father Dan entered from the sacristy to our right carrying a prayer book and wearing a long black cassock. He bowed briefly toward the cross on the altar, then turned to face us.

"Grace to you and peace from God our Father and from the Lord Jesus Christ." His vanilla voice echoed off the stone walls as he read from Psalm sixteen: "I will bless the Lord who gives me counsel; my heart teaches me, night after night. I have set the Lord always before me; because he is at my right hand, I shall not fall."

Dan's face was impassive as he read a verse from Amos: "Seek him who made the Pleiades and Orion, and turns deep darkness into the morning, and darkens the day into night; who calls forth the waters of the sea and pours them out upon the surface of the earth; The Lord is his name."

Dan paused. I glanced up and was surprised to see him swallow hard. Was he struggling with his emotions? I couldn't be sure. And couldn't imagine why. Nobody else seemed to notice his brief hesitation. When he read John 8:12 his voice was strong again.

"Jesus said: 'I am the light of the world; whoever follows me will not walk in darkness, but will have the light of life.'"

As the service continued, my emotions were in turmoil. *God loves me... He loves me not.*

"We confess that we have sinned...by what we have left undone..."

I should have stayed home the night Annie died. Her death—and Grampa's—had left a yawning emptiness in my soul.

My foul mood persisted during the Old Testament lesson—Isaiah, Chapter five—read by the woman wearing the half-moon glasses. That passage ends with God throwing a fit: "I will make it a waste; it shall not be pruned or hoed, and briers and thorns shall grow up; I will also command the clouds that they rain no rain upon it."

This is the kind of stuff that always makes me wonder about God. He seems so capricious, unpredictable, petulant, and unfair. I made a mental note to ask Father Dan about it.

"The word of the Lord!" Half-Moon declared.

Yeah. Right, I said to myself.

Everyone else read the more appropriate "Thanks be to God" response.

There were more prayers, but my mind wandered. I thought about my parents and what they would have been like had they lived. What would our lives have been like together? I tried, but the only image I could latch onto was me as a baby in a car seat. My mother—but not father—looked down on me adoringly.

The crinkling of paper brought my thoughts back to reality. Everyone but me had turned in unison to the final page of the Evening Prayer service. I had to turn two pages quickly to catch up.

Father Dan looked at me and, as he recited the benediction, I felt he understood my doubts and confusion.

"May the God of hope fill us with all joy and peace in believing through the power of the Holy Spirit. Amen," he said with great enthusiasm, his face radiant.

As soon as the service ended, Wig Man nodded curtly at me and darted out the side door as I put on my coat.

Father Dan stepped toward the two women in the front pew. Smiling, he extended his hand.

I picked up my backpack, slung it over one shoulder, and walked slowly toward them, privately hoping for an invitation to dinner, or a walk. I didn't want our time together to end just yet.

"...we just think it's the proper thing to do," Half-Moon was telling Father Dan.

"Well, I wish you had come to me first before you began circulating your petition," Father Dan said to the woman. He was still smiling, but it looked tight, like he was trying with all his might to be patient.

"I don't see what good it would have done," Half-Moon said indignantly. She was shorter, and plumper than her companion, Miss McLaine. "You would have denied it and tried to cover things up."

"Denied what?" I interrupted.

"Oh nothing," Miss McLaine interjected, avoiding my glance. "Clarissa," she said quietly to Half-Moon, "I don't think this is the appropriate place to bring up those accusations."

"What accusations?" I asked, looking back and forth between them.

"Miss McLaine is right, Lark. I'll tell you about it later," Father Dan said.

"Are you Lark Chadwick?" Half-Moon asked, turning her full attention to me.

"Yes. And you are...?" I decided not to hold out my hand.

"Clarissa Banks." She announced, examining me defiantly. "And this is Emily McLaine."

My third grade Sunday School teacher looked uncomfortable and continued to avoid my eyes.

"We're circulating a petition to oust Father Dan. The congregation will vote on it next week," Clarissa said.

"Lark, I think we'd better go." Father Dan took me firmly by the arm.

"You can't try to keep the truth from her by spiriting her away, Father Dan," Clarissa said loftily.

"What are you talking about?" I asked.

Clarissa ignored my question. "I'd like to hear it come from your mouth, Father Dan."

"I'm sure you would," he said under his breath. He let go of my arm and walked into the sacristy to take off his vestments.

"What do you two have against him?" I asked, slinging my backpack down and placing it on the floor next to me.

"He's unfit to be a priest," Clarissa hissed. "He's nothing like Father Vincent."

"Is that so bad?"

"I'm not surprised you don't think so," Clarissa spat.

"What's that supposed to mean?" My voice was brittle, wary.

"I would expect you would be one of his staunchest defenders."

"Why's that?" I felt my face redden.

"You're..." she paused, "...seeing him, aren't you?" She chuckled.

I flushed, then exploded. "Come on. You've got to be kidding. I can assure you that nothing is going on between Father Dan and me."

"Just like there was nothing going on between him and Anne?"

"There was nothing going on between them."

"They were having an affair," Clarissa announced, folding her flabby arms in front of her, her beady eyes taking aim at me through the crescent-shaped lenses and down her nose.

"I don't believe you."

121

"It's true," Clarissa nodded. "She even told some of us she was going to try to get him into bed."

"You heard this with your own ears?" I tried to keep my voice from trembling.

Clarissa Banks smiled smugly, and nodded. "It was last February at the pancake supper. I heard her tell Laura Nelson she'd like to be able to lure him to her bed. You were there, Emily. You heard it, didn't you?" Clarissa looked up at Miss McLaine for reinforcement.

My mouth hung open as I looked incredulously at Miss McLaine.

My old Sunday school teacher nodded. "I couldn't believe my ears when I heard it. And right in church, too. And then his car was frequently seen at her house late at night."

"Seen by whom?"

"Several people," Miss McLaine went on. "He wasn't even subtle about it."

My blood turned to ice.

"We kept a log of the times he was there and the duration of his visits," she said with pride. Then, the *coup de grace*: "And all of this going on while he's engaged to someone else," Clarissa said, shaking her head.

I froze.

My mind started shouting doubts at me: *Why does Father Dan seem to feel so strongly that Annie's death is a suicide? Did he somehow drive her to suicide as a way to cover up their affair?*

My mind flashed back to another time and place: Ross Christopher's cozy, candlelit bachelor pad and its honeyed sax arpeggios oozing from the CD player. Now the trauma of that awful night was back with the power of a tsunami.

Just then Father Dan emerged from the sacristy. Was that sheepishness and embarrassment I saw in his face? Guilt? Or was that half-smile the sneer of a powerful man, used to getting his way?

At that moment I realized the person standing before me no longer deserved the honorific title "Father." He was just "Dan." Dan the man...*and not much of a man, either*, I sneered to myself.

"Are you ready to go, Lark?" he asked.

"Yeah. I've heard enough," I said. I picked up my backpack again, turned on my heel and, without another word, marched out the door.

Chapter Twenty

I was already down the four stone steps and at the sidewalk before I heard the church's side door open and Dan's feet scraping on the steps. I didn't know what to think...or do. I was confused, hurt—and angry. I wanted desperately to believe Dan wasn't a pig, or worse, a murderer, but, as much as my mind didn't want to believe any of it, my gut was telling me otherwise.

"Lark, wait..."

I walked faster, slinging my backpack over my right shoulder. The music of Sade's "Smooth Operator" began playing in my head.

"You don't believe them, do you?" he called plaintively.

"Leave me alone," I shouted.

"Lark, I can explain..."

"I'll bet you can." I began to trot toward Pearlie, parked in front of Dan's Corolla on Regent Street.

He caught up to me on the boulevard next to Pearlie. I stopped, my back to him.

"Lark," he said softly, "I don't think it's wise for you to leave." He was breathing hard. White blasts of condensation shot over my shoulder, then dissolved into the darkness.

I whirled around. "And I don't think it was wise for you to have had an affair with Annie." I spoke just as softly, but vehemently.

"I didn't." His voice sounded pathetic, no longer the voice of authority from God I'd heard only a few moments earlier guiding my prayers.

"Well, it doesn't look good, buddy. And what's this about you being engaged?"

His jaw dropped.

"And how am I supposed to interpret that kiss on the cheek the other night? I thought you cared about me."

"I did. I mean, I do."

I turned away because I didn't want him to see my trembling lower lip. I put my backpack on Pearlie's front fender and leaned on it with my forearms.

"Will you let me explain?"

"Yeah. Maybe. Someday. Not now. I need to have some space." I was having trouble catching my breath.

He sighed. "Are you sure you'll be all right on your own? You're at a very fragile time in your life right now." His voice was barely a whisper.

"I'll be fine."

"Are you sure?"

"Stop patronizing me."

"I care about you, Lark," he said earnestly. "Promise me you won't do anything…drastic." Gently, he rested both his hands on my shoulders.

I stiffened, shook him off, then turned to face him. "Drastic, like go to the Bishop?" I shouted.

"Why would you want to do a thing like that?" He actually had the nerve to smile.

"Maybe I could tell him about your counseling sessions with Annie—in the sack," I yelled.

It began to sleet.

I retrieved my backpack from Pearlie's fender and tried to push past him.

He stopped me, gripping my shoulders firmly with both hands. "Lark, don't. Please." His teeth were clenched, his face red, his voice a mix of panic and anger.

It felt like being in the jaws of a human vise. Then Dan squeezed. Hard. His fingers dug into my flesh, bruising my arms. The pain from Dan's grip was the same as that night three years earlier when I'd been flat on my back, pinned against a sofa.

My breath caught in my throat. Dan had me pressed against Pearlie's fender.

I'm trapped!

I felt lightheaded.

You can't faint. You have to fight!

I lifted my backpack and, with all my might, slammed it into Dan's solar plexus.

Instantly, the vise digging into my shoulders released. Dan doubled over, gasping for air.

I dashed around the front of Pearlie, yanked open the front door and tossed my backpack onto the passenger seat.

Dan struggled to catch his breath, his face contorted in pain and anger.

"Lark, stop!"

I lunged behind the wheel and fired up Pearlie. As I floored her away from the curb, I saw Dan fumbling for his keys in the front pocket of his jeans as he ran toward his car.

As I made a quick right turn at the end of the block, I frantically looked back toward the church. I saw Dan's car pull away from the curb. To my surprise, a second pair of headlights came around the corner and followed Dan.

Are two people following me?

I thought I saw Dan's headlights make the turn off Regent Street, coming down the side street after me.

Quickly, I made another right at the next street, then a sudden left into an alley, where I pulled over, cut my lights and motor, yanked up on the emergency brake, and ducked down.

Seconds later, I heard a car race past the alley, followed quickly by the whoosh of another car.

I held my breath and tried to calm myself.

Sleet clattered on the roof.

Soon, I mustered enough nerve to lift my head and look around. The alley was dark and deserted. I pictured Dan combing the back streets near the church, looking for me.

And who was driving the second car? A stalker? Or am I just being paranoid?

I waited a few more minutes before starting the engine, releasing the emergency brake, and creeping, lights off, down to the end of the alley. The street in both directions was quiet and empty. I flipped on Pearlie's lights and turned left onto the street, swiveling my head in every direction, afraid one of my pursuers would reappear at any second.

I zigzagged down side streets until I came to a stoplight. The overhead signal cast a crimson smear on the wet pavement. Heaving a sigh when the smear turned green, I palmed Pearlie into a right turn, heading south on Park Street. Now that I was apparently in the clear, I drove aimlessly.

Soon, the rain stopped, but hot tears of anger and self-pity streamed down my face.

Chapter Twenty-One

I was too agitated to go home, plus I knew that would be the first place Dan would look for me, so I just drove, replaying the confrontation with him in my mind. My driving was automatic, no direction or destination in mind.

"Engaged?" I roared at the windshield. "How could you be such a ninny, Lark? You ditz! You actually believed he cared about you. What a joke! You pathetic, needy little girl." I pounded my fist against the steering wheel.

I kept driving—and seething. Soon, I was in the country.

My thoughts turned to Dan and Annie.

Could it really be they had been intimate? The thought sickened me. An image of them frenziedly coupling on Annie's bed kept creeping into my mind.

The nerve! How could he do such a thing?

I struggled to think things through calmly.

It's no wonder Annie was attracted to him—he's good looking, sensitive, attentive. They were about the same age. Was he attracted to her? A lot of guys were. She was, indeed, beautiful. He'd said so himself in his eulogy. And she was certainly capable of seduction. Did Dan give in to her temptations?

It's possible.

And, if he did, it's also possible he feared the affair was about to be revealed. *There's gotta be some law against screwing one of your parishioners.*

Maybe he was afraid Annie wouldn't keep quiet about it. She was a shameless gossip. Dan would have had so much to lose—his fiancée, his church, maybe even his priesthood. He'd been counseling Annie, so he knew she was unstable. Could he have manipulated her by using guilt as a goad to make her feel worthless? And, if she felt worthless, could suicide be far behind?

Half way to Pine Bluff I realized I was traveling a familiar road. A few miles outside town, I heeded an impulse and turned left onto the winding, crumbling blacktop of Old 58. It went down a hill and curved right, toward Pine Bluff. I slowed for the railroad crossing—the same crossing, I realized, where my parents died a quarter century earlier.

I eased Pearlie across the rails, then made a U-turn and rolled to a stop on the shoulder in front of the signal lights. If Vern Strozier was to be believed, this must be the spot where Dad parked while waiting for the train to come and kill him, Mom, and me.

I shut off the engine and lights, letting the quiet of the darkness enfold me. Soon my eyes became accustomed to the darkness and I could see a sky full of scudding clouds and brilliant stars.

The "accident" was beginning to make sense: they sat here, top down, gazing at the night sky. It would explain why the car lights were off when Vern Strozier and Max Labelle first saw the Mustang creeping toward the tracks.

I glanced at my watch. Ten-thirty—just about the time of the crash twenty-five years ago. At first, Mother probably didn't suspect what was in Dad's mind. Maybe the moon and stars transfixed her. By focusing on me in the back seat, concerned the whistle would awaken me, she didn't realize until too late that Dad had crept onto the tracks. She trusted him.

Big mistake, Mom.

Shouldering open my door, I stepped into the cool, rain-refreshed night. The strong stink of road-killed skunk mingled with the stench of manured earth.

All was quiet.

I took a deep breath. It cleared my head and made me feel a little better. Exhaling, I watched the white cloud of my breath float toward the stars.

I slammed the door and took a few casual steps toward the crossing signal. It towered over me, lights dark, bells mute. My coat and sweater felt warm around me, but my ears tingled. The air was brisk and bracing. Orion twinkled just above the southern horizon.

"Where are you, God?" I yelled at the silent sky. "Why is the universe so beautiful and I feel so ugly? If you're so powerful and creative," I sneered, "why can't you help me?"

The sound of my voice retreated across a field and dissolved into the darkness.

I wandered along the tracks in the direction of the Highway 58 overpass. On my left were trees—probably hundred-year-old oaks—standing just on the other side of a low fence of wood and barbed wire. On the right was an empty field where head-high corn cushioned my fall one hot July night long ago.

Now, as a lonely, mixed-up "adult," I surveyed the scene.

"Why? Why'd you die, Annie?" I cried to the empty sky.

Also welling inside me, relentless as an incoming tide, the flotsam of self-loathing.

Why didn't you pick up on it? Why didn't you see it coming?

I thought back to the last time I'd seen Annie alive, exactly one week ago. She'd seemed restless, almost pleading with me to skip work and go to a movie.

You didn't really need to go to work, did you? an inner voice taunted. *You could have stayed and been with her if you wanted to,* the voice sneered. *If you'd just gone to the movies with her, you could have kept her from killing herself. Maybe you could have talked. Maybe you would have said something to give her a reason to live.*

My thoughts continued to darken. There was a chill in the air, but no breeze. In the distance, the insistent barking of a dog. I walked onto the tracks, chose a rail, and teetered south toward the overpass, thinking again about Dan, about Annie, about my parents.

I balanced some fifty feet down the tracks to the point opposite the place in the field where my car seat had come to rest. As I stooped to pick up a stone from the roadbed, I smelled the sweet creosote coating the ties. The rock felt jagged as I rolled it over in my palm before tossing it into the field.

The stone thudded and bounced on the hard ground.

I hopped off the rail and trudged toward the place where the stone landed—the same place Sheriff Miller told me I'd been found. Once I got to the spot, I looked back toward the crossing.

In my mind's eye, I watched the accident:

Dad's car perched on the shoulder, where Pearlie is now.

A white light flickers in the distance.

Red signal lights flash and I hear the persistent *ding-ding-dinging*.

The car, lights off, slowly rolls toward the tracks.

The train thunders closer.

Mom, still unsuspecting, looks at me in the back seat.

The train's horn blasts.

The car inches onto the tracks.

Dazzling light drenches everything.

Staccato whistle-shrieks drown my mother's screams.

Impact!

Sparks.

Hunks of metal explode into the sky.

The car—and my parents—all disintegrate.

My little body, strapped snugly in the car seat, hurtles through the air, then comes to rest at my feet.

Shaking the awful images from my head, I found myself looking at the muddy ground in front of me. Tears streamed down my cheeks and dripped onto the dark dirt.

My Dad really did mean to kill me, didn't he? What could it have been that made him feel so...desperate?

"Miracle Baby," I jeered. "What a joke."

Maybe it would have been better if I'd died that night.

A car on Highway 58 *ca-thunked* across the bridge, but soon the hum of its wheels on the pavement evaporated into the night. An owl hooted in the woods. A slight breeze whistled past my ears.

My lip quivered and tears drenched my cheeks. I searched the sky and sighed.

"God, are you even there? Do you care?"

The night seemed to smother my voice.

I surveyed the spacious field where I was found. "I wish I'd never been born," I wailed.

Wiping the tears from my cheeks and eyes, I shuffled back to the tracks. Gravel crunched as I made my way up onto the roadbed and stepped onto one of the sturdy steel rails. I took only a few steps along the shiny-smooth platform before swaying, almost losing my balance. Pausing to right myself, I continued, unsteadily.

The dog in the distance had stopped barking. The breeze kicked up more. I thought about Dan, Annie, the accident. Life with its anguish and unanswered questions now seemed meaningless.

Maybe Dad did the right thing.

Just then—echoing through the night—I heard the long, mournful note of a train whistle.

Chapter Twenty-Two

When I first heard the whistle, the sound went through my soul like the thrust of a sword. I stopped abruptly. The locomotive's searchlight was just visible, shimmering around the bend some two miles down the tracks.

A surge of electricity seemed to pulse through me. I'd never felt more alive. In a jolt, I now understood exactly how Dad must have felt: eager excitement that soon his pain would be over. I still didn't know what weighed on him so heavily that he'd choose a hideous, but certainly decisive, way out. Yet he must have been tremendously excited his anguish would soon end—forever.

I resumed my slow walk toward the crossing, flirting with the possibility of a new goal—an oncoming train.

It whistled again, sounding as if someone was playing F-sharp on a huge outdoor pipe organ. The note echoed among the hills, as the faint hum and distant rumble of the engines drifted steadily toward me.

Figure-eight patterns of light scoured the tracks.

I took a deep breath. My footing on the rail was solid—I didn't need to look down. With each step, my hiking boot clamped onto the smooth steel as if a strong magnet sucked the sole to the track. It trembled slightly. I looked steadily ahead at the tunnel of light extending from the onrushing train.

So this is what it must have been like for Dad.

I felt the rail vibrate. It gave out a thin, high-pitched metallic screech. My whole body seemed to resonate with the rumbling power of the train as it lumbered toward me. I took a deep breath, realizing I didn't feel fear or terror, only exhilaration. Exhilaration and a profound respect for the raw force speeding toward me.

Steadily, the light got bigger and the sound got louder. This train sounded like a freight, straining to pull a heavy load. Two bands of silver reached toward me from beneath the headlight, widening. One streak passed me on the left, the other bisected me. The silver rails glistened against a black velvety background.

My pain will be over in an instant.

As I walked calmly toward the intensifying light, images of my mixed-up life assailed me: A Technicolor lava flow of dried wax caking the neck of a wine bottle at Ross Christopher's bachelor pad; the anger-contorted face of Mr. Green berating me after I'd forgotten to bring drinks to a table of big-spending businessmen; eagerly tearing open an embossed envelope from the New York literary agency, only to read a terse condemnation of my "screed"; the horrible image of my grinning father and screaming mother; Annie's cold hand sandwiched between my two warm ones; the peck on the cheek from Father Dan that once tingled, but now burned.

The silent crossing signals came to life, emitting pulsating red stabs of light. The bells clanged loudly.

Ding, ding, ding, ding, ding...

I kept walking.

The rail creaked and shifted slightly. The train got louder, closer, its searchlight a huge, dazzling orb. The train's two ditch lights took turns winking at me.

I kept walking.

Maybe it'll be better this way.

The grumbling of the engines was like rolling thunder. The rails in front of me glowed a bright silver, as did the tall trees on both sides of the tracks. Gravel speckled the shadows between the ties.

The train whistled again, two long blasts, as the engineer went through his routine of sounding the horn at a grade crossing. Then, suddenly, the blasts came in short bursts.

I'd been spotted.

I walked steadily toward the light.

The noise was deafening—horn blaring, engines rumbling, signal bells clanging. I felt the noise in my gut and let it envelop me.

The throbbing of the engines lowered, as the engineer throttled back. There was a loud *whoosh* of air when he engaged the emergency brake. A shower of sparks poured from beneath the train.

The sudden braking caused the trailing boxcars to violently buck and bunch as they *slam-bammed* into each other.

A high-pitched screech pierced the night, punctuated by the ringing of the locomotive's bell. The train was slowing, but I knew momentum would carry it through me. It would never stop in time.

I felt strangely at peace.

The brightness of the train's rotating searchlight bleached away the crimson flashes coming from the crossing signal. The train shrieked past the tower, which suddenly disappeared into the blackness, the warning bells now sounded like tinkling wind chimes.

The rail shook.

The light was blinding.

I could feel the whistle blasts.

In seconds, my pathetic life would be over.

Obviously, Mizz Chadwick, suicide runs in your family.

Chapter Twenty-Three

In that nanosecond, as I balanced in front of the onrushing freight train, I thought of my father as he stared unflinching—even grinning—at death. But, just as a smile began to curl my own lip, an insight dawned on me—a realization as bright as the brilliant beams of the train's searchlight: I was about to commit an act that would make me responsible for yet more misery in the world.

The misery had a face—Vern Strozier's.

The train whistle crescendoed to a deafening scream.

I leaped off to the side.

As the engine pounded past, a blast of wind buffeted my body, which was still in mid-air.

I hit the ground hard and rolled down a slight embankment into the tall weeds alongside the tracks. Tons of steel clanked past me as I lay on my back, gasping for breath, my heart pounding, the earth shuddering.

After a moment, I shook my head, checking to see if I was alive and unhurt. My shoulder was sore and I was a bit disheveled, but I seemed to be fine. A sense of relief and surprise washed over and through me.

I was glad to be alive.

I lifted my head and twisted around to watch the train as it slowed. The engine was just getting to the overpass, bathing the concrete pilings with a blinding light, then the bridge seemed to blink off as the locomotive passed beneath and beyond it.

I lay there for a while, breathing heavily, then I slowly got to my feet. My hair blew wildly around my face as I stood in the tall weeds and watched the boxcars rumble and rattle past.

After a minute or two, the caboose glided by, going so slowly I could have hitched a ride. A man stood on its back platform controlling an extremely bright searchlight. The beam panned back and forth along the tracks and roadbed. For a second, the light fell on me, drifted away, then suddenly returned, holding me steadily.

I shielded my eyes from its glare.

The man shouted something at me as he passed. It sounded like, "You okay?"

"I'm fine. Sorry," I shouted, my whole body shaking.

He snarled something at me about "trespassing," then spoke into a walkie-talkie in his hand.

The train moved on, gradually picking up speed. At the crossing behind me, the signal lights stopped flashing and the bells fell silent. Soon, the train was just a receding red light. Once again, in the distance, I heard the baleful notes of the train's whistle, sounding its warning at yet another grade crossing on its way to Chicago.

I brushed dirt and dried grass from my jeans and jacket, then crunched through the roadbed gravel and back onto the tracks, resuming my return trek to Pearlie.

I plodded along, head down, thinking, the smooth steel rail now warm on the soles of my feet. What did it mean to have made the choice to live? I couldn't be sure. The emotional pain was still there, but I had chosen to accept it, endure it, overcome it.

Is the pain there for a purpose? Is it some sort of inner barometer— a mechanism to guide, rather than a dictator to compel?

Choosing to live, I discovered, was an act of courage that made me just a little bit stronger inside. Strong enough to keep trying to track down the truth, no matter where it led. Strong enough to find out why my father made his fatal choice. Strong enough to search for what it was that had so agitated Annie.

As I drew closer to the crossing, just a few steps away from the blacktop, I glanced over at Pearlie. What I saw caused me to stop abruptly and gasp.

The shadowy figure of a man stooped beside Pearlie, shining a flashlight through the driver's window.

My blood turned to ice.

Has Dan followed me?

Chapter Twenty-Four

I held my breath. It was too dark to see clearly. All I could tell was the person was burly, wore a hat of some sort, and a bulky overcoat.

Another car—a dark sedan, much bigger than Pearlie—was parked with its lights off, directly behind my car.

I was perhaps twenty-five feet away from the man, too close to try to slink away. Any movement, I feared, would make noise and attract his attention. But before I could decide just what to do, I began to teeter on the track, lost my balance and, although I tried to land quietly, I crunched onto the gravel.

The man turned, swinging his light in my direction. The beam caught me in the face.

"Oh!" My hand sprang to my mouth.

"Lark? Lark Chadwick? Is that you?" The voice didn't belong to Dan, but I couldn't quite place it.

"Y-yeah…"

"What are you doing out here alone at this hour?" The big man began to stroll toward me.

"I, ah…who are you?" I stepped backward.

"It's me. Roy Miller." The sheriff laughed and turned the light onto himself, highlighting his chin and cheek bones. The light cast deep shadows into his eye sockets—a somewhat macabre effect. Flashes of gold glinted off the badge on his chest and Smokey Bear hat.

"Oh, Sheriff! Thank God. I thought you were someone else." I took a few confident steps toward him.

As I got closer to him, he snapped off his flashlight. "You sound glad it's not whoever you thought it was," he chuckled.

"That's for sure."

"You in some kind of trouble?" His huge frame towered over me.

"Maybe. I had a little, um, disagreement with somebody tonight."

"That must have been some disagreement."

"Believe me. It was."

"Do you think you might be in some kind of danger from this person?" His voice became gentle.

I remembered seeing an angry Dan running toward his car to pursue me.

"Maybe."

"Has he been stalking you?"

"Not exactly. I said and did some things to him that might have made him afraid enough or angry enough to try to stop me."

"Do you think he's capable of hurting you?"

I remembered the anger in Dan's voice. Saw the panic in his face. Felt the bruises of his vise-like grip.

"Yes, and it's entirely possible he's followed me."

The sheriff flicked on his flashlight and pointed it up and down Old 58 and along the railroad tracks. His light fell on a deer that had ventured onto the rails. Startled, it bounded soundlessly into the woods.

"Tell me about this guy," the sheriff commanded. He dug into the breast pocket of his coat and brought out a notebook and pen.

With the Jovial Giant looming in front of me, ready to be my protector, I gave Sheriff Miller Dan's name, told him Dan lived in the rectory next to the church, and described his car, all of which the sheriff relayed to the dispatcher over a portable radio.

"Thanks, Sheriff," I said after he'd completed his radio transmission. "What brings you out here?"

His deep laugh made me think of a kettledrum. "I was on patrol and found your car abandoned, so I stopped to investigate. Haven't totally given up my day job y'know...heh, heh."

We stood a few feet apart in the center of the road by the crossing. In the darkness, I could barely discern any of his features, just his massive frame blotting out a mammoth swath of stars.

I liked the sheriff, felt safe with him. And there was a special kinship, a closeness I felt, too. It was probably because he was one of the few living links to my parents I'd found, so far—a tie between the present and my past. Plus, he'd been kind enough to bring me out here the other day so I could get a strong sense of the accident and my survival.

I also was relieved and grateful he wasn't Dan.

"How's your research coming along?" Sheriff Miller asked.

"Okay, I guess." My emotions had not yet settled following my confrontation with the freight. My mind (or was it my soul?) was restless. "Sheriff?"

"Yeah?"

"Have you ever thought about suicide?"

"Whoa, you sure get right to the point, don't you?" His booming laugh echoed through the night.

"I'm serious. Have you?"

He was silent a moment, weighing his answer. My eyes were slowly becoming accustomed to the starlight, but I couldn't see him well enough to gauge his expression.

"I have." His voice was quiet—almost a whisper—but matter-of-fact.

The answer surprised me. So did my question. I'd had suicide on the mind. Now that someone I considered to be a friend stood next to me in the dark, I had instinctively decided to reach out. I needed to talk. His sudden assertion may have been because, like me, he felt darkness enhances intimacy. When you can't see the other person very well, you can't be daunted by their expression.

"You have?"

"Well, not about actually doing it, but I can understand why a person would do it. Sometimes life seems awfully meaningless."

"I know." I thought a minute. "How did you come to see life that way?"

He leaned against the front headlight of his patrol car. "Oh, I dunno. It came gradually, I guess. My dad was a hero in World War Two, but he drank himself to death. My older brother was sort of a John Wayne. I looked up to him, but he could always do stuff better'n me. When we both enlisted in the military, he became a Marine; I became an MP in the Army."

"MP?"

"Military Police. Both of us went to Vietnam, but he never came back."

Sheriff Miller became quiet for a moment, then continued. "I think that's when I began to think there's no God out there to be the Great Avenger. Figured it's pretty much up to the individual. Survival of the fittest and all that."

"Sounds awfully predatory."

In the dim light I saw his shoulders shift. A shrug. "Maybe. Depends on how you look at it. I'd say my mission—whether as Sheriff of Bluff County, or as a U.S. Congressman—is to fight predators. And it's worked pretty well. My younger brother looked up to me and he went on to become Bluff County District Attorney. Served something like thirty years in that position, 'til he died last year of a heart attack." He sighed. "We were a great team."

There was a pause. Roy Miller continued to lean against his car. He seemed in no hurry to leave. "What about you?" he said, finally. "You ever think about suicide?"

"A lot, recently."

"About doing it, you mean?"

142

"Not exactly," I lied. "In my research, I've come to believe my dad drove onto these tracks deliberately."

Roy Miller pushed himself up from his leaning position. "No. Isn't possible," he said with finality, once again rising above me.

"How can you be so sure?"

"Nothing like that came up during the investigation. Whoever told you a thing like that?"

"Any chance I can take a look at the accident report?" I asked.

"Oh, I suppose, if we can find it. We've changed our filing system a couple times since the accident."

"Mind if I stop over Monday and try to find it? I've got some hunches I want to check out."

"No problem. But don't get your hopes up. It could be buried under a lot of stuff. I've got some campaign appearances Monday morning, but I plan to be back in the office in the afternoon. If you can wait 'til then I might be able to help you unearth what you're looking for."

"That would be great. Thanks."

We stood a minute longer, looking at the stars. "How's the campaign going?" I asked, filling the silence.

"Oh, pretty good. I may be way ahead now, but things will probably tighten this week as we close in on election day. I'm trying to keep the tone positive, but it isn't easy."

"What do you mean?"

"For some reason, and I've never been able to figure out why, Reggie Lange seems to dislike me intensely, and personally, yet he's never had a run-in with the law, or with me."

"Is he hostile to you?"

"Nope. Just the opposite. He basically ignores me. He's always cordial in public, but even though there's never been a blowup, I can just tell that he's harboring some sort of deep animosity against me. I'm wondering if he might be planning some eleventh hour bomb."

"You think so?"

"Naw. I'm probably just being paranoid," he laughed.

"It's getting cold," I shivered. "I better get going." I dug into the front pocket of my jeans, feeling for my car keys.

"You take care, Lark. Sorry if I scared you."

"That's okay, Sheriff. My heart's about back to normal now—but barely."

The Jovial Giant chuckled as he lumbered toward his unmarked car. "Night, Lark."

"G'night, Sheriff…I mean…Congressman." Giggling, I ambled toward Pearlie. "Glad it was you I stumbled onto tonight."

"Me too, Lark."

"I'll stop by Monday to get that accident report. Maybe I'll see you then."

"Okay," he called. "Have a good weekend."

We slammed our doors simultaneously and revved our engines, but my revving sounded much less impressive than the sheriff's because Pearlie's power is measured more by hamsters than Clydesdales.

The sheriff did a swift U-turn, his tires kicking up a few stones as he rocketed off toward Pine Bluff.

As Pearlie bumped across the tracks, heading for Madison, I felt a renewed commitment to find out how and why my parents were killed and why the truth had been hidden from me. My quest, I realized, was what was keeping me going. I didn't like what I was learning, but I found the search and discovery process was liberating and fulfilling.

A definite purpose animated me. Who would've thought a year ago, or two weeks ago, for that matter, I'd be getting to know two candidates for The House of Representatives? Who would've thought a Pulitzer Prize-winning former *New York Times* editor would be mentoring me?

Old 58 came to a T intersection with the main highway. Nobody was coming from the left, so I turned right onto Route 58 and pressed the accelerator hard toward home. I like the drive between Pine Bluff and Madison because it's straight and flat and gives me a lot of "decompression time"—time to think, to turn over in my mind the events of the day.

I was exhausted, wearied by the weight of the past several hours. As I shifted through the gears, I glanced in my rearview mirror and saw a pair of headlights in the distance. Slowly, they drew closer until the other car was right on my tail. Suddenly, the high beams flashed on, bathing Pearlie's interior in bright white light.

Chapter Twenty-Five

Wham!

The bump from behind jerked my head back against the seat. Terror clawed at me. I gripped the wheel with both hands to keep from losing control.

Wham!

"What the—" I pressed the accelerator to the floor to gain some distance, but Pearlie's engine was already whining.

Wham!

He wants me to stop. He wants me to stop. But I knew it would be foolish to stop in the middle of nowhere.

Frantically, I looked ahead, hoping another car was coming so I could flash my lights at it, but the road ahead was dark and empty.

Wham!

"Oh, God!" I tightened my grip on the wheel and mashed the accelerator into the floor. Pearlie moaned in protest, refusing to lurch ahead. I was trying so hard not to lose control that I wasn't even worried about damage to Pearlie's back end.

Wham!

I tried twisting around to look behind me, but things were too jumbled. I glanced at the speedometer. Fifty-three. Fast for Pearlie.

The car behind me made contact again. Pearlie shuddered. But this time it wasn't a bump. This time it felt like my attacker's front bumper had welded itself to Pearlie.

I'm being PUSHED!

Pearlie's speedometer edged toward sixty.

I stamped on the brake to slow the sudden slide forward.

Pearlie pulled to the right, toward the shoulder. I smelled burning rubber.

The car was locked onto my rear bumper. I had the sick feeling I was no longer in control.

We hurtled down the highway, the car behind me pushing us faster. I fought the wheel, but my right tires slid off the road and onto the gravel shoulder. Looming ahead, I saw the concrete balustrade of a small bridge over a creek.

Fear bolted through me.

He's trying to kill me, my mind screamed.

Thirty minutes earlier, I'd stood in front of a freight train, welcoming sudden death. Now, I was fighting for my life. Desperately, I searched for approaching headlights.

Nothing. The road ahead was ink.

My panic-sweaty hands were slippery on the wheel. I stood on the brakes. Pearlie pulled more to the right, onto the shoulder—I was being bulldozed toward a solid slab of concrete.

I cursed myself for not wearing a seat belt.

Gravel hammered against Pearlie's undersides.

"Oh, Jesus…help me." My prayer was a whimper.

The bridge abutment was straight ahead, shining brightly in the beams of my headlights.

You have to get out from in front of this maniac. Do something!

Holding my breath, I closed my eyes, mashed the brake pedal and yanked the wheel hard to the left.

Pearlie went into a spin.

My body lurched toward the passenger door. I clung to the wheel with all my might. It felt like a stomach-churning ride at a sadistic amusement park.

Rubber squealed on cement.

Metal scraped against metal.
I screamed.

Chapter Twenty-Six

Pearlie spun to a stop and I opened my eyes. She'd twirled at least once and was now pointing, more or less, in the general direction of Pine Bluff—engine stalled, sitting at a cockeyed angle, blocking portions of both lanes.

To my left rear I saw a crimson blur, already too far away to recognize, racing down the highway toward Madison.

Still shaking and nearly hyperventilating, I turned the key. Pearlie wouldn't start.

In the distance...headlights?

He's turned around! He's coming back!

I felt sick to my stomach. I fought a strong urge to scream. My hand trembled as I twisted the key in the ignition a few more times.

Nothing happened.

The headlights were getting closer. I was just about to jump from the car and run away into the night, when I noticed I could still see the taillights of my attacker. The receding red specks went past the approaching pair of white lights.

I tried to start Pearlie again. The engine groaned, but that's all. I turned on my emergency flashers and scrambled out of the car.

As the oncoming lights neared, I loped toward them waving my arms. The lights flicked to high beam and the vehicle, a pickup truck, slowed and pulled to the side of the road.

I dashed to the driver's side of the cab.

"You all right?" the driver asked as he rolled down his window. He was a man in his fifties, wearing a feed and seed cap. Country music twanged from the radio.

"That car just tried to run me off the road," I shouted breathlessly, pointing wildly down the highway. "Did you get a good look at the car or the driver?"

"No, Ma'am, I didn't. Sorry." He spoke with maddening slowness. "What about you? Are you okay?"

"I think so, but my car won't start." I pointed at Pearlie flashing forlornly just shy of the bridge.

"Let's take a look."

He put on his emergency brake and flashers and climbed down from the cab, his heavy boots clumping on the metal running board. He ambled to Pearlie. The lights from his parked pickup illuminated Pearlie's rear end, which, I could see, was marred by an ugly horizontal gash.

"Try starting it once more," he instructed, glancing worriedly over his shoulder to make sure no traffic was coming.

Quickly, I jumped behind the wheel and tried to crank the engine again. This time, after some hesitation, it started.

"Must've been flooded," he said, sympathetically.

"I'm going to drive to the sheriff's office in Pine Bluff," I called, leaning out the window. "Will you please follow me to make sure I get there safely?"

"Be glad to, Miss."

His glacial gait eventually returned him to his truck. As he swung himself into the cab, I gunned Pearlie's engine decisively to make sure she wouldn't stall again.

Still agitated, I eased her into gear and began heading toward Pine Bluff. I was afraid whoever attacked me would come back. I kept checking the rearview to make sure the farmer was keeping up. He wasn't. Annoyed, I slowed to keep from getting too far ahead of him.

Although frightened and shaken, my anger was growing. Dan became my target: I'd hit him with my backpack and threatened to go to the Bishop. He'd chased me—and apparently found me.

He is not going to get away with this.

Rage fueled the drive to the parking lot behind the sheriff's office. When we got there, I was livid.

"You gonna be okay now?" the farmer asked from his cab as he pulled next to me while I parked the car. A stark security light blazed down on us.

"Yes, sir. I think I'll be fine now. Thanks for your help. I don't have much money, but I'd be glad to pay you," I said.

"Nah, that's okay," he said, waving me off. "I'll just wait here 'til you get inside."

"Thank you!"

I locked Pearlie, trotted to the entrance of the sheriff's department, and buzzed a doorbell next to the glass and chrome door. After a few seconds, a uniformed sheriff's deputy entered the lobby. He was in his thirties, had a kind face, and was in excellent physical shape. His muscles bulged beneath his tight, brown uniform. The name tag he wore over his left breast pocket identified him as Carl Olson.

He must have noticed how disheveled and upset I was. "What's the matter?" he shouted through the glass.

"Somebody just tried to run me off the road," I yelled. "I want to file a report and get you to try to find the guy."

As he unlocked the door, I waved to the farmer. He returned my wave and *putt-putted* out of the parking lot.

When the door opened, I rushed inside.

"Are you okay?" Deputy Olson asked.

"I think so. Can you try to reach the sheriff?"

"He's in the back." The policeman wore a wedding band, gold-rimmed glasses, and had thinning red hair.

"What do I have to do to get this guy captured?"

"Follow me," he said.

Deputy Olson led me into a dimly lit room filled with radio equipment. The floor was slightly raised and sounded hollow beneath our feet.

Sheriff Miller stood talking with the dispatcher. He did a double take when he saw me, his smile changing to concern. "Lark, are you okay? You look terrible." He took a step toward me.

"After I saw you at the crossing, somebody tried to run me off the road."

"The Houseman guy?"

"I-I think so."

The sheriff spun around and sat quickly in front of the computer next to the dispatcher and, as I watched over his shoulder, he typed Dan's name into the computer.

"This taps into the records of the Department of Motor Vehicles," the sheriff explained. "In just a second, we'll be able to find out what kind of car your friend drives."

"He's no friend of mine," I muttered.

The screen flashed, then filled with yellow type.

"Here we go," he said, ignoring my scorn. He took the mic from the dispatcher, keyed it, and broadcast Dan's description, a description of his car, and a summary of what happened to me.

"Looks like Houseman made his move, Lark."

His investigation still not over, Sheriff Miller contacted the Dane County Sheriff's Department and the Madison Police Department to get them to look for Dan's car. Then, he took me outside to examine the damage to Pearlie. He found no obvious paint from another car, but he scraped some small paint flecks from around the gash, explaining it would be used to "compare with marks on any suspect vehicle."

I dreaded getting back on the road and was grateful when he offered me a police escort home. I declined, however, because I was also afraid to go back to an empty and vulnerable house.

I called the Stones. Their phone rang three times before Muriel answered.

"Hi, Muriel. It's Lark Chadwick."

"Lark...what a pleasant surprise." She sounded genuinely pleased to hear me.

"I hope I'm not calling too late." I glanced at the clock on the wall and winced.

Eleven-thirty.

"No, not at all. Lionel and I were just sitting by the fire reading."

The scene sounded inviting. "I have a favor to ask," I began, timidly.

"Why, of course, dear. What is it?"

"I really don't want to impose. I'm at the police station right now."

"Oh dear. Here in Pine Bluff?"

"Yes. Downtown. The Sheriff's Department, actually."

"Is anything the matter?"

"I'm all right now, but someone tried to run me off the road a little while ago."

"Oh my goodness!" She spoke to Lionel. "It's Lark. She says someone tried to run her off the road."

Lionel came on the line. "Lark!" It was a command, not a question. "Are you all right?"

"Hi, Lionel. I'm sorry to be calling so late. Yeah. I'm fine...now...but I really had a scare a little bit ago. I think someone's trying...to kill me...."

Until that moment, anger and fear had kept deeper, more virulent emotions at bay, but now the terror and powerlessness of feeling hunted overwhelmed me. I began to cry.

"Where are you now?" Lionel barked.

"At the sheriff's office," I managed to choke.

"I'll be right there."

"No—" I began to protest, but he'd already hung up.

I handed the phone back to Roy Miller.

"Lionel is coming to pick me up," I said sheepishly.

Five minutes later, Lionel's Volvo squealed into the parking lot. Muriel was with him. They got out and hurried to the door where I was waiting for them with Sheriff Miller.

I'd just managed to regain my composure, but when I saw them, I began to cry again.

"I feel like such a wimp," I sniffed as Muriel's embrace surrounded me.

As she held me, Lionel fired questions at me: "What happened? Who did this? Do you know?"

"Dear," Muriel said to him, sharply, "can't you see she's upset? Do your interview after she's calmed down."

"I'm sorry I'm such a mess," I cried. "I really don't want to be a bother. All I need is a place to spend the night."

"And that you shall have, my dear," Muriel said firmly, holding me tightly in her arms.

"She's already filed a report, Lionel," Roy Miller said. "We've got our units, plus the police in Dane County and in Madison looking for the person she suspects."

"That's great. Thanks, Roy." Then Lionel turned to me, "So, you think you know who's trying to kill you?"

"Lionel!" Muriel said, sharply. "Not NOW. Let's get her home first. There's plenty of time for a debriefing, but only when Lark's good and ready."

"Right. You're right, dear." He turned to me. "Sorry, Lark. I got carried away."

"It's okay, Lionel. I don't blame you. I have more questions than answers, too."

"Come along now, let's go," Muriel guided me toward the door. "Lionel, you drive Lark's car home. She can ride with me."

Muriel didn't speak during the drive, but gently stroked the back of my neck with her right hand. I felt comforted by her strength and compassion.

Sighing, I leaned back and closed my eyes.

When we arrived at the Stone's house, Muriel pulled to the curb, rolled down her window, and signaled for Lionel to pull alongside.

"Lionel, put Lark's car in the garage where it'll be out of sight, and close the garage door. I'll park ours on the driveway."

Dutifully, Lionel complied.

Hmmmm, I thought, *The Bear can be a pussycat?*

The house was warm and cozy inside.

"Lark, how about having some hot apple cider or maybe some hot chocolate while you curl up on the couch? Then, if you feel up to it, you can tell us what happened," Muriel said.

I could smell the cinnamony cider. "Apple cider would be great. Thanks."

Sitting on the end of the couch, I slipped out of my hiking boots, and tucked my feet beneath me.

"Here, let's put this over you," she said, laying a quilt on my lap. She sat down next to me.

Lionel came in the back door from the garage.

"Honey," Muriel called from the living room, "would you please bring Lark some cider? And pour some for you and me, too. Then you can have your news conference." She winked at me.

I couldn't help but chuckle.

In a moment, Lionel came in carrying a wooden tray with three steaming mugs of cider and set it on the coffee table by the fireplace. He wore a dark blue pullover sweater and khaki slacks. It was the first time I'd seen him without a suit.

Muriel handed me a mug. Lionel put another log on the fire, poked and stoked it until it roared, then sat in an easy chair to my right.

"Captain, may I?" Lionel said, eyebrows arched as he glowered at Muriel.

"Yes, you may," she smiled, "that is, if Lark doesn't object," she looked questioningly at me.

"It's fine," I nodded.

"Well, then," Lionel began, "ah . . ." His mouth was open, but nothing came out. He looked like he was groping for the right word.

"What the Pulitzer Prize-winning former National Editor of the *New York Times* wants to know…" she grinned at Lionel, then turned to me. "What happened?"

I laughed, amused at their repartee.

"Right. What happened, Lark?" Lionel asked, glumly.

For the next several minutes, as we sipped our cider, I told them the whole story.

Well, not the whole story.

I sidestepped mentioning my confrontation with Dan. That incident had ignited long-suppressed raw emotions of rage and shame embedded in my psyche like a land mine when I'd been attacked and nearly raped by my English professor. Those toxic emotions now mingled with feelings of resentment and jealousy over the sordid allegations against Dan and Annie. And I was still confused about the revelation of Dan's engagement to some mystery woman, and embarrassed I'd allowed myself to believe that something romantic might have been developing between us.

I felt uncomfortable traversing this deeply personal emotional terrain with Lionel and Muriel, so I jumped ahead in my story to the meeting with Roy Miller, followed by the attack.

"What did you and the sheriff discuss at the crossing?" Lionel asked.

"I told him of my hunch the crash that killed my parents might be a murder-suicide."

"Did you tell him why you thought so?" Lionel sat on the edge of his chair, leaning forward aggressively.

"No."

"Good. What else did he say?"

"What does this have to do with the attack on Lark?" Muriel interrupted impatiently.

I wondered about that, too.

"I'm not sure, yet" he replied. "So," he said, turning to me again, "what did the sheriff say when you told him your hunch about the crash that killed your folks?"

"He discounted it right away. Said there was never any evidence of suicide."

"I see…" Lionel said, rubbing his chin, thoughtfully.

"Oh! I just remembered! I also asked him if I could see the accident report from that night."

"Good idea," Lionel said. "He have any problem with that?"

"No, he didn't seem to."

"Uh huh." Lionel gazed for a moment at the fire.

"What are you thinking, dear?" Muriel asked.

"Silkwood." He said, simply.

"What's Silkwood?" I asked.

"Karen Silkwood. She was a worker at a nuclear facility in Oklahoma back in the seventies," he explained. "She was exposed to some radioactivity and was going to blow the whistle on lax standards at the plant. She'd made an appointment to talk about all of that with one of my reporters, but never got to the meeting."

"What happened?" I asked.

"She died in a car wreck. It happened one night along a stretch of lonely road—a road a lot like Route 58 between Pine Bluff and Madison. It's always been my hunch she was deliberately run off the highway, but we could never prove it. Hollywood made a movie about it. Meryl Streep played Karen Silkwood."

"Who would want to kill her?" I asked.

"Someone with a lot to lose."

"Who would want to kill me?"

"Same kind of person."

"And who might that be?"

He didn't answer.

"The sheriff?" Muriel asked.

"Maybe..." Lionel answered.

"But why?" Muriel and I both asked simultaneously.

"Maybe he's got something to lose if the truth is known about the accident that killed your folks, Lark."

But Dan has plenty to lose, too.

I felt torn. I didn't want to let Muriel and Lionel probe too deeply into my personal life, yet I didn't want them to mistakenly suspect my friend the sheriff, either.

"Oh, I dunno, Lionel," I said, finally. "That's not what I told the cops."

"What did you tell the cops? Do you think it might be someone else?" Lionel asked, incredulous.

"Well, kind of..."

"Kind of? Either you do or you don't." He was becoming his irascible, on-deadline self.

"I think it might be Dan Houseman, the priest at my church," I kept my eyes riveted to my mug of steaming cider.

"Oh come on, Lark. What'd ya do? Skip confession?" Lionel got up and began to pace.

"I got into an argument with him earlier in the evening. I think he followed me."

"What did you argue about?" Lionel stood over me, but I couldn't bring myself to look up into his eyes.

"Lionel," Muriel cut in, coming to my defense. "Don't press her. Maybe she doesn't want to tell us. It's none of our business, really. The point is, she doesn't agree with your theory and she's told the police who she thinks might be after her. Let's leave it with them," she said.

I shot her a grateful glance, but could tell by her worried expression she was uneasy—not sure, herself, why I suspected Dan and not Roy Miller.

"Well..." Lionel grumbled, stuffing his hands into his pockets, "you know how I feel about leaving it to the officials."

"I know, dear." It seemed like Muriel was torn, too.

"Tell you what, Lark," Lionel said. "You get a good night's sleep. Spend the weekend here, if you want. Monday you can try to track down the accident report. That might give us more to go on. How does that sound?"

"That's sweet of you. Thank you." His offer was very tempting. The thought of having to make the long back-and-forth drives to Madison, and sleeping in the empty house on Dale Drive, made me cringe. But I was determined not to let my fears control me. "Tell you what. I'm exhausted, so I'll take you up on your offer tonight, but let me try to get back to normal at my own place tomorrow night. If it looks like it's not gonna work, could I take you up on it later?"

"Sure. That's fine."

"Let me show you to the guest room," Muriel said, springing to her feet.

I followed Muriel upstairs. From the linen closet she pulled out a fluffy white towel for me, then she poked around in a drawer by the bathroom sink.

"Ah! Here it is." She held up an unopened box containing a toothbrush. "We always have one of these in case of an emergency."

"Oh, this is wonderful. Thank you, Muriel."

She disappeared into her bedroom, returning quickly with a flannel nightgown, a blue cotton shirt, underwear, and a pair of wool socks.

"I figure you can wear your jeans again tomorrow. If you're like Holly was, jeans are a permanent part of the ensemble."

I laughed. "You're right about that." I took the clothes she handed me, then followed her into the guest room. "This will be fine, Muriel. You're so kind. Thank you."

I put the clothing down on one of the twin beds and hugged her.

"I know you don't want to talk right now about this Dan person," she whispered as we hugged, "but if you ever feel like talking, I'm more than willing to be your sounding board."

"Thanks," I said. "I might take you up on that. I just don't want to talk about it with Lionel. I'm not sure he'd understand."

"You might be surprised. He can be very understanding, but I know what you mean. Sleep well, Lark. You'll be safe here tonight."

She backed out of the room and gently closed the door.

Safe? Will I ever feel safe again?

After shedding my clothes and slipping into Muriel's nightgown, I snapped off the light. Doubts and fears pressed against me. As I lay in the darkness, I remembered the vague feelings I'd had all week of being followed, and realized with a start that the first time I'd seen a shadowy sedan was at dusk when I was at the crossing with the sheriff.

"God, if you're there, I really need you," I prayed—then cried myself to sleep.

Chapter Twenty-Seven

SATURDAY, OCTOBER 26TH

DAY 8

When I awoke, bright light streamed through the white sheer curtains of Muriel and Lionel Stone's guest room. I looked at my watch on the bedside table. Ten-thirty.

I sat up, alarmed I'd slept so long, yet grateful for the opportunity to sleep. I stretched, but lay there awhile, letting my thoughts roam.

Soon there was a light knock on the door.

"Come in," I called.

The door opened slightly and Muriel stuck her head in. "How are you feeling this morning, Lark?"

"Better, I guess. Thanks." I yawned.

"Want some breakfast?"

"That would be wonderful."

"How does hot oatmeal, toast, coffee and juice sound?"

"Great."

"It'll be on the table whenever you're ready."

"Thanks. I'm gonna take a shower first."

"Okay. Lionel is out running a bunch of errands. See you in a bit."

"I'll be ready in a few minutes."

She smiled and closed the door.

I threw back the covers and forced myself out of bed. I felt as if I'd been run over.

What might happen this day?

After my shower, I dressed quickly. When I entered the kitchen, Muriel was just finishing setting the table. She wore a camel-colored cardigan sweater, white blouse and gray wool slacks.

"How'd you sleep?" she asked brightly.

"Rough at first, but I feel better now." I tried to sound chipper, but knew it would be hard to fool Muriel. In the bathroom mirror I'd seen my red, swollen eyes.

I ate in silence.

Muriel joined me, but maintained a respectful reserve.

"Want a section of the paper?" she asked, nudging the *Wisconsin State Journal* toward me.

"Sure. Thanks." I reached for the front section, but merely scanned it. My mind kept wandering to the night before. I detested feeling exposed and unprotected against the talons of a ferocious predator—a predator still on the prowl.

The world seemed to be closing in on me again.

"Lark?"

"Yes?"

"What's bothering you, sweetheart? I don't mean to pry, honest I don't, but you've been through so much, I can't help but worry you're having a difficult time sorting it through."

"Oh, Muriel," I jammed my spoon into the half-eaten bowl of oatmeal. "My life just keeps getting more and more complicated."

"Maybe we should try to unwrap things and look at them one by one. Where should we start?"

"Even doing that's hard to do. Things have been so topsy-turvy. First Annie, then beginning to learn the truth about my parents, then almost being killed. It's a mess."

"I know what you mean. When Holly died, I thought it was the end of the world."

163

"How did you get through it?"

"I'm not sure I have, yet, or Lionel, either. It's like trying to hold an inner tube under water. Just when one of us thinks we've succeeded in keeping the pain submerged, something happens and the thing shoots to the surface again."

"That sure sounds familiar."

Muriel took a sip of coffee and looked out the window for a moment, a faraway look on her face. "But it seems to have gotten better with time, the pain isn't as intense. I can only attribute it to being able to focus on other people and duties and not merely on myself or how bad I feel."

She sighed, took another sip of coffee and looked at me. She smiled and shrugged. Her eyes looked as though she had seen much pain, yet she was willing to go on.

"Did you ever think about killing yourself?" I asked suddenly.

"Oh, my, no. Not seriously, anyway, although the thought did flit across my mind once a long time ago, when I was much younger. I think anyone who's thoughtful has wondered about it, but, no, suicide is not for me."

"Why not?"

"It's just not in my makeup. Seems too selfish."

I felt the rebuke even though none was intended. Yet I had to agree. Last night, when I'd been so close to suicide, I was only thinking of my own pain. I admired Muriel for her ability to see the choice so clearly. I'd almost allowed myself to miss that lesson altogether—and forever.

"What about you?" she said, returning her gaze to me.

"What about me?"

"Have you ever thought of suicide?"

"Less thinking than acting," I said, looking at the bubbles in my coffee cup twirl as I swirled the spoon in the brew.

"You mean you've actually made an attempt?"

"Sort of." I kept studying the coffee bubbles, refusing to look at her.

"Dear me! What happened? Do you mind if I pry?" Muriel Stone had always seemed to me to be the antithesis of prurient prying. I sensed her only motive was to help me.

"No, I guess not," I sighed. "I feel I can trust you."

"When did you try it?" she asked, her voice barely a whisper.

"Last night."

"What happened?"

"I stood in front of a train."

"Lark!"

"Pretty stupid, huh?" I looked at her timidly.

"Why did you do that?"

"I don't know."

"I think you do." Her tone was gentle. "Don't you?"

"Yeah. I guess." I could feel her eyes bore into my head.

"What's the matter?" she pressed.

I toyed with my oatmeal.

"Does it have anything to do with Dan?"

"Partly, I think."

"What part?"

I fought to hold back the tears, but it wasn't working. Powerful emotions from my self-pity-stew were bubbling to the surface again.

Muriel pulled her chair alongside me and stroked my back with her hand. The gentleness of her touch was all I needed to allow the emotions to come unleashed. I buried my head in my arms and sobbed.

Muriel kept kneading my neck and shoulders as wave after wave of tears flooded from deep inside—tears of regret about my parents, tears of grief for Annie, tears of anger and distrust at Father Dan, tears of terror that my life was now in danger. Finally, after at least five minutes, the surges of emotion became less frequent and intense, as if a severe thunderstorm had passed through with only its trailing remnants on the scene.

Muriel stopped rubbing my back and set a box of Kleenex tissues in front of me on the table. She pulled one tissue out with a *foop* and held it in front of my eyes. I sat up and accepted it.

As I blew my nose, she pulled out another tissue and handed it to me. When I sullied that one, she pulled out another and another and another—*foop foop foop*.

I giggled at how deftly Muriel was able to transform my grief to…well…a giggle.

"Now talk to me, Lark," she smiled. "You need to get it all out. Maybe I can help."

As I dried my tears, I told her of my feelings of drift and purposelessness, of finding Annie and my desperate attempts to revive her. I told Muriel of my doubts that Annie had killed herself and of the humiliation I'd felt at Coroner Sculley's condescending verdict that suicide runs in my family. I told her of the allegation that Father Dan had been having an affair with Annie, and told her of my suspicion that he goaded her into killing herself to cover-up their affair. Then I snorted and sniffed again as I recounted how my fight with Dan had revived powerful, unresolved emotions lurking just out of view for three years since nearly being raped by my professor. My story ended with the aborted showdown with the freight train.

Muriel sat patiently, listening, and administering more tissues whenever an emotional squall interrupted my narrative. She remained quiet for the half hour it took me to tell my story. When I'd finished, Muriel sat shaking her head, tears in her eyes.

"Do you think I'm a bad person?" I asked her.

"No, dear. You're a hurting person, trying desperately to come to grips with a heavy, heavy burden."

"So what should I do?"

"About what?"

"About everything."

"Well, the police are looking for Dan. Maybe they've already found his car, found the yellow paint on it, and made their arrest. About your whole life? Can we at least agree it's worth preserving?"

"How can you see things so clearly? So black and white? There are a lot of gray areas, wouldn't you agree?"

"Yes, but perhaps not as many as you think. I prefer to see the world not in blacks, whites and grays, but in rainbow colors. The contrasts can be stark, and there can still be room for individual expression, but there are boundaries, too. Choosing the right colors for the painting of your life can be an adventure."

"But what if the painting gets messed up?"

"Color over it. Try something new. Don't just let the problem sit there. And for God's sake, don't destroy the canvas. Rework what's on it."

I sat quietly, mulling over what she'd said. Finally, I nodded. "Killing myself would be selfish. I know that now. But knowing why my life's worth preserving is another matter."

She smiled. "Articulating lofty pronouncements on The Meaning of Life isn't my specialty, I'm afraid, dear, but I do believe life itself is a gift. And we each need to make the best of it. I've found—and I'm speaking strictly for me—curiosity and the pursuit of what's true are very life affirming."

I perked up as I remembered the exhilarating anticipation I'd felt the day I returned to Pine Bluff to poke into my past. I remembered the burst of energy I'd felt when I read about the accident I survived, and remembered my enthusiasm when Lionel hired me to write the follow-up story.

"Yes," I said. "I see what you mean. Trying to find answers to all these nagging questions has really been stimulating. I guess it just seemed overwhelming there for a while when I couldn't focus on one of them at a time."

"More coffee?" Muriel asked.

"Thanks."

She got up from the table as I went to the sink and rinsed off my plate and cereal bowl.

After pouring me another cup of coffee, she came to my side and put her arm around me. "Thanks for talking with me, Lark. I know it wasn't easy."

I put my arm around her waist. "Thanks for listening."

"You know we're here for you."

"I know that, Muriel. Thanks."

"We love you," she whispered.

It had been years since anyone told me that. I cried again.

So did she.

Chapter Twenty-Eight

The newspaper office was empty when I arrived, so I used a key Lionel had given me to let myself in. I felt purposeful again. I was pursuing My Quest.

For several hours I worked steadily. I listened to the interviews I'd done with Roy Miller and Vern Strozier and chose quotes to incorporate into the story. I also transcribed their interviews, and then wrote a rough—very rough—draft of the follow-up feature story.

Peppered throughout, I made notes and questions to myself whenever I realized I needed to find out more information. One note urged me to track down Harlan Bell, the minister who'd officiated at Mom and Dad's funeral. I thought he might have some insights about their marriage—or might point me toward someone who did.

My mind was throbbing when I left the office. The sun was just setting—my favorite time of the day—a perfect time to stop by the cemetery before returning to Madison.

Pearlie's tires crunched on the gravel as I wound through the placid setting of the Oak Grove Cemetery. Suddenly, panic jolted through me like a shock wave. Am I being followed? I'd been so wrapped up in my work all day that I'd forgotten to pay attention. I made up for my carelessness by jamming on the brakes and worriedly looking all around me. Finally, convinced I was safe, I continued driving.

Soon I came to the base of a small hill. The Chadwick family plot was laid out at the top of the hill in the middle of a copse of oak trees. I stopped the car and got out. Looking around, I saw no one. The place was quiet. Dead quiet. The pun made me smile...and relax.

I slammed the car door, locked it, and walked up the hill. A light wind made the air feel cold. Frigid flower arrangements shivered in a heap atop a mound of fresh earth that covered Annie's markerless grave. Annie was buried between her parents (my Gramma and Grampa) and Mom and Dad. The five of them were buried in front of a massive ebony slab of granite, into which was carved CHADWICK. At its base were the graves of my great-grandparents, who'd died before World War II.

I shifted my attention to Gramma and Grampa's graves. I'd always enjoyed coming to visit them on their farm. Gramma was a happy, energetic woman. She had organized a kazoo band of some women at the church. Every Friday night, they'd perform at a nursing home "to make the old folks feel better," she'd explain, yet she was probably older than most of the so-called "old folks."

Grampa was laconic, but always had a big teasing smile. And he was a great hugger. It occurred to me Grampa had been the only man I'd been close to as I was growing up. I'd stick to him like glue and I realized now I had always deeply missed the presence of a father figure in my life. It was an emptiness that became a gaping hole when Grampa had his fatal heart attack back in May.

I looked at the graves of my parents. They remained a mystery to me, and their gravestones—identical gray granite markers, slightly rounded like small pillows—yielded only the barest information. They'd died the same day. Together. And she was so young, only twenty-four.

Questions. I've got so many questions.

I thought back to the day when I was only five or six and the drive to Gramma and Grampa's farm when Annie'd made her first cryptic mention of the accident that had made me an orphan. Not long after we'd arrived, I was sitting in Grampa's lap out on the concrete side porch steps.

"Grampa?" I'd asked as I watched a robin hop across the lawn.

"Yes, sweetie?" He wore my favorite flannel shirt, the blue one that made me feel all snugly.

"Will you tell me about the car accident that killed my mommy and daddy?"

When he didn't answer right away, I'd turned to look up at him. He looked stricken, almost fearful.

"Who told you?" he whispered.

"She did." I pointed at Annie who was walking with Gramma toward the clothesline with a wicker basket full of clothes.

"What else did she tell you?" His voice was strangely soft.

"Just that they died in a car crash when I was a baby and that my daddy was her brother."

He sighed heavily. "Isn't that enough to know?"

"I dunno. What were they like?"

Grampa was quiet a long time. We watched as Annie and Gramma pinned shirts and sheets to the clothesline. They flapped in the breeze like blue and white flags.

"Well? What were they like?" I'd persisted.

Big tears filled Grampa's eyes and trickled down his cheeks.

His tears frightened and confused me. I'd never, ever seen Grampa cry. I knew what I felt like whenever I cried: weak, powerless, angry, sad—usually all mixed together.

"I'm sorry, Grampa. I didn't mean to make you cry."

"That's okay, sweetie." He reached into a pocket of his overalls, pulled out a big white handkerchief, and blew his nose.

"I don't mind that Annie's not my real mother," I said, hurriedly, trying to make him feel better. "I think it's kinda neat."

"Well, you may think it's neat, sweetheart, but to your Gramma and me, it's very painful. George was our only boy."

I stroked his sleeve.

171

"It still hurts," he sniffed. "It really does."

After supper, while Grampa was smoking his pipe on the side porch, I began pumping Gramma for more information as we did the dishes. She'd cried, too, but then she hugged me—even asked me if I wanted to see pictures of my parents.

I was thrilled.

We let the dishes soak in the sink. Gramma went to a bookcase in the living room and got out a photo album. It was big, with a thin line of gold trim. She took it to the couch in the living room and sat down. Annie and I sat on either side of her. Slowly Gramma turned the pages.

Lila had dark wavy hair like mine. She wore it parted down the middle. It rested on her shoulders. George had a crew cut and glasses—geeky by any standard. I was particularly entranced by a shot of me as a newborn being held by Lila. She was sitting on a sofa, smiling, holding me on her lap. George crouched in front of her. I looked closer at the picture and realized, with a little gasp, that the doilies draped over the back of the sofa were the same doilies Gramma had on the couch where we were sitting at the moment. Gramma was sitting right where Lila'd been when the picture was taken.

"Gramma? How come none of you ever told me about my mommy and daddy?"

I'd asked.

"You were too young, dear," she answered, turning a page.

Just then, the screen door in the kitchen banged and Grampa came into the room.

"What are you doing?" he asked.

"I'm showing Lark pictures of George and Lila. And look—" She held up the album. "Here's one of them with Lar—"

"Put it away," he said harshly. His face looked like a thundercloud.

The smile on Gramma's face froze. Slowly she lowered the book of pictures to her lap.

Grampa's voice got louder. "I said, put it away!"

"But—"

"Now!"

I put my hands over my ears. I'd never heard Grampa shout before. Annie got to her feet. "Dad—"

"And don't ever bring that thing out again."

In one smooth motion, Gramma closed the book, stood, and placed it back in the bookcase.

"They're gone." Grampa shouted. "There's no need to go diggin' up the past." He turned abruptly and stormed through the kitchen and out the side door.

No one moved until we heard the door bang closed. Gramma stood by the bookcase, wiping her eyes. Annie stood next to the sofa, hands on her hips, mouth agape.

"Why was Grampa yelling?" I asked from my place on the couch.

"Grampa's upset because he misses your daddy," Gramma said, trying to smile. "C'mon, let's finish the dishes."

Lesson learned. That subject is off limits. It makes Grampa mad and everyone cry.

On our next visit to the farm, when nobody was watching, I remember looking for the photo album, but it had been removed from Gramma's bookcase—safely shunted down Orwell's *1984* memory hole.

I looked sadly at the flowers as they lay dying on Annie's grave. The yellow, white, pink, and red petals were fading. Soon they would be brown and decaying. Slowly shaking my head, I gazed at Annie's grave. My eyes welled with tears as I silently asked God to take good care of her.

"I miss you, Annie," I cried. "Why didn't you ever tell me anything?"

Then, I wiped my cheeks with the back of my wool glove and sighed. I was doing a lot of that, lately. Sighing had become a reflex.

"What a waste," I said bitterly.

As I sat on the cold stone bench in front of the graves, I reflected on what I'd learned so far, and brooded about the direction I wanted my research to take. I thought about the difference between the sheriff's theory that Dad raced the train, versus Vern Strozier's emphatic belief Dad's act of driving onto the tracks was deliberate. Surely Roy Miller, as chief investigator, had talked with Vern Strozier that night. It would be interesting to see the official record of what happened. Wouldn't Strozier's eyewitness account have been enough to convince the sheriff the accident was a murder-suicide?

Or was the sheriff merely trying to spare my feelings? Roy Miller doesn't want me to be tormented by the truth, I reasoned. And that made me angry.

All my life I'd been kept in the dark about my past by people who wanted to protect my supposedly delicate psyche. But if this research project was teaching me anything, it was teaching me to develop a thick skin.

"I can take the truth!" I declared to the mute graves. "I might not like the truth, but I can take it."

As I stood to leave, I realized I now had the courage to face the truth about anything. When I slid behind the wheel for the drive back to Madison, twilight had just given way to darkness. I kept an uneasy eye on my rearview mirror all the way home.

Chapter Twenty-Nine

My cell phone was ringing just as I arrived at the house on Dale Drive about six o'clock. I picked up as I was unlocking the front door.

"Hello?"

"Is this Lark Chadwick?" The voice was anxious. A young woman.

"Yes."

"This is Betsy Wells. I'm Dan Houseman's fiancée."

I froze.

The voice continued before I could hang up. "Look, I know you're upset with Dan. I'd like to talk with you, if you don't mind. Just the two of us. It's very important."

I hadn't been home alone for two seconds and already fresh fears about Dan were making me feel uneasy. Maybe leaving Stone's wasn't so smart after all.

"I...I don't know what to say," I stammered.

"I know this is a difficult time for you," the Betsy-voice said, "and I wouldn't be a bit surprised if you're feeling awkward and uncomfortable hearing from me."

"You can say that again."

"Frankly, I feel kind of awkward myself."

"Did Dan put you up to making this phone call?" I challenged.

"He suggested it, yes. But I agree with his suggestion. I think it's important that we meet. Have you eaten yet?"

"No, I just got in."

"Why don't we meet at the Camp Randall Café, by the stadium?"

"Um...where's Dan?"

"He'll be home. It'll just be you and me. I promise."

Pregnant pause from me.

"My treat," she nudged. "There's something I really need to tell you."

"Okay," I heard myself mumble. *What's that adage about curiosity and the cat?*

***

The Camp Randall Café is a greasy spoon hole-in-the-wall across Regent Street from the football stadium, and two blocks from St. Stephen's. It's not unlike The Korner Café in Pine Bluff, but a little smaller and has wooden booths instead of tables and chairs. The food is excellent.

A petite, nervous woman of about thirty was waiting just inside the door. She wore a buttoned down blue and white striped cotton blouse and a khaki skirt.

"Lark?" she asked, as I entered.

I nodded.

"I'm Betsy." She held out her hand.

I looked at it, but couldn't bring myself to touch it.

She let it drop, ignoring my slight.

The restaurant wasn't very crowded. She led the way to a booth near the back, but when she began to sit I stopped her.

"I'll sit there," I said. "I want to keep an eye on the door."

I'd been looking around nervously for Dan, but so far at least, Betsy'd been true to her word—there was no sign of him. Yet.

Betsy sat across from me, her back to the door. She had an open, pretty face. Tastefully coiffed black hair rested gently on her shoulders.

She smiled.

I waited.

"Dan's told me a lot about you," she began.

"He didn't tell me anything about you."

"Well, then, let me bring you up to date," she said pleasantly. That's the way her voice sounded—pleasant, earnest, sweet.

I listened impassively as she talked. She told me she's a member of Grace Church, the historic Episcopal church on Madison's Capitol Square. She said she'd just gotten her Masters in Clinical Psychology at the university. As she talked, I couldn't help being reminded of Melanie, the charitable character played by Olivia de Havilland in *Gone With the Wind*. I had to admit it: Betsy Wells looked like an angel. I hated her.

After the waitress brought coffee and took our orders, there were a few moments of uncomfortable silence.

"So, how long have you and Dan been engaged?" I asked, trying not to be blinded by the rock on her ring finger.

"Since the end of the summer." She smiled, but then caught herself, when she realized I probably didn't share her joy.

"How'd you meet?"

"At a diocesan leadership workshop last spring," she said simply.

"When's the big day?"

"Soon." She couldn't help but beam. "A couple months, actually."

I shrugged and sighed.

"Lark, I know you're upset with Dan, but there are some things you need to know."

"I'm listening," I said, then took a sip of the coffee. My hand trembled slightly. I couldn't help thinking about Dan and Annie—that Dan might be responsible for manipulating Annie into suicide.

"I'm not exactly sure how to put this," Betsy began.

I was surprised to see uncertainty in her. She had seemed the master of above-it-all, cheerful in the face of adversity. Now, her face was drawn, her brow deeply lined.

For the first time, I noticed bags under her eyes. In spite of her beauty, it looked as though she'd been under tremendous stress.

I didn't know what to say, so I waited. And listened.

"I know you're upset with Dan," she repeated. "And I know that on the surface it looks bad, but there's more to the story than you know."

"Go on."

"The way Dan told it to me, you . . . " she paused, groping for the right word, "left the church, upset with him because you believed he had been involved with Annie, is that right?"

"That's about the size of it," I said, my anger building. I remembered the strong emotions of betrayal I'd felt as I flew out of the chapel. I wondered how she could talk about this so directly. I glanced nervously at the door, fearing Dan would walk in at any minute.

"I want you to know, Lark, I was aware he'd been going over to see Annie. Nothing was going on between them."

"Look, Betsy, I really don't want to try to convince you that your fiancé may have a serious character deficiency. If you don't think so, that's fine."

I knew I was being harsh, but I couldn't help it if she had agreed to marry someone who might have abused her trust, then possibly steered Annie toward suicide to cover up their affair. Betsy, apparently, was as innocent and naïve as I had once been.

Betsy coughed nervously before continuing. "You're right. It all comes down to character. If the parishioners vote him out because they believe he's some sort of reprobate—when I know he's not—his ministry will be ruined, unfairly."

"Yes. I understand that, and it's too bad, but what does it have to do with me?" I folded my arms.

"I— we need your help."

"What could I possibly be able to do?" I said to her. *And why should I do it?* I said to myself.

"I need your help convincing the rest of the parish Dan was not having an affair with Annie."

"First you need to convince me of that."

"I know." She looked down at her plate.

"So, go ahead, convince me. I'll be open-minded." I sat back in the booth, arms locked across my chest.

The waitress came with the food, which both of us ignored.

"Convincing you is the hard part," Betsy said.

"Hard because it's so unbelievable?"

"No…hard because there are some things about Annie I'd have to tell you that are…um…unsavory."

I waited, stone-faced.

"Are you willing to hear the story?" She looked at me timidly.

By agreeing to listen to Betsy's story, would I once again be learning something sick and twisted about my own family? Could I handle it? Could I believe it?

"I'm willing to listen…I think," I said softly.

"Maybe I shouldn't tell you," she said, suddenly. "I'm just being selfish." She stabbed her meatloaf with a fork and took a bird-like bite.

Her quick switch didn't add up. Selfish would be the last word I could think of to describe her. Gullible? Maybe, but definitely not selfish.

As I watched Betsy Wells pick at her food, I felt sorry for her. It must be terribly lonely when the whole congregation is gossiping about the man you love. I felt selfish, shallow and mean. I'd been harboring a grudge against Dan—perhaps it was justified—but Betsy, no matter what the truth about Dan and Annie, seemed an innocent victim, caught in the vicious crossfire of church politics.

"No, you're not being selfish, Betsy. You're hurting." I reached out and touched her hand with much the same tenderness Muriel had shown to me that morning.

Betsy squeezed her eyes shut. Huge teardrops dripped down her cheeks and her face contorted into a grimace. Her fork clattered onto her plate and she put both hands to her face. As she sobbed silently, her whole body shook.

I looked around, nervous for her privacy, but the few people in the place weren't looking. After a moment, she dabbed at her eyes with a paper napkin I handed her.

"I'm sorry," she said after she'd blown her nose. "I didn't mean to do that."

I stroked her sleeve and waited. "I'm sure this has been a painful time for you, Betsy. How can I help?" This time my voice was gentle.

Betsy regained her composure and took a sip of water. "Okay," she said finally. "Let me tell you the rest of the story."

Too apprehensive to look at her, I began to eat my salad, bracing myself for the next awful truth about the Chadwick clan.

"As you know," Betsy began, "Annie was a very troubled person."
I nodded.

"Shortly after Dan became the rector at St. Stephen's, Annie became increasingly active in the church, volunteering for this and for that."

"Right…" I remembered Annie's burst of ecclesiastical enthusiasm.

"And, she also scheduled a lot of personal counseling sessions with Dan, which," Betsy hurriedly added, "is all perfectly normal and above board."

"Okay…"

"But then, Annie began coming over at all hours of the night, upset, distraught. Dan told me that once she came to the rectory in hysterics at four in the morning."

That I didn't know. "What was she upset about?"

"Different things. She said she couldn't cope—she said life felt like it was closing in on her." Betsy took a deep breath. "Dan was concerned she was going to kill herself if he didn't have an affair with her."

"What made him think that?"

"Because she told him."

"And Dan told you this?"

"Yes."

"At the time?"

"Yes."

"Why would he do that?"

"Because we trust each other and he wanted my help."

"How did he want you to help?"

"He wanted me to be present, whenever possible, when Annie was around. He told Annie I had some expertise in psychotherapy and he wanted her to have a woman's perspective on the areas where she needed counseling. He also told her he wanted me present so it would be clear he was not interested or available to her in any way other than as a priest."

"So, when his car was at our house…"

"I was there too." She paused.

I considered this for a moment.

She went on. "Dan and I kept urging Annie to get professional help. We recommended several psychiatrists and psychologists to her, but she never took our advice."

I sat in silence for what seemed a long time to me, and must have seemed an eternity to Betsy. I was beginning to like Betsy and felt terrible for her. On one level, even though I didn't want to believe Annie was as desperate as Betsy said, her story seemed in character with the manic Annie I knew.

But my doubts about Dan persisted. He could be just as desperate as Annie supposedly was—perhaps more so. What kind of pressure might Dan now be putting on Betsy to keep me from doing something "drastic?" Could I afford to believe Betsy's story?

Betsy placed her hand on my arm. "Dan was not in a sexual relationship with Annie, Lark, and the rest of his congregation needs to know that. They might believe you, if you could convince them."

"I've got a lot on my mind right now," I said.

"The meeting's Tuesday night at seven." Her fingers pressed, urgently. "Can you be there? Will you come?"

I pursed my lips. "I don't know yet."

Chapter Thirty

MONDAY, OCTOBER 28TH
DAY 10

First thing Monday morning I was in the sheriff's office, talking with Nina, a neatly coiffed fifty-ish secretary.

"Let me see . . ." She twisted her mouth, trying to think. "I remember that accident, but where might the report be? Just a minute." She turned to another woman in the office. "Trish? Where are the accident reports that are fifteen years old and older?"

"Didn't they get moved to the basement?"

Trish, an efficient-looking woman in her forties, looked up from her typing. "Remember? About five years ago we put all those old reports in boxes and stacked them in the basement. It's a real mess. I don't think anyone's been down there in years. Good luck finding what you need," Trish smiled.

"Could I go down and take a look?" I asked Nina.

"Be my guest. Follow me."

She picked up a ring of keys from her desk. Her high heels clicked on the marble floor as she led me down a long hallway to the rear of the building. We went through a door marked "stairwell," down a flight of concrete steps and through a couple narrow passageways. Nina stopped in front of a closed door and selected a key from the jangling key ring.

"There." The lock clicked and she pulled open the door. She flicked a switch and a single bulb, hanging from a wire, cast dim light into the room. "There are the files." She gestured at stacks and stacks of cardboard boxes.

"Thanks."

"Have fun," she said. "I'll be back at noon to lock up when we close for lunch."

"Thanks," I said, looking at my watch. Nine-oh-five. Plenty of time.

The warm room was a dusty, gritty mess. I shoved a few boxes aside. Someone had used bold magic marker to note the year on the side of each one, but it took awhile to find the right box. It was hidden behind several others, all of which appeared to have been slung into the room haphazardly—an extension of Roy Miller's messy office.

I shuffled through the files until I came across the month of July. I opened the July file and flipped through the pages, which, I discovered, were not in perfect order. A report from July 5th came right after a report from July 17th. The paper was musty, dirty and slightly yellow. I paged through them all, but couldn't find the accident report I was looking for.

After burrowing through every other box in the room—a feat which ate up the rest of the morning, as well as my patience, I slammed the last carton shut in disgust. I got up to leave—but couldn't. Roy Miller's massive frame filled the doorway. He was in uniform—and grinning.

"Oh!" I froze, startled.

Is Lionel right? Is it the sheriff who tried to kill me Friday night?

I was trapped.

Instantly, my mind sketched a grisly scenario: In a second, he could spring at me, clamp his enormous hand over my mouth before I could scream, then he could either strangle me, or—more likely—snap my neck. Killing me would only take a couple seconds. Apparently, nobody ever uses the room, so he could lock my dead body in here until after dark, then come back and dispose of it late at night.

He could kill me and get away with it!

I considered screaming and trying to push past the grinning monster. *But that would be foolish. Wouldn't it?*

Before I could do anything, the sheriff—still smiling—took a step toward me.

I stepped back.

"I'll bet you're looking for this," he said, holding up a manila folder.

"Y-yeah. I guess so…" I stammered.

"I came in over the weekend and decided to poke around down here to see if I could find it. I lucked out and made a copy of it for you to keep," he smiled, his voice even. "Here you go."

He held the file toward me. In his other hand he held a few sheets of white paper stapled together.

"Th-Thanks," I said. My hand trembled as I took the folder from him. "I thought I was going to have to hire an archaeologist to find it," I laughed, nervously.

"One other thing, Lark," the sheriff said, turning serious.

"Yes?"

"We ran a little check on your…ah…friend. The Madison Police say Dan Houseman's car checks out—no yellow paint on it and he apparently has a good alibi, so it doesn't look like Houseman is the one who tried to run you off the road."

"Then who could it have been?"

"It might just have been some lunatic. Maybe a drunk, or somebody who wanted to rob you or attack you—a random thing. You know, nothing personal, just wrong place, wrong time."

"That's reassuring," I said, still spooked that someone wanted me dead.

"At least it doesn't look like anybody has some sort of vendetta against you personally. It was probably a coincidence and will never happen to you again in a million years. I think you can rest easy, Lark. We'll keep our eyes open, though, okay?" The sheriff's manner was nonchalant—almost light-hearted.

I wasn't sure how I felt. If not Dan, then who? And would they try again? I knew Lionel suspected the sheriff, but I wasn't so sure.

The sheriff's my friend. Isn't he?

"Well, Sheriff, I'll get out of your way," I said, edging toward the door. "Thanks again for the report."

Roy Miller didn't move.

Our eyes locked.

Just as my panic began to return, we heard the *click-click-click* of Nina's high heels as she came to lock up.

The sheriff stood aside. "Sure thing, Lark. Hope it helps."

I barely heard him. I was already past Nina and halfway to the stairwell.

Chapter Thirty-One

"I got it, Lionel." I waved the folder at him as I barged into the office. "Hi, Muriel."

Muriel leaned on the counter where a copy of the newspaper was opened wide. She looked up and smiled.

Lionel was at his desk going through the mail. As usual, the sleeves of his starched white shirt were rolled above his elbows. Swiftly, he inserted a letter opener into the top of an envelope, slit it open, scanned the first few lines, then tossed the news release into the trash.

I went around the side of the counter, plunked down at the desk next to Lionel, opened the folder and read the accident report.

My eyes scanned the pages, noting the bare facts: time of accident, weather conditions, lack of skid marks, measurements, and a diagram of the accident scene. Then I settled down to read the sheriff's narrative:

> Accident occurred approximately 10:50 p.m., July 25 on Wisconsin State Road 58 about two miles west of Pine Bluff where the road crosses the Burlington Northern railroad tracks.
>
> Vehicle driven by George Chadwick, 1124 Garden Avenue, was hit broadside by an Amtrak passenger train.
>
> Train crewmen Vern Strozier, Engineer, and Max Labelle, Fireman, both of Aurora, Illinois, witnessed the accident.
>
> Strozier stated he was traveling approximately fifty (50) mph when he

spotted the car off to his left speeding
toward the crossing. Engineer stated
that it appeared the car was trying to
"race" the train. Strozier stated he
reduced speed rapidly, applied his
emergency brakes, and began to sound
the train's horn in an attempt to get
the attention of the car's driver and
possibly get him to stop.

Fireman Labelle agreed with Strozier's
account.

The report went on to document the details about how far the car was pushed down the tracks and told about how I was found "crying in a cornfield alongside the tracks."

"Something's wrong here, Lionel."

"What is it?" He continued to slit, scan, and toss press releases.

"Look here," I held the report toward him and pointed to the sentence containing Strozier's quote.

Lionel's eyes studied the sentence. He frowned. "Let me see that." He took the report from me and quickly read the whole thing. "This is incredible," he said, looking up at me.

"Somebody's lying," I said.

"Looks that way."

"But who? And why? Remember how adamant Strozier was about the accident being deliberate?"

"I certainly do," Lionel said, scratching his chin.

"I can't think of any reason why Strozier would lie."

"It's possible the report contains his first impression," Lionel said slowly, "the one he gave the sheriff that night, but then, over the years, as he thought back over events, he came to believe that it was deliberate.

Give Strozier a call and read him the report. And call back Labelle's widow and read it to her, too."

I dialed Mrs. Labelle's number first. When she answered, I reminded her of our past conversation and thanked her for putting me in touch with Vern Strozier. Then I got to the reason for my call.

"I've just come across the official accident report and I want to read part of it to you to see if it corresponds with what you remember your husband telling you about the accident. Would that be all right?"

"That's fine, although I'm not sure I'll be able to be very helpful," Mrs. Labelle answered.

I got her permission to tape the call and started the recorder. "The first question is easy," I said. "What's your first name?"

She laughed. "It's…" There was a pause. "Oh, dear, I'm so flustered I almost forgot," she chuckled. "It's Mildred."

I read Sheriff Miller's report to her. When I came to the line about Max Labelle agreeing with Strozier's account, I heard her exhale sharply.

"Is the police report accurate, Mrs. Labelle?"

Long silence.

"Mrs. Labelle? Are you there?"

"I'm here," she sniffed. Her voice sounded husky, as if she'd been crying. "No, Miss Chadwick. The report is most certainly not accurate."

"What's not right about it?" I asked.

"It was your parents who were killed in the crash, is that correct?" she asked.

"Yes, Ma'am. That's right."

"When you called the first time, I didn't want to tell you all that Max had told me because I didn't want to upset you, but I can see now that you're determined to learn the truth. That report you just read me does not contain it."

"What did your husband tell you happened that night?"

"He was emphatic until his dying day that the accident was a deliberate act of murder-suicide. The car crept slowly onto the tracks with its lights out." The words tumbled out of her. "And the thing that drove him mad, really, was the image seared into his mind of the woman turning toward the train and seeing it bear down on her. He said she became wildly hysterical. He could clearly see her scream and then turn toward the back seat as she struggled to get out of the car. And he told me how eerie it was that the man—the driver of the car—was calmly looking directly at the train and grinning."

Tears were in my eyes as I scribbled down her words. Her account was so vivid.

Even though she didn't witness the event, it was obvious to me her husband did, and that she had heard him repeat the story over and over as he'd tried to purge the scene from his memory.

I thanked Mrs. Labelle and then called Vern Strozier. As soon as he got on the phone, his heavy wheezing told me every breath had now become a major effort. After getting his permission to tape the call, I quickly got to the point.

"The official police report of the accident quotes you as saying my dad's car was racing the train. Are you sure—"

"That report's a bunch of buzzard pucky!" he spat.

"But is it possible that's the way you thought it was at first?"

"No. No. No. The car was crawling, not racing. There's no doubt about it in my mind whatsoever." He gasped a few times, then continued without losing his intensity.

"What brought him to our attention was the fact that his lights were out and he was just creeping closer and closer to the tracks. He was timing it to make sure he got onto the tracks just as we got there. Are you sure there's nothing in there about that?"

"Positive. Did you make a statement to police that the accident was deliberate?"

"Yes. Yes. Absolutely. I was emphatic about that. How could he get it wrong? Come to think of it, though, the cop cautioned us about talking to reporters and actually made it seem like he was doing us a favor by keeping us sealed away from everyone else. Me and Max spent a lot of time in the back of a police cruiser like we was under arrest or something. At the time I didn't mind—I wasn't really interested in talking more about it anyway, but maybe I should have told my story to the newspaper guy who was there taking pictures."

"Somebody's lying," I said again to Lionel as I hung up the phone.

"They stand by their stories, eh?"

"Stronger than ever. But why would the sheriff get the facts so wrong?"

"The question is: What doesn't the sheriff want us to know?" Lionel got up and paced. "If the report is a lie—and not just a case of getting the facts wrong, or mixed up—if it's a lie, what's Roy Miller's motive for lying?"

"To cover up the truth," I answered. "But we now know the truth. It was a suicide. Big deal. Why cover that up?"

"Maybe to protect you and the parents of the victims," Lionel suggested. "Or maybe…"

"Maybe what?"

"Maybe to keep people from asking why George Chadwick committed suicide."

"That would mean the sheriff knew the answer."

"Exactly," he smiled.

Chapter Thirty-Two

A few minutes later, Lionel and I were standing by the railroad crossing. He wanted to photograph me there to use alongside the "Miracle Baby Follow-up," as he called my article.

The air was cool and calm. Lionel, wearing his homburg and overcoat with a Nikon dangling from a wide nylon strap around his neck, walked a few dozen feet down the tracks toward the Highway 58 overpass. Every few feet he turned and took aim at me standing by the semaphore signal lights.

"Nope, that's not right," he said, squinting through the viewfinder. "Come a little closer."

I shuffled toward him, my mind preoccupied with unanswered questions.

"Lionel?"

"Yeah?" His right hand twirled the focus ring on the camera lens as he peered at me.

"Do you think I should just go to Sheriff Miller and confront him with what we know and what we suspect?"

Lionel let the camera drop so it swung from the black strap. "Absolutely not!"

"Why not?"

"It's premature. You need to dig around more first and try to come up with something concrete. To talk to Roy Miller too soon might raise his defenses so high we might never find out why he's covering up the truth about your dad's suicide."

Lionel stepped off the tracks, almost lost his balance on the loose roadbed gravel, and stutter-stepped into the tall grass next to the tracks.

"Come this way a little bit," he directed, waving me toward him.

I obeyed.

"That presumes, of course, Sheriff Miller knows why my dad did what he did," I said. "I'm still not totally convinced the sheriff knew why, or that he's the one who tried to kill me the other night."

"Oh?" Lionel seemed surprised. "What's your thinking on that?"

"First, I still think someone other than the sheriff has been following me, but I'm willing to chalk that up to raving paranoia. Look. If he'd wanted to, he could have killed me Friday night at the crossing. It was dark; we were alone. Why risk an attack on the open road? And this morning he had another opportunity to kill me. We were alone in an out-of-the-way storage room at the Sheriff's Department, but he'd been his usual helpful, jovial self—not menacing at all, really."

I paused, remembering my panic. "Okay, I'll admit I was a little spooked being trapped in there with him, but I think it's at least partly because you're the one assuming he did something sinister, when he might have covered up the cause of the accident for purely humanitarian reasons."

Lionel grunted. "Humanitarian reasons?"

"You know. Trying to spare our family the embarrassment that a ruling of suicide would bring. Believe me. I'm having enough trouble accepting that Annie killed herself. Maybe the sheriff thought murder-suicide would be too much to bear."

He sighed. "I suppose it's good you're keeping an open mind, Lark. You've got good instincts. But as Ronald Reagan used to say: 'Trust—but verify!'" Lionel shook his head. "Geez—I can't believe I'm quoting Reagan," he muttered. He fiddled with the settings on the camera, then raised it to his eye. "Move a little to your left."

***

I paid a visit to Michael Gurst, a distinguished man in his seventies, who had been the president of the bank where Dad had worked. Although retired, Gurst wore a snazzy, dark blue pinstripe suit when I interviewed him in the wood-paneled den of his palatial country home. I felt a little uncomfortable dressed like a slob in jeans, while Mr. Gurst was the epitome of distinction.

"Tell me about my parents, Mr. Gurst," I began once I'd secured his permission to tape record the interview.

At first, Gurst sat rigidly in his rocking chair and seemed preoccupied by the small recorder between us on a mahogany coffee table. He stumbled and stammered, giving curt one-line answers. So, I tried a new approach. Instead of just asking questions, I engaged him in a two-way conversation, telling him a little about myself and how I'd only recently discovered that I'd survived the accident. That seemed to work. Soon he was rocking gently and talking easily about my parents.

"Your mother was a beauty." Gurst smiled broadly, remembering. "She was charming. A delightful conversationalist. I must say, a real asset to your father's career."

"Oh? How do you mean?" I took a sip of tea from a delicate china cup.

"Your dad was rather reserved. It was your mother who was the charmer. It seemed to me to be the perfect case of opposites attract."

"Did you know them well?"

"Fairly well. My wife and I gave frequent dinner parties and George and Lila were regular guests here. Lila was delightful to talk with. She came from up North somewhere," he said, scratching the bald spot on the back of his head.

"Peshtigo," I said.

"That's right. As I remember, both of her parents were in their forties when she was born and they'd already been dead a few years when she and George met in college."

He paused, a smile on his face as he gazed at the fire crackling in the fireplace. "Yes, it's really true what they say about a good woman behind every successful man. My wife—bless her—was the same way. She died last year," he said, looking at me, tears shining in his eyes.

"I'm sorry to hear that," I said, gently. I paused until he looked ready to continue.

"So, you say my father was successful in his work?"

"Oh, my yes. He worked hard. George Chadwick was conscientious and dedicated. I had high hopes for him."

"What was he like?"

"He was shy, but once you got to know him, he could be warm and friendly. He was also very careful and attentive to detail."

"Can you describe what he was like on the day he died?"

A cloud seemed to darken Michael Gurst's face. "Something was definitely wrong," the retired bank president began. "He seemed to be a completely different man—very morose and withdrawn. Disheveled, too. Looked like he hadn't slept a wink."

"Did you say anything to him?"

"I inquired about his health. Asked him if everything was all right."

"What did he say?"

"Nothing much. He apologized. Said he thought he was coming down with the flu. He was such a conscientious man. Never took a sick day. It was early afternoon, and I insisted he take the rest of the day off. He thanked me, apologized again, and said he hoped he'd be better on Tuesday, once he'd gotten some sleep." Gurst sighed. "It was the last time I saw him alive."

***

Next, I interviewed The Rev. Harlan Bell, rector of Redeemer Episcopal Church in Pine Bluff. He was the minister who buried my parents and, as I learned from Mr. Gurst, also performed their marriage ceremony.

Rev. Bell, an energetic man in his mid-fifties, with a blond mustache and metal-framed glasses, met with me in the cramped, book-lined office of his church. He wore his priest's collar, a gray shirt, and black sport coat. He didn't want the interview recorded, and asked me not to take notes.

"I'll be able to talk more freely if you just let me tell you about your parents," he explained, as we sipped Cokes. "As a priest, I don't want to get a reputation for blabbing in the newspaper about people's personal lives."

At first, I was a little irked I couldn't use his comments in the article, but I'm glad I agreed to talk informally because I came away feeling I knew my parents better. I liked Rev. Bell. We clicked. He was plainspoken and unselfconscious. He simply told it as he saw it.

"Their relationship was doomed from the beginning," he said bluntly—and we were off. "Your father was obsessed with your mother. When I first came to this church, your dad was just out of college and was getting started at the bank. He came to see me. Sat in the chair you're sitting in, as a matter of fact. He told me that all through high school, he never dated. Girls thought he was square, he said. But then at college he met a wonderful girl he wanted to marry. Asked me if I'd perform the ceremony. I told him I wanted to meet the bride-to-be first. So he brought her by."

"What was she like?"

Rev. Bell took a sip of his Coke. "A real sweetheart. Not a raving beauty, but cute, and very friendly. As outgoing as he was reserved."

"But why do you say the relationship was doomed?"

"During the meeting, it was obvious to me your dad was crazy about her—he held her hand, put his arm around her, couldn't keep his hands off her. It was almost like Linus and his blanket. Anyway, a day or two after our meeting, Lila came to see me by herself. She was...not distraught, really, but concerned. That's the word: Concerned."

"What was bothering her?"

"She said she was having second thoughts about getting married."

"What did you tell her?"

"Nothing at first. Asked a lot of questions. Tried to scope things out."

"What did you learn?"

"I learned that she genuinely liked your dad, but just wanted time to think about it. Yet when she told that to him, she said he freaked."

"Freaked?"

"The way she described it, he came unglued. Went into an emotional tailspin. Wouldn't eat. Called her at all hours begging her to reconsider. Told her he couldn't live without her. Said he'd kill himself."

"Weird."

"That's what I told her."

"What did she say?"

"She cried. Said she couldn't break his heart, because she felt sorry for him."

"So she married him?"

"Yep. I tried to get her to listen to her heart. She said she would, but within two months, they were married."

"How come you performed the ceremony if you had such serious doubts?"

He looked me right in the eye and shook his head. "That's a good question and unfortunately, I don't have a good answer. Back then, I was still pretty inexperienced. I met with them again just before the wedding and they seemed to have worked things out, but they fooled me, Lark. Maybe they fooled themselves, too."

"And you buried them?"

He was silent for a long time. "Yep. Less than two years after I married 'em, I buried 'em." He bit his lip and his voice broke. "That was a sad day. Haven't thought about that in a long time," he said, more to himself than to me. He took another swig. You're sure bringing back the memories."

"Can you give me any insight about the accident?"

He looked at me thoughtfully, and shrugged. "Hunches, but that's all."

"Suicide?"

His eyes widened. He sat up, then leaned toward me, speaking excitedly and stabbing a finger in the air for emphasis. "That's exactly what I've always thought, but you're the first person I ever heard who said it out loud. Everybody said your dad was trying to beat the train. They didn't know what I knew about the so-called courtship of your mom—but it wasn't my place to blab about that."

"What about Grampa? What did he have to say?"

"Nuthin'."

"Not a thing?"

"Nope. It was as if he encased his heart in protective concrete so that nothing would ever hurt him. He never, ever, talked about his son again."

"Was this Gramma's reaction, too?"

"Your Grampa ran a tight ship, Lark. I couldn't get either of them to discuss the accident, to get their grief out and examine it. To my way of thinking, it's very unhealthy, but a lot of people just put a lid on their emotions and go on—even if it leads to an early grave."

I told him about my interview with Vern Strozier and how it differed with Roy Miller's account. "Why do you think the sheriff still insists the accident wasn't suicide?"

Rev. Bell shrugged. "Suicide is a heavy burden for any family to bear. I don't know, but I would guess that Roy is motivated by compassion. He probably reasoned it was bad enough that your parents were killed, why make it worse for your grandparents by saddling them with the stigma that a horrible accident like that was caused by their son's mental illness. Sometimes the truth can cause excruciating and lifelong pain. Maybe the sheriff was trying to protect them—and now you."

"But why?" I asked. "Why did my dad do it?"

The priest was silent a very long time. Finally, he shook his head, sadly. "I can't explain it, Lark. I'm not surprised that something caused him to snap. Maybe Lila's doubts were surfacing again. Maybe she wanted something as innocuous as a little space—not even a separation or a divorce. If someone's unbalanced, it doesn't take much to push them over the edge." He stroked his mustache and thought for a moment.

"I never had an inkling that anything was amiss, though. She seemed thrilled when you were born. We were even making arrangements for your baptism." He shook his head again. "Why did he do it? I don't honestly know—and probably never will."

Chapter Thirty-Three

By six Tuesday morning, I was fully awake, my mind throbbing with thoughts and questions. Before heading for home after talking with Rev. Bell, I'd gone to the office, where I transcribed the Gurst, Labelle and Strozier interviews and updated the rough draft of my article, which was due Wednesday.

It was an interesting enough piece. The "lead" was that the car-train collision appeared to be a murder-suicide, a conclusion disputed by Sheriff Miller. Soon, I would need to interview the sheriff, tell him what Harlan Bell and Vern Strozier said about my father's mental instability. That, I reasoned, would force the sheriff to explain why he had covered up the accident all these years. I presumed he would, as Rev. Bell suggested, profess a desire to spare our family more pain, and that would be it. End of story.

But what continued to gnaw at me was the unanswered question of why? Why did Dad—to use Rev. Bell's word—snap? Being mentally ill is one thing. But what is it that can cause a person to go over the edge? Already, I could see the makings of another story. It seemed to me that hiding the truth about mental illness and suicide does more harm than good. I made a note to ask Lionel if I might be able to begin researching a follow-up story on the subject.

I couldn't lie in bed any longer; I had to get going. By seven Pearlie and I were cruising down Main Street in Pine Bluff. The town was just beginning to stir. A yellow milk truck and a few pickups were the only vehicles moving on the street.

As I squinted at the orange sun rising at the far end of town, I decided to begin my day at the cemetery. As I passed beneath its wrought iron entryway, I had my choice of narrow roads that would eventually lead me to the Chadwick family plot. Usually, when the road forked, I would bear right until I came to the base of the hill containing the Chadwick graves, but on this morning, feeling the need to jog my thinking, I chose to bear left, deciding, on a whim, to try a new route.

The road—cinder trail, actually—wound among trees of oak and pine, and gravestones of polished granite. Finally, I came to the Chadwick hill and parked just off the road.

Frost was still on the grass. I tramped across the crystalline blades and up the hill to the graves, where I stood shivering for a moment with my hands stuffed into the pockets of my jeans. As I surveyed what had become a familiar scene, I paused first at the fresh mound of dirt covering Annie's grave. It hadn't yet been two weeks since she'd died—it seemed longer. I sighed. In the past few weeks, I'd come to realize how terribly desperate and alone she must have felt.

"I miss you, Annie," I breathed.

Missed her, yes. Ached to have her back? Of course. But no longer did I feel the malaise I'd felt the night she died. My Quest—my search for the truth—was like a small sprouting seedling of hope. My life was finding a purpose. For that I was grateful.

Next I edged over to the graves of Gramma and Grampa, now silent forever, just as silent as they'd been about my past when they were alive. I'm sure they'd thought I was too fragile to handle the truth about the accident. Did they suspect their son had committed suicide? Had he written them a note? Were they too ashamed talk about it? Maybe they'd been right to shelter me when I was so young, but now that I was more mature, they were gone, and I'd never be able to get answers from them about Mom and Dad.

I shook my head sadly.

Next my eyes swept over to the graves of my parents. They were becoming less mysterious to me, less distant. I felt I was beginning to get to know them better. I cried for Mom. Apparently, she was an innocent victim of what seems to have been Dad's tunnel vision. He was probably so fixated on his own pain—whatever the cause—he was oblivious to the consequences his actions would have on Mom and me.

After my own showdown with that freight train the other night, I now understood better how easy it could be to feel death is preferable to life. But what triggered the hopelessness that overwhelmed Dad?

The tall pine trees encircling the clearing at the top of the hill towered protectively over the graves. I sat down on a stone love seat sheltered by several large trees. As I sat there meditating at the graves of all the Chadwicks who had gone before me, I realized how close I'd come to duplicating Dad's act of desperation and how much I now wanted to choose life—life, with all its pain, fears, uncertainties, challenges, and epiphanies.

As I sat thinking, I heard the thump of a car door. The sound came from my right rear—on the opposite side of the hill where I'd parked Pearlie. A moment later, Mayor Reginald Lange walked into the clearing. He didn't see me as he passed because I was hidden by a tree next to my bench.

He wore a dark blue topcoat and bright red muffler. His head was uncovered, his thinning hair slicked back. The white condensation of his breath came in fierce bursts because of his hike up the hill. The mayor walked to the grave of my father and stood there a moment, oblivious to my presence, his back to me.

I watched in stunned surprise as Mayor Lange crossed himself and bowed his head. After a moment, he crossed himself again, then stood looking down at Dad's grave.

Heaving a sigh, he turned to leave, but when he saw me sitting on the bench, he stopped suddenly.

"Good morning, Mayor." I stood.

"Oh!" he said, startled. "Good morning, Miss Chadwick. I...ah...I didn't see you there." He seemed uncomfortable.

"Looking for votes Chicago-style?" I smiled.

"Heh, heh. I get it," he laughed, his mouth a tight smile. He walked toward me holding out his hand.

It was cold and limp as I gripped it. "Do you come here often?" I asked.

"Sometimes I start my day by walking in the cemetery. It's quiet and helps me put things in perspective. I find that I'm less likely to take myself too seriously if I realize I'm just passing through this life."

It occurred to me he hadn't been "walking" in the cemetery—he had driven to this grave purposefully.

"I know what you mean," I said, keeping the observation to myself. "Since I began my project, I've been coming up here regularly, too."

"How is your project going?" he asked, seemingly relieved the subject had changed.

"It's been very interesting. Not at all what I expected."

"Oh?"

"I've learned some astounding things about myself and my parents—especially my father."

"Oh really?" He paused, then plunged ahead, speaking in that fake British accent of his. "Do you mind if I ask, or is it premature for you to reveal your insights?"

"Seeing that you're here, I've got a question for you."

"Yes?" He was wary.

"Do you remember my father's mood in the days leading up to his death? Did he seem different...or troubled by anything?"

"It was a long time ago. All I can say with any certainty, Miss Chadwick, is that your father was usually a very warm, caring, shy person. But on the day he died it seemed like a veil came over him—an invisible, impenetrable shield. Quite frankly, he seemed depressed."

"Did you know him well?"

"Not as well as I would have liked. I was just coming to know and appreciate him more."

"You do know what caused the accident, don't you?" I said softly.

He thought a moment, considering his answer carefully. "I have a hunch, Miss Chadwick, that it was not an accident," he said, gravely, his eyes looking deeply into mine.

"I already know it wasn't," I responded.

"You do?" His eyebrows went up in amazement—and confusion.

"Yes."

"B-But how?"

"I've talked with one of the witnesses—the engineer of the train. He says it looked as though my father drove the car onto the tracks deliberately."

The mayor gasped.

"You didn't know?" I asked, surprised.

"No. It was just a feeling, an intuition. It hurts to know that, if it's true. The newspaper reported it was an accident and the talk around town was that your dad tried to beat the train to the crossing."

"I've heard that, too," I said, "and I'm more than a little troubled about that. The official accident report quotes the engineer as saying he thought my father was trying to race the train. But that's a direct contradiction from what the engineer told me personally."

"Racing the train doesn't sound like the George Chadwick I knew," Mayor Lange said. "He wasn't a risk-taker like that." He paused. His thumb lightly stroked his lower lip. "Very interesting," he said to himself.

"What is?"

"Roy Miller was the chief investigator that night, as I remember."

"Right. He took me out to the scene and showed me how he thought the crash happened, plus he gave me his accident report."

"Hmph." It was a dismissive harrumph.

"What made you think Dad committed suicide?" I pressed.

Mayor Lange was silent, seemingly lost in thought.

"Do you have any idea why he would deliberately drive his wife and infant daughter directly into the path of a speeding locomotive?" I persisted. "Please, if you know, you've got to tell me. The question is driving me nuts."

Reginald Lange seemed on the verge of tears.

I tried again. "Why do you think it was suicide? Being depressed is one thing, but why was he depressed? What could it be that would drive my dad to commit murder-suicide? Do you have a hunch about that?" My voice was urgent.

The mayor's face contorted as if he had just eaten an extremely sour lemon. He was quiet a long time. I could hear the *swoosh* of traffic in the distance as the people of Pine Bluff slowly began another day.

"You do know why he was depressed." I paused. "Don't you?" I added gently.

"Yes," he barely whispered.

"Is it more than a hunch?" Time seemed to stand still.

He said nothing, but the pained look on his face now seemed fixed.

"Look, Mr. Mayor. In the past week and a half I've had to face some tough truths. Believe me, nothing you could say can shock me anymore. I just need to know the truth. I can take it."

He studied my face with his sad, brown eyes—the eyes of a grief-stricken puppy.

"You do know why he killed himself, don't you?" I nudged.

He nodded slowly and sighed. "I think so."

"Will you tell me?" I breathed. "Please?"

A major battle was being waged behind his eyes. Finally, he spoke: "Very well, but not here," he said, nodding at Dad's grave. "Follow me."

Chapter Thirty-Four

Mayor Lange suddenly turned away from me and took long strides toward his car parked at the bottom of the hill.

"Where are you going?" I called after him.

"Not far. I'll drive you."

Something told me I might need my car. "That's okay. I'll follow you." I scampered down the other side of the hill, slid behind the wheel, and followed the road as it looped around the hill.

Mayor Lange was just completing a U-turn when I caught up with him. I stayed on the tail of his dark blue Chrysler sedan as it left the cemetery, then turned right onto County Road N.

As we drove, I couldn't imagine what the mayor might tell me, but I certainly didn't want to miss it.

He drove at what seemed like an extremely slow speed. We paused at the intersection of Highway 58, crossed the road and continued on County N for about five miles into the country. Finally, he made a right turn into Bluff County Park. We passed dozens of picnic sites before the mayor pulled over and stopped at the center of a dirt and cinder parking lot. The park was deserted.

We got out of our cars and walked to a cluster of picnic tables in a covered pavilion. Mayor Lange sat atop a green wooden table and rested his feet on the seat. I sat next to him. To our right was a softball field. Straight ahead stood a large stone building containing bathrooms.

"Why did you bring me here?"

"I'm going to tell you, but on one condition." His voice was firm, authoritative.

"Sure. What's that?"

"It must be understood that what I'm about to tell you is off the record."

Off the record. I'd heard the term. I wasn't sure what it meant, but I didn't like the sound of it. It sounded like he would tell me things germane to my newspaper article which I'd never be able to print.

"Wh-what's 'off the record' mean?" I asked, fearing the worst.

He exhaled in disgust as if I'd just asked the dumbest question imaginable. "It means," he said, trying to remain patient, "you cannot use my name if you print what I tell you."

That didn't sound so bad. "But I can still use the information, right?" My hopes brightened.

"That is correct. You just can't say where you got it."

"Okay. Off the record. Sure. That's fine," I shrugged, relieved.

"I want to be clear about this, Miss Chadwick." He turned his whole body and drilled me with his eyes. "I must have your word you will not use my name in connection with the information I'm about to tell you in any story you might write about your father and mother's deaths. The information is very explosive and must, I repeat: must be handled prudently and discreetly. I must have your word of honor you will not use my name. Do we understand each other?" He looked at me sternly.

"I understand, Mr. Lange," I looked into his eyes with more steadiness than I felt. "You have my word," I said solemnly and with no small amount of repressed impatience.

His gaze held mine as he seemed to scour my soul for any hint of insincerity.

"Very well," he said after an excruciatingly long pause. He looked away and spoke in a slow, precise manner as if dictating a letter. "What I am about to tell you, I have never told to another living soul. I'm only telling it to you now so you will have a better understanding of the circumstances which I believe led to the deaths of your father and mother.

I should add," he went on, turning to look at me "you might find the information personally painful. It's certainly painful for me to share it with you. And while it's difficult for me to tell you this, it's been eating away at me for more than twenty years."

His hands were clasped in front of his knees. He dug his right thumb into his left palm.

The suspense was killing me. It was all I could do to keep from jumping up, grabbing him by both lapels, shaking him and shouting "Tell me! Tell me! Tell me!" But I forced myself to be patient.

It wasn't easy.

He looked off into the distance. For a second, I feared he'd changed his mind. I decided this wasn't a good time to ask if I could tape record the conversation. Finally, he spoke.

"A week before the accident— No, let me start earlier than that," he began. "I knew your dad through my business. I was in real estate back then and he was a loan officer at the bank."

Yeah. Yeah. I know all that. Will you just get on with it?! I screamed inside my head.

"Had he lived," Mayor Lange continued, "I'm sure he one day could have become the bank's president. He was always honest, discreet, friendly, sensitive."

Right. I know this!

"Your father cared about people. I can't come up with enough adjectives to describe how much I respected him."

Don't try. Pleeeeze. Don't try!

"And I still respect him to this day, in spite of—well, I digress."

I'll say you do. Get on with it!

Reginald Lange continued with his dictation. "Anyway, I would see your father occasionally during the week, usually at the bank and at least once a week at Rotary. But my admiration was mostly from a distance.

Then, late one night—" His voice quavered. His eyes welled with tears. He took a deep breath and continued. "About three in the morning, I came here." He nodded toward the stone building.

"The bathroom?"

He nodded curtly.

"But why here? And why in the middle of the night?"

"It was summer. I was hot and restless. You see, Miss Chadwick, the park after dark was a gathering place for, um, people like me."

"People like you? I don't get it."

"Oh, dear. You are naïve, aren't you?" he said, shaking his head. "The park is where people like me came back then to find, ah . . ." he swallowed, "sex with other men."

My jaw dropped.

"I've never told anybody before," he said, massaging his eyes, "but I feel you need to know this and I feel I can trust you." He looked at me with haunted, sad eyes.

I continued to stare at him, my mouth agape.

"If this ever gets out, my political career will be ruined," he said. "Times were different back then and homosexuality wasn't as accepta-ble as it is now. Yet even now, especially in places like Pine Bluff, ho-mosexuals are still held in contempt."

I did my best to recover, trying to look stoic, but my stomach was doing flip-flops. I'd always considered myself to be a fairly open-minded, tolerant person. But that was before the issue became personal. Now, I was confused.

"What does this have to do with my father?" The question popped out of my mouth, despite my fear I was going to hear the answer—and wasn't going to like it.

"The accident happened on a Monday night. The previous Friday, as was my habit back then, I came to this park very late at night, long after the park was officially closed. I'd hang around, waiting. That night I saw the figure of a man looming in the shadows over there." He pointed to a grove of trees off to our left. "I entered the men's room and waited. A moment later, the man came in. It was your father."

"Oh no…" I said, half under my breath.

"I'll spare you the details, but it gets to the reason why I believe he took his life."

The mayor turned to look at me. "I'm sorry to have to tell you this, Miss Chadwick."

His fingers brushed my leg, a feeble attempt to be soothing.

I felt my flesh crawl.

"That's okay, sir," I lied, "I wanted to know and now you're telling me. Go on," I said. I felt like crying.

"While we were in there, somebody with a flashlight suddenly came in and pounced on us. I was able to get away without being recognized, but your father wasn't so lucky." Mayor Lange pointed to the front door. "That's the door I ran out of, scared to death, not sure what I should do. When I got outside, I crept around that side of the building."

My eyes followed the sweep of his arm as it extended along the wall in front of us.

"I stood beneath that window on the end," he continued. "It's the window to the men's room."

The closed window stood about five or six feet high. A metal grate protected the frosted, textured glass.

"The window was open that night," Mayor Lange said. "I wanted to find out what was going to happen to your father. As I crouched beneath the window, I could hear every word echoing off the tiles."

In my mind, I saw a frightened young man in his mid-twenties, cowering breathlessly beneath the bathroom window straining to listen to the voices reverberating inside.

"The person began to taunt your father. Called him vile names." The mayor's eyes were glazed as he relived that hot summer night. "'Would you look at this,' the man teased in a condescending singsong voice, 'George Chadwick is a faggot—a little fairy.'" The mayor had begun to breathe heavily. His eyes were moist. "The man toyed with your father awhile, talking about how Pine Bluff needed to be rid of scum like him."

"Did the guy hit him?" I couldn't contain myself any longer; I had to ask a question.

"No, although I was afraid he might. The torture was purely psychological. Diabolically psychological."

"What happened next?" I teetered on the edge of the picnic table, my eyes riveted on the mayor's face. He looked toward the stone outhouse, but he saw twenty-five years into the past. Although the chill of this October morning was still in the air, sweat beaded on Reginald Lange's upper lip.

"This humiliating torture went on for at least ten minutes. It seemed as though the person was trying to decide what to do with your father. Then suddenly it came to him. He said, 'You wouldn't want your wife and the rest of the community to know that you're a no-good faggot, would you, George?'

"And your Dad whimpered, 'No. No. Please. I'll do anything. Anything.'

"As I listened," the mayor continued, "the man finally said, 'there might be a way to keep your name out of the papers, and keep your wife from finding out what a degenerate you are.'

"Your father said he'd do anything, anything. He was pleading, crying. Finally his tormentor said, 'You work at the bank don't you? Responsible for a lot of money, aren't you? You wouldn't want to lose that prized position, would you?'

"'No, no,' came your father's pitiful whimpers.

"'Well, maybe there's a way out after all. Maybe you can skim some cash off the top on a regular basis. You know, appreciation payments so that I keep your dirty little secret from getting out.'

"Your father was really in a bind over that one. 'No, no, I couldn't possibly do something like that,' he said. 'It would be wrong.'

"To which the man bellowed with great glee, 'Wrong? Wrong? You have a lot of nerve to tell me what's wrong! You're the pervert who picks up other faggots in the county park men's room in the middle of the night, not me.'

"'But I might get caught. Somebody might find out,' your father pleaded.

"But the man said, 'You're creative, George. If you know what's good for you, you'll come up with a way to make it work.'

"So, as I stood listening beneath that window," the mayor said, nodding toward the building, "I was stunned and saddened as I heard your father promise to find a way to embezzle money for the sheriff...er...man."

"The SHERIFF!?" I nearly shrieked.

"Shhhh. Not so loud," Mayor Lange said, looking around, frightened.

A bright orange Bluff County Parks Department dump truck had stopped nearby.

Two county workers were rounding up trash containers and emptying the contents into the back end.

"Are you saying the sheriff, Roy Miller, was blackmailing my father?" I asked in a stentorian stage whisper.

The mayor seemed genuinely flustered. "Well, ah, I really didn't intend to reveal the sheriff's identity to you, but yes, I heard Roy Miller blackmail your father just a few days before he drove in front of that train."

"This is incredible." I shook my head, trying to comprehend the monstrous news.

"It was Roy's first term," the mayor continued. "His brother was the District Attorney. The two of them were arrogant and power-hungry back then. Roy still is, really, but he's mellowed a lot. I actually believe he's haunted by what ultimately happened."

"Have you ever talked with him about this?" My ears buzzed.

"No, he never got a good look at me that night, so he doesn't know who the other person is who was with your father, and he doesn't know that I hung around listening."

This was incredible. My adrenaline was pumping. I had a sudden urge to jump up and run to tell Lionel, but I needed to know more.

"Do you know if my dad actually gave any money to the sheriff? Did you talk to my dad about it later?" I grabbed his sleeve. "What happened next?"

The mayor pulled away, took a rumpled handkerchief out of his overcoat pocket, and blew his nose. His eyes were red and puffy.

"I didn't know what to do. I didn't know if I should let your father know that I knew. I felt so ashamed. I remember going by his office to talk about it on Monday, but he was very withdrawn, quiet. And I lost my nerve. Twelve hours later, he was dead." A tear rolled down Reginald Lange's cheek. He turned to look at me. "I'm so sorry, Miss Chadwick."

Gently, I touched his arm. "It's all right, sir. I understand."

My emotions were roiling. I was overcome with sympathy for the mayor. In less than two weeks I'd absorbed one emotional body-blow after another. Pain had become my intimate friend. Now that I recognized the same pain in someone else, all of society's taboos didn't seem to matter. The man now sitting next to me crying, for all of his authority and prestige, was just a man, a fellow human being. He, too, was coming to grips this day with some very hard truths.

As I thought those things, I continued to stroke the mayor's arm. "This is incredible," is all I could manage to whisper.

"That it is, my dear," Mayor Lange said, sadly, "that it is."

Chapter Thirty-Five

I gently rubbed the sleeve of Reginald Lange's dark blue overcoat. He was emotionally spent; I was breathing hard.

I have to get back to the office.

After a moment, I hopped off the picnic table.

"Remember your promise," Mayor Lange said sternly, but I saw the desperation in his eyes.

"Right. Off the record." I thanked him profusely for sharing what had obviously been very painful for him.

As I drove away, I saw the mayor in my rearview mirror, still sitting on the picnic table, head in his hands, his shoulders heaving violently as a fresh wave of emotion overtook him.

In the few minutes it took to zoom to the newspaper office, I turned Reginald Lange's story over in my mind. I'd resolved to follow the truth wherever it led, never expecting it would lead to a park bathroom in the dead of night. It felt like my nervous system was on Novocain.

At least I can use the information.

It was actually two bombshells: one about my father, but an even bigger one about Sheriff Roy Miller. Perhaps if I'd known my dad personally, it would have been more difficult to be willing to reveal his secret. But I felt compelled to use the mayor's story because—regardless of how unsavory—it was the root cause of the crash. Yes, it hurt to know that my father was apparently living a double life. But it hurt even more to know he'd been victimized—tormented and humiliated into doing something illegal in order to keep from being publicly shamed.

No wonder he snapped.

But Roy Miller an extortionist? I felt a sense of personal betrayal. We genuinely liked each other, or so I thought. Yet what Mayor Lange told me made sense. It would explain why the sheriff would concoct a phony police report to lead everyone away from a conclusion of suicide. He probably did his best to spread the lie by word of mouth. Of course, to be fair, I'd call the sheriff for a comment, he'd deny it and then we'd go with it.

No doubt: this had become a very compelling story.

Another realization hit me like a punch. Lionel could be right: It could have been Sheriff Miller who'd tried to run me off the road. The sheriff didn't want me digging into the cause of the crash because, if I found out it was a suicide, then I'd try to find the reason. And Roy Miller knew all too well what that reason was.

I thought back to Friday night, standing at the crossing with Sheriff Miller. I'd just told him I suspected the accident was a suicide and wanted to see the accident report. Even though we went in separate directions on Old 58 when we parted, he could have turned right when he got to the main highway instead of left toward Pine Bluff. He drives like a maniac, so he could have overtaken me easily in his souped up unmarked car, run me off the highway, then zoom down back roads to be at the police station before anyone could report the accident. He had to kill me to keep the cover-up going.

"Lionel will be ecstatic," I said out loud as I swooped into a parking place in front of the *Pine Bluff Standard*.

***

"You promised to go off the RECORD?" Lionel screamed. He was definitely not ecstatic.

He loomed over the desk where I sat, glowering at me, his face red with rage.

217

"He said I could use the information," I argued. "What's the big deal?" My ears were ringing.

"The big deal," Lionel spat out the words slowly and with great vehemence. "The big deal," he repeated, gritting his teeth, "THE... BIG...DEAL," he roared, "is that now you cannot use the information!"

"Why not?" I asked, bewildered. "He explicitly said I could. Otherwise, I never would have agreed to keep his name out of it." My voice sounded like a plaintive squeak.

Lionel heaved a sigh. "Lark, don't you get it? Think about it: Reginald Lange is twenty points behind in a race for Congress against his longtime political rival. It's the last week of the campaign. The last issue of the *Standard* before the election comes out day after tomorrow. Lange has just accused his opponent of a felony which, at least indirectly, led to the horrible and unnecessary deaths of two people and almost the death of an infant."

"Yeah...So?"

"So?" He was bellowing again. "So?" The tendons stuck out of his neck and his face flushed a shade darker.

"I'm sorry, Lionel, I don't understand why you're so upset. You're the one who wanted me to use Lange and Miller in the story. Now you're so obsessed with some little technicality that you don't care about me or my feelings." My lower lip trembled.

Do not cry, I ordered myself. *You will not cry.*

"Don't you get it?" Lionel's voice softened and he spread his arms, imploringly. "Lange's using you. It's the oldest trick in the book. He gives you all kinds of dirt about his opponent—at the eleventh hour, I might add—and then hides blithely behind anonymity."

"I thought you'd be thrilled. This is a big story," I said, weakly.

"You're right, Lark. This story is a giant, it's a monster...and we can't use it."

"But why not?" I pouted.

"What if it's not true?"

"Lionel, you should have heard him. He'd tried to keep the sheriff out of it, but his name just slipped out…inadvertently. And, for the first time in his life, Lange revealed his homosexuality."

"Right. Big deal. To you, but to nobody else. If you ever repeat the story, he'll deny it, call you a liar, maybe sue. And people will believe him. Or—and this is probably more likely—he'll revel in coming out of the closet. He's probably already booked to be on Oprah. And I'd say *Time Magazine* is about due for another 'Yep, I'm Gay' cover story like they did when Ellen DeGeneres came out on her TV show."

"But why would he tell me?"

"He…wants…to…win…the…ee-LECK-shun," Lionel said through gritted teeth.

"He probably made it all up and knew you'd be gullible enough to buy the whole story and run with it." He shouted the word gullible with all the derision he could muster.

His words stung. I was a nanosecond from bursting into tears, but I was so furious at Lionel I didn't want to give him the satisfaction of seeing me dissolve.

"But—"

"No buts. We're handcuffed. And you are the one who handcuffed us." He swore, kicked a wastebasket across the room, and began pacing.

My anger flared, too. I stood and faced him. "I truly don't understand you, Lionel. Just the other day you were convinced the sheriff was trying to kill me. Now I've come across evidence that it's probably true—evidence he tried to blackmail my father. What do you want?" I shouted.

He stopped pacing and turned to face me, his hands on his hips. "I want us to be sure we know what the facts are. We can't be sure the evidence is reliable if the person giving it to us doesn't have the guts to put his name to it. We can't run with this unless we have independent confirmation that what the mayor is telling you is true."

"And what kind of independent confirmation did you have in mind?" I sneered as I bent down to the keyboard, pounded the keys, and logged myself off the system.

"I don't know. And I don't think we're going to get it. That is, unless you can find the janitor who just happened to be cleaning out the john at three o'clock in the morning on a specific July night twenty-five years ago. Nice going, Lark."

My lower lip undulated as I stomped to the door. "I just don't get it, Lionel." My voice quavered. "You've suspected all along the sheriff is crooked. Now I've found proof, but you're too chicken to print it." I knew I sounded juvenile.

"Chicken? You think I'm chicken?" His voice boomed. "Listen to me, you little snot." He shot toward me menacingly until his face was almost in mine. "In Vietnam, I was scared to death. Guys died in my arms. And then there's Watergate. You think it's easy being on Nixon's enemies list? Enemies list…you're too young to even know what I'm talking about. Can you imagine what it's like to go up against the President of the United States, the guy who can sic the IRS, the FBI and the CIA on you all at once? Don't you dare call me chicken." He was trembling with rage.

"You're right, Lionel," I said in a steely-soft voice. "You're not a chicken. You're a bully. I can see why Holly didn't want to go into journalism."

I turned my back on him, stomped out of the newsroom and slammed the door, knowing it was one of the dumbest things I'd ever said or done.

Chapter Thirty-Six

During most of the drive to Madison, I cried and cursed myself for being so stupid.

I keep burning bridges. Why do I always fly off the handle? Why do I hurt the people I love?

As Pearlie and I turned off Route 58 and sped north on U.S. Highway 14, I began a ruthless self-examination. As nearly as I could discern it, my anger tended to burn when I felt morally superior—or hurt. Lionel's tirade had frightened and angered me. He made me feel foolish, and in my embarrassment, I'd once again lashed out at someone I loved and respected and who had cared for me—just as I'd lashed out indignantly at Dan because I believed Emily and Clarissa's gossip.

It was still unbelievable to me that Mayor Lange was purposely trying to use me to bring down Sheriff Miller. It really did seem Lange was willing to be vulnerable with me because he honestly wanted me to know the truth about Mom and Dad. And didn't Lange himself say he now thinks Roy Miller has remorse for what had happened?

Yeah, Babe, but you also thought Roy Miller was your friend.

My crying had almost stopped by the time the alabaster capitol dome came into view on the horizon. I thought over the implications of Mayor Lange's allegations about Sheriff Miller.

The sheriff was power hungry, a bigoted bully, an extortionist, and quite probably an attempted murderer. He had to be stopped. But how would I ever be able to independently confirm any of what Lange had told me? The prospects seemed bleak.

Although it was almost noon when I got home, I threw myself onto my bed and slept for five hours.

Supper was lonely: A baloney sandwich and a bowl of soup. As I ate, I sorted through the mail. It included the phone bill, a past due electric bill, and a letter from Nicholas Davis, the attorney handling Annie's estate. In the envelope, Davis enclosed a court document officially appointing me Annie's personal representative. He instructed me to take the document to the bank so I could gain access to Annie's safe deposit box.

"Gather any important papers (insurance policies, etc.) and bring them to me, so I can finalize her affairs as quickly and expeditiously as possible," Davis wrote.

I tossed the Davis letter aside. Now that I'd ruined my relationship with Lionel—and, most likely, any chance of completing my newspaper article—I decided that tomorrow I'd go to the bank and get all that boring financial stuff out of the way.

Also in the mail: the weekly bulletin from St. Stephen's. I was about to throw it into the trash, but an item caught my eye—an announcement about the parish meeting and vote on Father Dan's future. I'd forgotten about it. The blurb said the meeting was at seven o'clock… tonight.

I checked my watch. Six-forty-five.

***

So many cars were parked by the church that I had to park two blocks away and walk. There was no place to sit in the basement meeting hall, so I stood at the back of the room.

The tension was electric.

There must have been more than a hundred people crowded into the little room. Dozens of subdued conversations produced an excited buzz. Slicing through the noise was the orotund voice of Leo Manes, the

Senior Warden, a florid and pompous surgeon at University Hospital. He stood at the front of the room behind a lectern.

"All right. Let's get started. This special parish meeting is now in order." Dr. Manes waited until the room fell silent. He didn't have to wait long.

"For the record, we're here tonight to take a vote on whether or not we want our rector, Dan Houseman, to continue in his current capacity."

Clarissa Banks waved her hand aggressively from the front row. "Shouldn't someone be transcribing these proceedings?" she said, looking over her half-moon glasses.

"Yes, Clarissa, that's already been arranged," Dr. Manes smiled tolerantly. "Now, then, the question before us is a serious one, and requires sober examination."

Before turning the meeting over to Bill McKloskey, a member of the vestry who had been designated to briefly outline the case for removing Father Dan, Dr. Manes outlined the procedure to be followed. "Father Dan will be permitted to witness the vote counting," the warden concluded. "If the vote goes against Father Dan, the Junior Warden and I will immediately report the results as a recommendation to the bishop in Milwaukee. Are there any questions?"

A young man standing along a side wall and wearing a double breasted navy blue suit spoke up: "Why is it necessary to go to the bishop? We hired Father Dan; we should have the authority to fire him, too."

His comments were greeted by murmurs of approval.

"The canons say the final decision is up to the bishop," Dr. Manes answered. "The purpose of tonight's meeting is advisory—that is, to get the advice of the congregation as the most Godly way to proceed in this matter."

Father Dan and Betsy sat in the front row. He slowly shook his head when Dr. Manes, the Senior Warden, referred to the meeting as the "Godly way" to proceed.

From my position at the back of the room, I couldn't see Betsy's face. Her head was bowed.

"Now, if there are no more questions," the warden said looking around, "let's proceed. Bill?"

A distinguished white-haired man stood and walked from his place in the front row to a spot in front of the lectern. He was immaculately dressed in a dark suit, stiffly starched white shirt with gold cuff links, and an understated Burgundy paisley tie. His huge head and wavy hair reminded me of a lion. When he spoke, his voice reached to every corner of the room.

"I'll be brief," Bill McKloskey began. "Let me quickly bring you up to date with the concerns that have been brought to the attention of the vestry: On September seventeenth, the wardens were informed anonymously that the rector was spending an inordinate amount of time at the home of Anne Chadwick, a divorcée. The vestry appointed a committee to investigate and, over a period of several weeks, determined that the charge has merit. In addition, there have been numerous complaints the rector devotes too much time to outside interests and not enough to the care and feeding of his flock. The vestry has determined the complaints contain enough validity to be brought before the entire congregation where the rector would have an opportunity to be confronted with the problem and respond to the concerns. Are there any questions or comments?"

At first, there was a hush. No one seemed to know what to do or say.

"No one?" McKloskey laughed.

"Yes. I have a question." It was Father Dan. Slowly, he got to his feet. "I'd like to know how the vestry conducted its investigation." His hair was trimmed and for the first time in my memory, he wasn't wearing jeans. He wore a dark gray suit, black shirt, and white collar. The image of Father Dan the funky priest was gone, replaced by The Rev. Daniel Houseman.

For the first time, McKloskey seemed uncomfortable. "We, ah, monitored the situation," he began.

"You spied on me?" Father Dan asked evenly.

"That's one way of looking at it," McKloskey conceded, but then his tone turned combative. "Another is, we observed your actions carefully because you are accountable to us and to this congregation."

"And what, specifically, did you observe?" Father Dan asked.

McKloskey shuffled through some papers in his hands and put on a pair of reading glasses. "Over a period of four weeks, your car was observed by various members of the committee to be parked at Anne Chadwick's. This occurred on several evenings, for extended lengths of time, and at times when it is believed Ms. Chadwick was home alone."

McKloskey removed his glasses and looked sternly at Dan. The two men stood only a few feet apart.

"It has also since been noted," McKloskey continued, "that Ms. Chadwick commented to several members of the altar guild that she was interested in having an affair with you."

Father Dan reddened.

The crowd buzzed.

"Sorry to be so blunt, Father Dan, but you asked," McKloskey smiled, magnanimous in victory.

"What were you doing over there so much?" Clarissa Banks demanded.

"Yeah," chimed in a few others.

Father Dan turned to face us. It looked as though he'd been crying, but I was too far away to be certain.

Betsy continued to bow her head, in prayer, I assumed.

"As you know by events that have since transpired," he began, "Annie Chadwick was a very troubled person. I was counseling her."

"Yeah, I'll bet," someone near me muttered. The comment was followed by some murmurs and chuckles.

"What about those comments that she was trying to get you to sleep with her?" someone called out.

"I'll let my fiancée address that," Father Dan said quietly. "Honey?"

The room became still, holding its collective breath as Betsy rose and turned to face the crowd. She wore a trim two-piece dark blue suit. When she spoke, her voice was so soft I couldn't hear her.

"Louder! Can't hear you back here," shouted a balding elderly man in the back row.

Betsy tried again in a voice still barely audible. "I said—"

"Speak up," the man hollered again, harshly.

My heart went out to her.

Betsy faltered a moment and shook the hair out of her face. When she tried again, her voice sounded high and quavering.

"I'm Betsy Wells. I'm Father Dan's fiancée, a member of Grace Church downtown on the square, and a psychologist. Very early on, Dan told me he was uncomfortable counseling Anne Chadwick alone because he was concerned she was trying to initiate an affair with him. Dan asked me if I would be willing to join his meetings with her."

A young man in front of me poked the guy sitting next to him. "Did she just say they had a *ménage a trois?*"

The other man snickered.

I felt my face grow hot.

"On those occasions when Dan's car was seen at Anne's," Betsy continued bravely, "I was there with him helping counsel Ms. Chadwick."

An undertone of whispering rustled through the crowd. Leo Manes, the Senior Warden, seemed exceedingly interested in the papers on the lectern. Bill McKloskey blushed.

"Any other questions or comments?" asked Dr. Manes.

Betsy sat down.

"I have another one," Father Dan asked, standing. "What specific evidence do you have that I've been neglecting my duties here?"

McKloskey gestured grandly. "Some of the specific objections come from parishioners who wish to remain anonymous so as to not call attention to their private needs."

Father Dan continued to stand, his eyes riveted on McKloskey.

"In general," McKloskey continued, "it's been felt the time you're spending as a volunteer chaplain chasing ambulances for Dane County is taking you away from parishioners who feel they have valid pastoral concerns which are not being met. Father Vincent was very diligent about making hospital visitations and bringing communion to shut-ins. But with you, apparently, those kinds of things have a low priority."

"Well," Father Dan responded softly, "I wish I'd been made aware of those concerns."

"You were never in your office," a woman said.

"Perhaps not," Father Dan said. "I'm truly sorry if there's a perception I haven't been as available to you as you feel I should be. But if that's the case, there are more constructive ways than a public inquisition to let me know. I can't respond to your concerns if I don't know about them." His voice was slow and firm. He seemed very angry, but under incredible self-control.

Everyone in the room was quiet.

Father Dan paused, but looked intently from one person to another. When he spoke again, his tone was gentle. "I hope it's not too late to turn around this perceived pastoral deficiency on my part. But at the risk

227

of being misunderstood, let me briefly explain that one reason I help the Dane County Sheriff's Department in notification of next-of-kin cases is to possibly gain referrals to the church. Perhaps an unchurched person who's hurting might see the need for Jesus."

"And just how many new members have we picked up due to your ambulance chasing?" Bill McKloskey wanted to know.

"None that I know of," Father Dan said, lowering his head.

"Let me say something about that," I heard myself say. My voice was powerful and filled the room.

Heads swiveled in synch to look in my direction.

"Some of you may not know me—I'm Lark Chadwick, Annie's niece. She raised me after my parents were killed when I was an infant. I came tonight not sure how I'd vote." I plunged ahead, not wanting to lose my audience, my momentum—or my nerve. "Regarding his county chaplaincy, let me just say this: You call it ambulance chasing," I said, looking sharply at Bill McKloskey. "Had Father Dan not been on call the night Annie killed herself, I might not be standing here right now."

Anger had brought me this far, but now I found myself struggling to keep from losing my composure. It would be a race to finish before my emotions overwhelmed me, rendering me totally ineffective.

"I discovered Annie's body that night," I said, pausing to keep my voice from breaking as I remembered the moment when I realized Annie was gone forever. "I felt so terrible. So...alone—"

Then the tears came.

"I'm sorry," I whispered, digging into my jeans for a hanky. After dabbing at my eyes, I continued. "And I felt so angry." My voice regained some of its strength and urgency. "I was angry with myself for not having done enough to help Annie."

"Your two minutes are up, Miss Chadwick," Bill McKloskey said.

"Let her finish," the pushy, elderly man in the back row shouted.

I went on. "When I saw Annie lying there...dead," I paused, my emotions strangling me. "If Father Dan hadn't bothered to chase that ambulance—" I groped for the right words, swallowed, and tried again. "Father Dan saved me from my anger and despair and self-pity, then helped me to find a path of hope and purpose, when all I could see were bitterness and despair."

My tears flowed freely again, stinging my eyes and cheeks. "When I heard the rumors about Father Dan and Annie, I believed them and, as a result, severed my relationship with Father Dan. That was a serious mistake. I threw away my friendship with him because I closed my mind. I believed the lies, rumors, and insinuations against him." I swiped at the tears, but barreled ahead. "I see now, probably clearer than I've ever seen before, what a real man of God Dan Houseman is, and how lucky—no!—blessed we are to have both him and, pretty soon Betsy, in our midst." My eyes found Father Dan's, and I spoke directly to him. "So, I want you to know, Father Dan, I was wrong. I hope you'll forgive me. I hope you'll forgive us."

"Let's vote," bellowed the old man in the back.

Chapter Thirty-Seven

A woman sitting near me got up and let me sit in her seat. She rubbed my back as I sat weeping with my head in my hands. I didn't stop crying until a ballot was slid under my nose.

Borrowing a pencil from a person sitting next to me, I made a very dark X in front of the sentence reading, "I do NOT recommend that Father Dan be removed."

The commotion in the room crescendoed as the ballots were collected. Many people stood in small clusters, talking. A few looked in my direction. The room was too crowded to easily move about, but I saw Betsy standing alone in the front craning her neck, searching the room with a slight scowl on her face. Then she found me, broke into a big smile and gave me a thumbs up. "Thank you," she mouthed.

I nodded and tried to smile.

"That was very moving, dear," an older woman said to me. "I never realized Anne had been so troubled. Thank you for being so brave to tell us your story."

"Thanks," was all I could say.

Soon Father Dan, Bill McKloskey, and Leo Manes returned from the kitchen next to the meeting room, carrying the counted ballots. Dan's face was impassive. I couldn't tell from looking at him—or the others—which way the vote had gone. He took his seat next to Betsy. She rubbed her hand across his back and leaned her head against his shoulder.

"May I have your attention?" Dr. Manes said from the lectern. He nearly had to shout to be heard above the din.

The room quickly hushed.

"Here are the results of the balloting." He turned to write with magic marker on a large sheet of paper attached to an easel. In large capital letters he printed the words FAVOR and OPPOSE. "The number of people favoring Father Dan's removal: Fifty-seven."

A hum of excitement rippled through the crowd as he wrote the figure on the paper.

"Opposed: sixty-three."

There was a burst of applause from some people; others seemed stoic.

"The majority of voters feel that Father Dan should be allowed to remain as Rector of St. Stephen's," Dr. Manes said, with a lack of enthusiasm.

"I'd like to say something, if it's all right," Father Dan said, getting to his feet.

Dr. Manes stepped away from the lectern and Father Dan turned to face us. "I just want to say," he began, "I'm well aware many of you have a low opinion of me and the job I'm doing. I want you to know I will do whatever it takes to earn your trust. All I ask is that you keep an open mind and an open heart. I pray we can be reconciled and that you will let me know of problems so I can work to correct them. To the rest of you, especially Betsy," he nodded at his fiancée in the front row, "and to Lark there in the back," he gestured toward me, "I want you to know how much I appreciate your support. Please, let's all continue to do what we can to reach out in love toward those with whom we disagree. Thank you."

There was a smattering of applause.

"Is there a motion to adjourn?" Dr. Manes called.

The rest of the formalities were drowned out by the drone of one-hundred-twenty people shuffling toward the exits. A few people nodded at me, or gave my hand a squeeze.

One woman said into my ear, "Thanks for what you said. I changed my vote because of your little speech."

"Thanks," I managed to say.

Father Dan was surrounded by well-wishers who pumped his hand.

I felt a tug at my sleeve. It was Betsy. Her face was tear-stained, but radiant. She threw her arms around me and wept. "Thank you, Lark. Thank you."

We stood embracing for a long moment while people went around us as if we were boulders in a rushing stream.

"I wish the vote hadn't been so close," I breathed.

"I know," she said, pulling back to look at me, "but now Dan knows where things stand. He's got a seriously divided congregation, but maybe he won't be shadowboxing any more. The charges are now out in the open and he can deal with them."

"It looks like he has a lot of work ahead of him," I said.

"Yes," she agreed, "but he's good at building relationships. Now he has a fighting chance. And it's all because of you, Lark. Thank you so much."

Father Dan came up behind her as she spoke and rested his hand gently on her shoulder. "I can't thank you enough, Lark, for what you said."

"I can't apologize enough for being such a jerk, Father Dan. Will you forgive me?"

"All's forgiven." He paused. "I need your forgiveness, too, Lark."

"Oh?"

"For that peck on the cheek."

I glanced at Betsy. I expected her to show surprise, or annoyance, but she was smiling at him.

Father Dan went on, his face slightly flushed, "I told Betsy about it. She was very, um, helpful—"

"Forceful." Betsy corrected.

"Right," he said. "That's probably a better word. Clear. She was very clear in explaining to me that dispensing little kisses probably isn't the wisest way to show support and encouragement to a member of the opposite sex."

I blushed. "That's okay." I paused, then laughed.

"What's so funny?" he asked, clearly wanting to be in on my private little joke.

"I was just thinking of something. I was going to apologize to you for misinterpreting your affection."

Betsy said, "But you honestly thought he was unattached."

"Exactly," I said. I turned to Father Dan. "But I'm glad we've gotten that kiss thing out of the way."

"Me too." he said. "I meant well, but it was a dumb thing to do."

"Still, I have a lot to learn about romance," I said.

"Don't we all," Betsy laughed.

"Y'know?" I went on, turning philosophical, "I think growing up with Annie helped warp my view of men and romance."

"How so?" Father Dan asked.

"She must have been a very unhappy person. In an era when women had been putting off marriage to have careers, she squandered her future. First, she married a man who didn't love her, then wasted her life desperately throwing herself at men. You wouldn't believe some of the lowlifes she brought home from the bars."

"Those are some of the same things Betsy and I were both trying to get her to see. It's really too bad what happened to her." Father Dan shook his head sadly.

No wonder I'm still a virgin! I thought. My role models—plus fear of AIDS and other sexually transmitted diseases—had taught me to fear intimacy. With Dan, it was good to realize I actually had a desire to be close to someone else, but it was also a lesson that I still had a lot to learn about romance.

Later, over pound cake and decaf next door at the rectory, I brought Father Dan and Betsy up to date on all that had been happening, including the stunning revelation about the sheriff blackmailing my father and the argument with Lionel about going off the record. But I was careful to honor the promise I'd made to the mayor, referring to him only as a "source."

"It looks to me like the story's dead," Father Dan said sadly.

"It sure does," I said, my indignation at Lionel resurfacing.

"It's not totally unlike the situation with Dan at the church," Betsy offered. "People have been allowed to make all kinds of unsubstantiated allegations that he hasn't been able to fight easily because the accusations have been made anonymously. It's easy for people to hide in the shadows and throw stones."

"Right," Father Dan said. "If people would just be more willing to take personal responsibility for their statements, there'd be a lot more truth and justice in the world than there is now. Sounds like Lionel is a man of integrity."

"You're right, I guess. Too bad I blew it with him. I think I really burned a bridge, perhaps irreparably."

"I hope not," Father Dan said, but not with a lot of conviction.

"Me too," I said softly.

Chapter Thirty-Eight

WEDNESDAY, OCTOBER 30TH

DAY 12

The white marble lobby of the State Bank of Madison was crowded and bustling. I got to the bank, an 1880s limestone structure on Capitol Square, shortly after three in the afternoon. I'd spent the morning moping around the house on Dale Drive, putting off my planned chore of inventorying Annie's safe deposit box.

As I stood in line in the crowded lobby, my mind was on yesterday's blowup with Lionel. Several times during the morning I'd picked up the phone to call him, but hung up, unsure of what to say. I wanted to apologize, but I feared Lionel's anger.

I also wanted to know if Lionel would accept at least a watered down version of my article since it was due in only a few hours. I'd already followed his advice and revised my rough draft several times, but, fearing his derision, I felt tongue-tied at the thought of even raising the question with him. So, the longer I put off calling him, the more resigned I felt that he'd already killed the story—and would like to kill me if given half a chance.

After a ten-minute wait, I finally made it to the front of the line at the bank. A plumpish woman of about thirty waited on me. I handed her the court document appointing me Annie's personal representative. She read it carefully, and checked my driver's license before allowing me to sign in.

The woman led me into a gleaming stainless steel vault lined on all sides with metal drawers. After finding the correct drawer, she instructed me to insert my key into one of the dual locks, while she slid her key into the other. She then slid the long metal drawer from its place and led me down a short hall to a claustrophobic cubical where she left me alone.

I opened the lid of the long rectangular metal drawer, bracing myself for the mind-numbing financial mumbo jumbo of insurance policies I was about to encounter.

My mind—and heart—was still on the story I'd been working on for Lionel. I decided that if there were anything Nicholas Davis might consider relevant to the handling of Annie's estate, I'd take it with me and drop it off at his nearby law office. After that, I'd grit my teeth and call Lionel to apologize and see if something could be done to resurrect at least some of my story.

Annie Chadwick's safe deposit box contained three silver dollars from the 1920s, a long string of pearls, and a small stack of envelopes. Carefully, I made a list of the contents of the box on a page of the narrow reporter's notebook I carried.

The first envelope I inspected was a $10,000 life insurance policy naming me as the beneficiary. Beneath that one was the insurance policy for Grampa's farm. Another envelope contained the birth certificates and Social Security cards for Annie and me. The same envelope also contained the death certificates of my parents and grandparents.

The final envelope was intriguing.

It was addressed to my grandparents. I opened the flap and retrieved a two-and-a-half page, handwritten note, penned on stationery of the First Bank of Pine Bluff.

I read it, astonished:

July 25, 1977
Dear Mom and Dad,
By the time you read this, I'll be dead.

Life is closing in on me. I've done some terrible things and can no longer bear the guilt. I'm sitting here at my desk at home, trying to explain why I plan to kill myself, but the words won't come.

I feel like I'm a green shoot, struggling for the nourishment of the light, but the underbrush of my deeds is suffocating me. It's my own fault; I'm my own worst enemy.

I've just poured myself a stiff drink. Maybe that will help.

What's brought me to this? Why isn't there a better way?

Simply put, I'm being blackmailed by Roy Miller, the county sheriff. He knows what a despicable, loathsome person I am. I can't afford to have him reveal to Lila and the community what I've done, yet I can't bring myself to do what he wants me to do, which is embezzle money for him from the bank.

I can't go to the authorities, either. The District Attorney, as you know, is Roy's brother, plus there would be all the negative publicity and gossip.

Even now, I'm too ashamed to tell you the truth about who I am.

There's no other way out. If I begin to embezzle for him, I couldn't live with myself. If he reveals my secret, I would be living in a constant, torturous hell. I would be so ashamed. Lila would recoil from me in horror and disgust. Little Lark would grow up with a disgrace for a father. I would be an outcast in this town that has been home all my life.

At this point, the handwriting became more careless. Some words—false starts of sentences—were crossed out. The ink was smeared in a few places. Apparently, the liquor was having an effect.

I'm weak. I can't fight this. The only way I can do anything at all constructive is to write this note and then remove myself and my family from the face of the earth and take us to the shelter of a loving and forgiving God.

I'm afraid of dying alone.

I wish I could be more specific for you. Please know that this is the only way.

I'm sorry to have caused you this pain, but it's not your fault—it's mine. This is the right thing to do. I wish I could have found a better way, but I'm weak and afraid.

This is best.

God, forgive me.

Love,

George

P.S.

I can't decide what to do about Lark. I think I'll put her in the back seat of the car, but not strap her in. That way there's at least a chance that she'll survive the collision with the train.

If she doesn't, then it's God's will to keep our family together in that way.

If Lark survives the crash, PLEASE DO NOT EVER TELL HER WHAT I'VE DONE.

By the time I finished, tears were streaming down my face. My hands trembled. I double-checked the postmark on the envelope: July 25, 1977, 10:15 p.m., Pine Bluff, Wisconsin—less than an hour before the fatal crash.

My pulse pumped. I had to get moving. No matter how angry Lionel was, I had to let him know about what I'd found.

I rummaged through my backpack and found my cell phone, but the battery was almost out of juice. I did my best to compose myself, prayed my cell phone wouldn't die, and called Lionel at the paper.

Muriel answered on the first ring.

"Muriel? It's Lark," I panted. "I have to talk with Lionel right now." My voice echoed off the vault walls.

"I'm not sure he's too keen on talking with you right now…or perhaps for a long while, Lark." Her voice was drained of its usual warmth. "You really hurt him yesterday."

Her rebuke hit me like a slap. "I know…"

Deafening silence came from Muriel's end of the line.

"Muriel?"

"I'm here," she said without expression.

"I don't know what to say."

"Why did you say that to him, Lark?"

"He went off on me. Called me a snot. I guess I felt hurt and embarrassed, so I wanted him to hurt, too."

"It worked."

I took a deep breath and let it out through pursed lips. "I'm such an impulsive dope," I said under my breath.

"It hurt me, too," she went on, her voice quavering.

I tried to hold back my tears. "Oh, Muriel, I never meant to hurt you." It felt as though the thirty-mile chasm between us was unbridgeable. "Muriel?"

"Yes, Lark?" Her voice was tired, but gentle.

"Can you ever forgive me? Is there anything I can do to make it up to you? To both of you?" I scraped my thumbnail back and forth along the seam of my backpack...and waited.

Muriel Stone sighed. "Yes. I can forgive you. Forgetting will take a lot longer, though. I can't speak for Lionel."

"Is he there? Can I talk to him?" I asked, eagerly.

"He just came in. He's been out all morning." She lowered her voice. "He didn't sleep much last night and he looks terrible, Lark. I won't pretty this up for you—he's very angry with you right now."

"I appreciate your honesty, Muriel, but I really need to talk with him. There's been a major break in the investigation I've—*we've* been working on."

"Just a minute." It sounded like she covered the phone with her hand. Her muffled voice said something to Lionel, but I couldn't quite make out her words. After a brief silence, she spoke again to him, the tone of her voice sounding firm and insistent.

After some clumping and shuffling, Lionel's gruff voice came on the line.

Yeah?" he barked, "what is it?"

"Look, Lionel, I'm sor—"

"Skip it," he said sharply. "What d'ya have? Muriel says it's something about the investigation."

"Right. I'm calling from the bank where Annie had a safe deposit box. I'm here going through some of her stuff for her estate."

"Yeah. So?" He sounded impatient, belligerent.

"I found a note my dad wrote the day he died. It's a suicide note," I added excitedly.

"Yeah?" His voice betrayed a touch of interest. "So?"

"Lionel, he writes that Roy Miller is trying to blackmail him."

"In so many words?"

"In so many words."

"Read it to me," he ordered.

I did.

"Wow…"

"Do we have a story?" I asked, my excitement growing.

"Just a minute, let me think." There was a pause. "We might have a story," he said, slowly. "Here's what I want you to do." He sounded like the old Lionel again. "How soon can you get here?"

"Half an hour. Twenty minutes, if I hurry."

"Hurry."

"I'll be there as soon as I can." I was about to hang up, but Lionel's voice stopped me.

"Wait!" he shouted.

"I'm still here." I tingled all over and my palm felt sweaty against the plastic of the cell phone.

"Just so you know, you need to do two things before we can go with your story."

"Okay. What are they?" No matter what, I was now ready to do things his way.

"I want you to call the mayor and read him the suicide note. Better yet, show it to him. You need to convince him that he must be willing to go on the record if his story is to be told."

"But he'll never do that, it'll ruin his career," I protested, despite my resolve to do whatever Lionel wanted.

"Maybe, but it will threaten the sheriff's career, too. Tell him that. Tell him to let the voters decide. Shoot, I've had a hunch he was gay since the day I met him. Miller's the real crook in this."

"Okay. What else?"

"Make sure he doesn't insist on approving the copy ahead of time. It'll be tempting for you to want to promise him anything, but we can't give editorial control to one of the principals in the story. Also, you've got to run this past Roy and get a comment from him. He'll probably deny it, but you never know. We've got to be fair."

"Okay. What if I can't get in touch with either of them?"

"Then the paper goes to bed tonight with a gaping hole in it. You've got to track 'em both down, get Lange on the record, get a comment from Miller, and file your story before six. That's only two-and-a-half hours from now—it's when I've got to get it to the printer. Now move!"

"On my way."

Just then my cell phone died. I stuffed it and Dad's suicide note into my backpack, slammed shut the lid to the drawer, hustled it to the woman who'd helped me, and bolted from the bank.

Chapter Thirty-Nine

My mind raced as I pressed Pearlie's accelerator to the floor. So many thoughts and ideas were colliding inside my head that paying attention to the road was an afterthought.

I took some deep breaths to help calm myself and focus my thinking, but I couldn't get Dad's anguished letter out of my mind. Ruthlessly, I pushed my emotions aside and riveted my mind on telling the story. But the familiar story I'd been constructing so carefully over the past week had unraveled, with no quick way to reweave it.

"What am I going to do? What am I going to do?" I whined to Pearlie.

The interior of the car seemed to close in on me, and my breathing was so rapid I feared I might hyperventilate.

"Come on, Lark, get a hold of yourself. Think!" I took more deep breaths.

By the time Pearlie and I entered Pine Bluff, I was actually turning specific phrases in my mind. I whisked past the newspaper office and skidded into a parking place across the street from Reginald Lange's campaign office. But when I burst through the door, I discovered that neither the mayor nor Eugene, his assistant, were there. Only a gum-smacking teenaged girl stuffing envelopes.

"This is an emergency," I said breathlessly. "I need to find Mayor Lange. Do you have his schedule? Do you know where he is right now?"

"Um...like I just got here? And, like, I don't have a clue where he is?"

I dashed back to Pearlie and raced down the street to City Hall. Clutching the envelope containing Dad's suicide note in my hand, I ran into the building. I stole a furtive glance at my watch. Almost four o'clock.

"Is he here?" I wheezed as I rushed into the mayor's office.

"No, I'm sorry. He's not," the surprised secretary said. "He's campaigning in…let me see," she flipped through some papers on her desk, "…Stoughton."

"I've got to see him right away. It's critically important."

The secretary continued to shuffle. "He's got a four o'clock speech at a nursing home there, and then—"

"Which nursing home?"

"The Bethany Home on Main Street," she said.

"Thanks." I spun and headed for the door.

Fifteen minutes later, I trotted through the front door of the Bethany Home and Rehabilitation Center in Stoughton.

"Could you please tell me where Reginald Lange is speaking?" I asked the receptionist. She was a young woman, no older than I am. A vase of silk flowers sat on her dark wooden desk.

She looked blank.

"He's the Mayor of Pine Bluff. The guy running for Congress?"

A light blinked on. "Oh, him! He's in the dining room. Go to that hall and turn right," she said pointing off to her right rear. "Second door on the left."

"Thanks." I'd barely stopped walking. Momentum carried me to the hall where several old people sat like figurines in wheel chairs parked along the wall. One ancient woman with a vacant face, stringy, gray hair and glasses clutched a teddy bear to her collapsed chest.

In the dining room, about fifty people, many of them in wheel chairs, listened to the mayor's speech. Eugene leaned nonchalantly against a far wall, and nodded to me as I entered.

Reginald Lange stood in the center of the room, his back to me, giving an informal speech. He wore a gray suit. A television cameraman stood in front of him, a bright spotlight mounted above the lens.

Impatiently, I glanced at my watch. Four-thirty-five.

The mayor wrapped up his speech and began shaking hands, pausing every so often to say a few words to someone.

The television camera, trailed by a big-haired blonde reporter, dogged his every step. She wore a bright red ankle-length coat and carried a slender reporter's notebook.

I caught the mayor's eye.

"Good afternoon, Miss Chadwick," he smiled and shook my hand. "Good to see you."

I'd never seen him quite this friendly.

"Mayor, I have to talk to you right now. It's of critical importance," I whispered.

"Sure. In just a minute," he said as he resumed his schmoozing. My blood pressure ratcheted up a notch. The crowd—and the TV camera—seemed to invigorate him.

Big Hair sidled up to Lange. "Mayor? Mind if I ask you a few questions?" she smiled, alluringly.

"Sure, Ashley. Be glad to," he said.

I thought I would have a stroke. I maneuvered myself between her and the mayor and leaned close to his face. "I'm on a very tight deadline," I said, "and I think you know just how important it is that we talk privately—and right now."

His eyes widened as if he was the deer and I was the Mack truck.

I turned to Big Hair. "I'll have him back to you before your guy is finished setting up lights." I nodded at her photographer who was busy rummaging through his light case.

Lange turned to a gray-suited woman hovering at his elbow. She wore black-rimmed glasses and her hair in a bun. The badge she wore identified her as Nursing Home Administrator. She reminded me of a stern librarian.

"Is there a place we can go to have some privacy, Jane?"

"Certainly. You can use my office. Come this way," Jane said, briskly leading us down the hall, past the receptionist, and into a cramped office.

"Now, what's so important?" Mayor Lange asked as I closed the door. He stood facing me with his arms crossed as we stood toe to toe in front of Jane's polished desk.

I breathed a quick prayer and plunged ahead. "First, let me say I appreciate how difficult it was for you to tell me the real story of why you think my Dad killed Mom and himself."

"And I appreciate your willingness to keep my name out of the story, Miss Chadwick," he said, his eyes lasering mine.

"That's why I'm here, sir," I said, lowering my eyes for an instant. "Lionel says I can't use any of the information."

"Oh?" he seemed surprised, but I couldn't tell if he was perturbed… or relieved. "Why not?"

Be diplomatic, I ordered myself. *For once in your life, be patient and diplomatic.*

My fingers felt moist as I clutched the envelope containing Dad's suicide note. "Lionel insists that, as a matter of integrity, we not print allegations that are this serious without independent verification of your information."

"I see," he said, stroking his chin. "Which means, you have no story, is that right?"

"Until an hour ago, yes, that's true, but I've made an important discovery I want you to see." I handed him the envelope.

He reached for it warily, as if I were handing him a letter bomb. Delicately, he plucked it from my hand and pulled his reading glasses from the breast pocket of his suit. First he inspected the envelope, then removed the letter. Slowly, his eyes scanned the pages. As he read, he eased himself into a half-sitting position against the administrator's desk. Every now and then a nearly imperceptible guttural noise, almost a grunt, escaped from his throat. Finally, he took off his glasses and tucked them away in his jacket as he handed the letter and the envelope back to me.

"So, why show it to me? It seems you now have your independent verification."

"I have one source—a critically important one—but it's not enough. It doesn't explain the reason for the blackmail."

The mayor said nothing. He waited.

I waited.

Mayor Lange broke the silence. "So?"

"So...in order to tell the story fairly and completely, without distortion, I'm here to ask you if you'll reconsider. Will you allow me to use your name in connection with the information you gave me yesterday?"

The mayor slid off his perch on the desk and ambled to the window. He thrust his hands in his pockets and stood with his back to me looking outside, saying nothing.

A grandfather clock ticked loudly in the corner.

Finally, he spoke: "And what will you do if I refuse to go on the record?" He swung around to look at me, hands on his hips.

I cringed inwardly, wishing he hadn't put me on the spot like that. *What should I say?*

"Then, the truth won't be known and justice won't be done," I said softly.

"Maybe that's just as well," he said, matching my tone.

"I don't think so." My voice gained strength as I put into words the intense feelings crystallizing inside me in the past few days. "I know that's what my dad thought. It's what my grandparents thought. And it's apparently what Annie thought. But my whole life has been lived in the shadow of a lie.

"But during these past several days, people like you have helped me to shine a light on my past. Now I have a better understanding of my history and myself. I can't say I know what it all means yet, but I feel engaged with life as the truth pokes me and prods me to make something of my life. I—"

"That's all very admirable, Miss Chadwick, but I'm not sure you understand what my going on the record would mean."

"Oh, I do—"

"As for me: I've known the truth about myself for a very long time. For years I hated myself; tried to change myself." He leaned closer to me. "Do you realize how painful it is to have people tell you faggot jokes, not realizing that unwittingly they're revealing their contempt?" The veins in his neck bulged as he spoke with great passion, yet all the while his voice was a low hiss.

"Don't you understand, Miss Chadwick, the truth is people despise people like me? You talk about truth as liberating. I see truth as my death sentence."

"But if you go public it really gives you the moral high ground."

He rocked back on his heels. "Oh? How so?"

"You would be labeling the sheriff as a blackmailer whose brutish ways led to a murder-suicide. By going public it would show that you are willing to risk your reputation to bring out the truth about the sheriff. You really don't believe he's morally fit to be in Congress, do you?"

"Of course not. But by telling the truth about myself, a lot of people would say I'm not morally fit for the office, either."

"Let the voters decide. Don't you remember? Steve Gunderson is gay and he was a Congressman from Wisconsin."

"Yes, but none of his constituents knew he was gay until long after he'd been in office. Then, once he was publicly identified—against his will, I might add—he didn't run again," the mayor shot back.

I refused to give up. "My hunch is the voters'll decide that what Roy Miller did to my father was much worse than anything you've done."

There was a knock on the door. Eugene pushed it open. "Sir, we need to go. We're thirty minutes behind schedule."

"Okay, Eugene. Coming," the mayor called.

Eugene backed away and closed the door.

"All right, Miss Chadwick. Let me think about what you've said. When do you need to know?"

I looked at my watch. Five after five—less than an hour to get back to Pine Bluff, write my story, track down the sheriff for his reaction, and give the finished piece to Lionel for him to edit and take to the printer.

"I need to know right now, sir."

Chapter Forty

Reginald Lange's smile fell. "Why now?"

"Because," I explained, "the deadline for the paper is six o'clock, less than an hour from now. The paper comes out tomorrow."

He walked past me toward the door, his face was dark and brooding. At the door he put his hand on the knob and turned to look at me. "I want to see the story before you print it," he said.

My heart sank as I shook my head sadly.

"I can't do that. You have my word it will be accurate, factual, and fair. Lionel Stone—a former Pulitzer Prize winner and *New York Times* Editor—will have the final say, Mayor, not anyone who's a principal in the story."

Reginald Lange sighed, bit his lip, and shook his head slowly from side to side.

I felt like crying. He'd made up his mind and his answer was no.

"You know," he said softly as he studied the design in the Oriental rug in the center of the room, "ever since I was a teenager, I've been living a lie. I was terrified that the truth would come out, that I'd be found out. But I've made an interesting discovery in the last day or so, Miss Chadwick."

His study of the Oriental rug pattern completed, he looked up at me and smiled serenely, a man at peace with his decision. "I took a chance with you. I told you about the real me. I knew what would happen if I went on the record: a lot of people would turn on me…reject me…hate me…whatever. And maybe others would do just the opposite. They'd want to co-opt me…use me as the poster boy for their own political agenda."

He looked down and shuffled his feet. "I'm ashamed of myself, Miss Chadwick. Ashamed because I didn't blow the whistle on Roy Miller when it could have saved the lives of your parents, or blown the whistle on Roy right after the accident. It seems that for my whole life I've been cowering in a safe cocoon of falsehoods."

He looked sad, deflated.

I felt guilty, responsible for wrecking this man's self-esteem while I so single-mindedly pursued my selfish Quest. I was about to walk out the door in quiet defeat when Reginald Lange said one more thing:

"But that's not all you've helped me to discover, Miss Chadwick."

I looked up, confused.

"I trusted you with the truth and you treated me with respect, honesty, and integrity. I feel stronger inside now. By telling the truth, I'm not afraid of the truth anymore. So, Miss Chadwick: Go for it and we'll see what happens."

I had to shake my head to make sure I'd heard him correctly. The pent up pressure from deep inside me escaped all at once in a huge whoosh of expelled air. I ran to him and gave him a big hug.

"Thank you, sir. I'll do my best to—"

"Now stop blubbering, Lark," he laughed, his hand awkwardly on my shoulder. "You've got a deadline to meet and I've got an election to win."

I dashed from the room—past Eugene waiting in the hall, standing next to Ashley, who seemed perturbed I'd dominated the mayor's time, not realizing the big story she'd just missed—that is, if I could get back to Pine Bluff in time to write it.

Chapter Forty-One

It was five-thirty-two when I banged through the front door of the *Standard*.

"Where have you been?" Lionel bellowed from where he sat at his desk across the room. Muriel was talking on the phone.

"I just got the mayor to agree to change his mind. He'll go on the record," I shouted excitedly.

"Outstanding! Now get writing." He shooed me over to a computer, where I sat with my coat still on as Lionel paced the floor behind me.

I sat scowling at the blank screen, my toes touching the floor, heels elevated, nervous energy causing my heels to bounce.

"Come on, come on," I goaded myself. I bit my lip. Panic tightened my stomach.

Things had seemed to flow so easily when I was driving in Pearlie, but now my mind was as blank as the screen.

"Just relax," Lionel coaxed.

"I know, I know. Don't read over my shoulder," I snapped.

"I can't. There's nothing to read," he muttered. He was about to turn into the on-deadline bear he'd been the day I met him.

The blank screen and I continued to stare at each other.

"You need to write something, Lark," Lionel said impatiently, but then, seeming to sense my panic, his voice took on the urging of a boxing coach. "Just get something down in writing. Anything. We can fiddle with it once we have something to rework. Loosen up," he said with a forced calm. "Just tell the story. Let the words flow. Don't feel like it's got to be perfect the first time."

"Good advice. Okay, just a second." Tentatively my fingers roved the keys, gradually gaining speed.

> At about 10:50 p.m. on a hot July
> night 25 years ago, an Amtrak passen-
> ger train slammed into the side of
> George Chadwick's 1968 Mustang at a
> crossing just outside Pine Bluff.
>
> Chadwick, 26, a local banker, and
> his wife, Lila, 24, were killed in-
> stantly.
>
> Their infant daughter survived the
> crash. Her rescuers called her "The
> Miracle Baby."
>
> They were referring to me.

Not great, but it's a start.

I decided to keep going. As Lionel said, I could go back later and clean things up. My feet bounced at a frantic pace as my fingers made the keys clatter.

Lionel continued to pace behind me. From time to time, the pacing paused as I sensed him peering over my shoulder at the screen, satisfying himself that something resembling English was actually being written.

Gradually the story took shape as I cut and pasted quotes from the various conversations I'd had over the past week. But then I hit a brick wall.

"Oh, no!" I exclaimed.

"What's the matter?" Lionel came running from across the room.

"I've still got to get a reaction from the sheriff," I whined, glancing at my watch.

Five-fifty.

"Right. Finish the story first, read it to him over the phone, then drop his reaction into the piece."

"Could you try to track him down? He might be in the middle of Timbuktu campaigning somewhere."

"Okay. You keep working. I'll try to find out where he is."

Lionel picked up a phone and stabbed the buttons.

Another phone rang; Muriel picked it up.

I tried to shut the newsroom din out of my mind as I turned my attention to the story unfolding on my computer screen. My heels bounced as my fingers pounded the keys.

"How you doing on finding the sheriff, Lionel?"

He motioned me to be quiet and continued speaking urgently into the phone.

"Right. We're breaking a story in the *Standard* tomorrow about him and I need to talk with him for a reaction. Right. Just a minute." He put his hand over the phone.

"How soon you gonna be done, Lark?"

"Just about done. Few more minutes. You got him?"

"Yeah. He's at a town hall meeting in Mount Horeb. It starts in the next few minutes. If we don't get him now, you'll have to wait at least two hours."

"Is he on the line?"

"No, but he's in sight of the aide I'm talking to on a cell phone."

"Okay. Just a sec. Almost done. Just keep him on the line."

I returned my attention to the computer screen.

Nothing would come. I skimmed what I'd written, hoping to regain my momentum.

"Oh, how stupid," I said. I'd almost forgotten to insert quotes from Dad's suicide note. Quickly, I typed them in.

"Okay, Lionel. I'm ready to talk to him. I'm going to read him what I have and get his reaction."

"I've got the tape recorder set up." Then Lionel barked into the phone. "Melvin? You there?" He paused to listen. "Nuts!" Lionel said to me, "he's just getting ready to speak." Back to the phone: "Is he on stage yet? No? Put him on." Lionel thrust the phone at me. "Here," he said. "He's all yours."

I put the phone to my ear. "Hello, sheriff?"

No answer.

"Sher—"

"Hello?"

"Sheriff Miller?"

"Yes."

"Lark Chadwick."

"Hi, Lark. I've only got a second. What's up?"

"Sir, I know you have to begin your meeting in just a minute, but I'm writing the story about the accident for tomorrow's paper and I have to get your reaction. I'm tape recording the call so I'm sure to quote you accurately. Okay?"

"Fire away," he said jauntily.

I read him the story right from the top. As I read him the mayor's account of what happened that night in the men's room of the park, Sheriff Miller muttered under his breath, "why that little weasel..."

I continued to read until I reached the last paragraph about contacting him in Mount Horeb.

"Your reaction, sir?"

"Are you going to print that crap?" he spat in a stage whisper.

"Uh, yes, sir. What's your reaction?"

"He's lying. He's desperate," Miller fumed.

Had Roy Miller not been surrounded by a roomful of voters, I'm sure he would have treated me to a blistering burst of profanity.

"He's so desperate, that at the eleventh hour he concocts something so incredibly outrageous that it would be laughable if it wasn't so libelous."

"Are you denying you attempted to use your position as county sheriff to extort money from my father after catching him committing a homosexual act?" I spoke as rapidly as I could for fear Miller would abruptly hang up.

"You catch on real fast, Lark," the sheriff roared, "Of course I'm denying it. It's a bunch of crap. Let's see you print that in Lionel Stone's rag."

"And do you have a comment about my father's suicide note?"

There was no answer. The line was dead.

I hung up the phone and began to type.

"What'd he say?" Lionel asked.

"Can I use the term 'crap' in the paper?"

"Is that what he said?"

"Yup."

"Go for it."

Contacted Wednesday night at a campaign function in Mount Horeb, Sheriff Miller vigorously denied Mayor Lange's account, calling it "crap" and referring to his opponent as a "little weasel."

Miller accused Lange of a "desperate" eleventh-hour tactic to win the upcoming Congressional election.

Sheriff Miller made no comment about
the suicide note.

"Okay, Lionel. Where do I go from here?"

He stood behind me, barking orders. "Go to the top and scroll down."

I obeyed.

He read out loud in a sort of stage whisper.

"Lemme sit there," he said, nudging me aside. Skillfully, his hands fingered the keys. He changed a word here and there, but did little wholesale editing.

"Good," he'd say now and then as he read, nodding occasionally.

He made several changes, mostly spelling corrections. A couple of times smoothing out the syntax.

"I think you've got it, Lark," he said, dragging and dropping my piece to another file. "You ended it just right." He grabbed his coat. "Gotta get to the printer."

At the door he paused with his hand on the doorknob and looked back at me.

"Good job," he said.

Before I could respond, he was gone.

Chapter Forty-Two

After Lionel dashed out the door to take my story to the printer, I slumped forward, my throbbing head in my hands.

"How are you feeling?" It was Muriel. She pulled up a chair and sat next to me.

She wore a fuchsia turtleneck beneath a light blue corduroy shirt, and tan twill slacks.

"Shot," I groaned.

"Lionel will be up half the night putting the finishing touches on the paper," she said. "Come on over. I'll fix you some supper."

Mechanically, I got up and followed her out the door.

Later, after a simple meal of chicken potpies, we sat by the fire in her living room. Dinner had been a very quiet affair—Muriel hadn't said much and I didn't know what to say.

"Muriel?" I said, breaking the silence.

"Yes, Lark?"

"You're being so nice to me. Does this mean you're giving me a second chance?" I shot her a shy glance.

"I think it does, yes," she smiled, pouring me a cup of tea and then one for herself.

"But what about Li—"

"Oh, he'll come around. In fact, I think he already has—I watched the two of you work together." Her voice caught.

She put the delicate pot on the coffee table and placed a tea cozy over it to keep it warm. When she recovered her composure, she spoke again.

"Lionel can be stubborn, but he doesn't hold grudges. You've been under tremendous pressure, dear." She sat back in her easy chair, saucer in one hand, and brought the cup to her lips.

I stared into the fire, grateful for second chances...and for love.

The yellow and orange flames were mesmerizing as they danced and flickered. My mind wandered.

"So much has happened to you in less than two short weeks, Lark. What have you learned?" Muriel asked, softly.

I looked at her, not sure what to say.

She smiled her dazzling smile. "I'm in my teacher mode, but don't worry—there won't be a test at the end of the evening." She paused. "What have you learned?"

"Hmmm. That's a tough one. Let's see . . ." I counted on my fingers. "There's Annie's death...researching the article...the showdown on the tracks with the train...the attack by the stranger on the highway...the move to oust Father Dan...I guess I've learned a lot."

"But out of all those experiences, what's the most important lesson you've learned?" Her prodding was gently relentless.

If I hadn't been so exhausted, perhaps my guard would have been up; perhaps I would've resented her question as intrusive. But all my defenses were leveled. And, because they were, it all seemed to click into place. There was a feeling of accomplishment brought on simply by relaxing and looking at the problem in a new, less frantic way.

"If I had to narrow it down to just a few words," I began, "it would be that getting into arguments and running away solve nothing, and usually make things worse. Facing life—no matter how frightening or unsavory it might be—is far better than fleeing from it."

Muriel nodded. "Interesting you would say that."

"Oh? How come?"

"I've seen fight and flight tendencies in you. It's good you've come to that realization on your own." She paused long enough to take a sip of tea. "Now, how have you changed?"

I laughed. "You're a good teacher. You're making me think. I wish I'd had you in high school." I stalled for time. "How have I changed? That's harder to answer. I don't think I can be objective about that, Muriel. What do you think? Have you noticed any changes?"

"Turning the tables on me, eh?"

I giggled.

"Yes, I have seen some, but I first want to hear what you think." She leaned forward and rested her chin in her hand. Her gaze looked serene and patient in the shimmering light.

I sighed. "I've come to appreciate second chances," I said slowly, squinting at the fire, "and forgiveness."

"Forgiveness?"

"Mmm hmmm. I've said and done some pretty stupid things, but Father Dan and you and Lionel never gave up on me—even though you all should have. It's simply amazing."

"I think you're becoming a stronger person, Lark. More mature, and definitely more purposeful." She held up the teapot. "More tea?"

"A little. Thanks."

She splooshed some of the golden liquid into a cup I held out to her. "I feel really good learning the truth about Mom and Dad," I said.

Muriel poured herself a refill. "By writing the story, you've brought an injustice into the open. That's very important." She put the cozy over the teapot again. "Maybe it'll be the first step toward reversing that injustice."

I leaned toward my steaming cup and inhaled. It smelled pungent, exotic.

Muriel took a sip. "That must be very satisfying."

"Yes, it is. But not knowing what the public's reaction will be is a little spooky."

"Oh?"

"It's sort of like the thrill you feel in your stomach when you're at the pinnacle of a tall roller coaster just as the downward plunge is about to begin."

Muriel chuckled, knowingly.

"I wonder . . ." I said, my mind idling.

"You wonder what?" Muriel asked, putting her cup into the saucer and placing them on the coffee table.

"I wonder what will happen now."

"Tomorrow your article will be the talk of the town."

"Right. But I wonder what effect it will have on the mayor and the sheriff."

"Those kinds of things are always hard to predict, but you can be sure Lionel will be watching, because that's where the next big story will be coming from."

"What do you suppose the sheriff will do?" I took a sip. It warmed my insides all the way down.

"He's the wild card, isn't he?" She stood and walked to the fireplace and laid another log on the fire. "What do you think?"

"I think…" I tried to envision the possibilities. "Actually, I don't know what I think."

I watched as Muriel stoked the fire with a metal poker. Brilliant sparks crackled, escaping up the chimney. The flames blazed higher and brighter.

Suddenly, in spite of the warmth from the fire, a chill crept over me.

"Come to think of it," I said with a shudder, "my life might be in more danger now than it ever was."

Chapter Forty-Three

The newspaper felt crisp and new in my trembling fingers. I let my eyes linger on the black ink spelling out "by Lark Chadwick" on the front page. My first byline. I was thrilled.

"That ought to attract some attention, Lionel," I said, slapping my hand across the banner headline:

MAYOR IMPLICATES SHERIFF IN FATAL CAR-TRAIN CRASH

Lionel grunted and slowly stirred his coffee. He seemed engrossed in thought. Or was he just eavesdropping on the hushed conversations going on around us? We sat next to each other on revolving stools at the counter, which ran almost the entire length of The Korner Café's left wall.

My story took up most of the front page. Below the banner headline were official head-and-shoulder pictures of Roy Miller and Reginald Lange, and below those was the 1977 picture of a much younger Roy Miller peering into the wreckage of my parents' smashed auto.

The story ended on the next page, adjacent to the picture Lionel had taken of me at the crossing as we discussed whether to confront Sheriff Miller with what we knew so far. The caption read, "At the scene of the crash, Lark Chadwick contemplates the accident she survived, but which killed her parents 25 years ago."

It was a flattering picture—windblown hair, dark eyes, confident chin. It was a fairly tight shot of me, with the crossing signal and tracks slightly out of focus in the background. Lionel had snapped the shutter as I'd looked pensively toward the field where I'd been found crying in my car seat.

Looking at myself in the newspaper, I was struck by how purposeful I appeared—much different from the malaise I'd felt nearly two weeks earlier as I left work, needing to talk with Annie.

At Muriel's urging, I'd spent the night at the Stones', then, this morning, I'd accepted Lionel's invitation to join him for breakfast at The Korner Café so we could gauge local reaction to the piece. The place was full when we got there about seven-thirty.

The sun was just coming up. Condensation on the front window clouded the view of Main Street. Although the restaurant was crowded, it was quieter than usual. Many people were reading the paper. Others talked quietly.

A few minutes after we arrived, people who'd already read the story came up to us one by one to talk. Lionel introduced them to me. Called me "the gutsy little writer who got to the bottom of it."

"You done real good, girlie girl," said a man who looked to be in his seventies with a face full of gray stubble and a mouth almost devoid of front teeth.

Our waitress, Millie Korner, interrupted with what I considered to be ominous advice: "Watch your backside, honey. No telling what Roy might do to get even."

"What do you think about that?" I asked Lionel when Millie took her coffee pot on a tour of the room.

"About the sheriff getting even?"

"Yeah."

The spoon clinked against the coffee mug as Lionel stirred his muddy brew. "I would think it's actually less likely to happen now that the story's out. To be sure, he's probably really upset, but now he knows everybody'll be watching. He also knows that if anything happens to you, he'll be the first one under suspicion." He blew the steam away from the surface of the coffee and took a tentative sip. "Roy could handle this a couple different ways."

"Like how?"

"The most extreme, of course, would be for him to come in here with a shotgun and blast away." Lionel looked teasingly over his glasses at me and smirked.

"Oh, that's a comforting thought." I made a face.

"I don't really think he'll go berserk," Lionel added quickly when he saw I thought his comment was neither far-fetched nor funny. "He's a pretty outgoing guy, Lark, not some sort of brooding recluse with no social skills." He set his spoon down. It clattered against the counter top. "I'm sure Roy's reaction will be more subtle."

"Oh?"

"If I were him, I'd realize I have a huge public relations problem on my hands. After I put the paper to bed last night, I sent your article to my old pals at the Associated Press in Madison. By now it's on the wire. Radio stations all over the state are probably running it. By the end of the day it'll be on television in Madison, Milwaukee, La Crosse, Green Bay, Eau Claire—all over. By the end of the weekend, voters will begin to reassess their decision. I'll bet this place will be crawling with camera crews and all kinds of reporters from Madison before the end of the day, maybe even by noon. Probably some Milwaukee press, too. This is a monster story, Lark."

Lionel was in full analysis mode, talking rapidly. "My guess is the statute of limitations has run out and Roy's legally in the clear. That is, unless we can prove he tried to run you off the road." Lionel turned to me again. "Attempted murder is a charge he might be sweating, assuming he thinks you suspect he's the bad guy who tried to do you in."

"We could check the front bumper of the car he was driving that night to see if there's any of Pearlie's yellow paint on it," I suggested.

"Good idea." Lionel pulled a ballpoint pen out of the breast pocket of his starched white shirt and made some scribbles in a small notebook he pulled from his back pocket.

My index finger traced imaginary doodles on the counter.

"Look at it this way, Lark," Lionel said. "You might have just done the sheriff the greatest favor of his life. Now he has the chance to face himself and maybe straighten out his life. Sort of like how Chuck Colson—Nixon's hatchet man—did after Watergate. He started a prison ministry. It never would have happened if Watergate had gone unreported."

The bell above the door jingled and I turned to see a handsome twenty-something young man walk in. He looked fresh out of an Eddie Bauer catalogue: clean-shaven, blond hair, blue eyes—outdoorsy. He wore a dark blue down jacket, jeans and hiking boots, and was accompanied by a scruffy man of about thirty carrying a TV camera.

They said something to Millie who stood near the door. She pointed to Lionel and me at the counter.

"Uh oh, Lionel," I said tugging at his sleeve. "It looks like we're beginning to see the first fruits of that wire story."

As Lionel turned to look, the man walked to Lionel and introduced himself. "Mr. Stone?"

"That's right," Lionel said, turning his stool a quarter turn to the left so he could face the visitor.

"I'm Jason Jordan with Channel 15 in Madison," he said, extending his hand to Lionel.

As they shook hands, I noticed Jason didn't introduce his cameraman who was also standing next to him, holding his camera at his side like a suitcase.

"We saw the story on the AP wire this morning about the sheriff and mayor," Jason Jordan continued, "and we wondered if we could get an interview with the reporter who wrote the story."

"She's sitting right here," Lionel said gesturing to me. "Why don't you ask her?"

I felt like sinking through the floor.

As Jason turned to look at me, our attention was diverted when the bell above the door tinkled again.

In the doorway, surveying the room, was the scowling hulk of Sheriff Roy Miller.

He wore a blue Milwaukee Brewers baseball cap, a blaze orange hunting vest over a tattered and faded red flannel shirt, baggy coveralls, and scuffed boots. He hadn't shaved and looked terrible, as if he'd been up all night.

Everyone stopped talking. The silence was broken only by the sizzle of eggs on the grill.

Roy looked sternly from face to face. Then he saw me and drilled me with his eyes.

"There you are," he bellowed.

I gasped and leaned back against Lionel as Roy stalked toward me.

Jason Jordan nudged his cameraman, who swiftly brought the camera to his shoulder, pointed it at Roy, and squinted through the viewfinder.

"Now, Roy…" Lionel began to say.

"You shut up, Lionel," Roy shouted. "This is between me and Lark." He didn't take his eyes off mine. His wild stare was frightening.

"No, it's between you and me," Lionel said, getting up from his stool and standing between us. "You leave her alone."

"And you," Roy said, grabbing Lionel by the shoulder, "get out of my way!"

Roy shoved Lionel as hard as he could into a table.

"Lionel!" I cried, jumping to my feet.

The table tipped over sending Lionel sprawling into a heap of broken dishes and spilled food.

"And you," Roy said, roughly grabbing a fistful of the back of my shirt collar, "are coming with me."

He held me so tightly with his massive hand that I could barely breathe. With his free hand, he reached beneath his hunting vest and produced the biggest handgun I'd ever seen.

He jammed the bore against my temple.

Chapter Forty-Four

Several people fell to the floor. Others, including Jason Jordan and his cameraman, backed away from us. I felt as if everyone had deserted me. Everyone, that is, except Roy Miller, and he, of course, was the last person I wanted to be close to just then.

Breathing heavily, he continued to hold me tightly by the shirt collar and looked fiercely around the room. His breath stank of stale beer. No longer the Jovial Giant, he'd become the Menacing Monster.

"C'mon," Roy growled in my ear and tugged me so hard toward the door that I stumbled. He merely tightened his grip and lifted me onto my feet as if I weighed almost nothing. The front of my shirt nearly strangled me until my top button popped off and bounced onto the tile floor. My legs were rubbery. I felt like I was going to throw up.

"Don't do this, Roy," Lionel shouted, struggling to his feet as we reached the door. Lionel's hair was mussed and his white shirt was blotched with coffee and a colorful palette of other food stains. He rubbed his left arm, which made me fear he might be having the beginnings of a third heart attack.

Roy didn't answer, but turned to look over his shoulder, making sure no one was going to threaten him. Everyone kept a respectful distance. Roy continued to press the gun against my head with his right hand as he held me by the collar with his left.

"Open the door," he ordered.

I hesitated.

"Open it!" He shook me. I flopped like a rag doll.

I decided this was not the best time to be impulsively rebellious. I pulled open the door. The bell above it tinkled merrily.

He shoved me ahead of him down two cement steps, and across the sidewalk past a few alarmed pedestrians. A rugged red pickup truck was parked haphazardly at the curb in front of Jason Jordan's white Bronco with the NBC logo emblazoned on the side. Roy nudged me between the two vehicles and around to the driver's side of the large pickup.

"Get in," he commanded, mashing me against the door.

I fumbled with the handle.

"Hurry up!" he shouted.

The door creaked open sluggishly.

"Slide all the way over," he said, pushing hard.

I stepped up and into the cab. For a split second, I thought about sashaying all the way across the front seat and out the other side, but as I slid along the seat's smooth vinyl, I turned to look at the gun. The gaping hole where a bullet would come out was an eloquent argument against doing anything foolish.

The keys were in the ignition. Roy put the gun in his left hand, started the truck, and squealed a U-turn in the middle of Main Street. Cars screeched to a stop and honked.

"Wh-where are you taking me?" I tried to sound brave, but my voice trembled.

"Shut up, just shut up," he snapped.

I could see he was right on the edge, so I decided to back off and give us both room to settle down.

Be calm, I told myself. *Be calm.*

I turned to look behind us and caught a glimpse of Lionel, Jason Jordan, and the cameraman piling out of The Korner Café and scrambling into the white Bronco.

Steering with his right hand, Roy threaded his way around traffic as we careened west on Main Street. The gun in his other hand was still pointing in my general direction.

For a moment I considered opening the passenger door and rolling out, but we were going too fast.

My heart was going fast, too. I tried to take deep, slow breaths.

What can I say to talk some sense into him? What can I say?

"Look, sheriff. I know you're upset." As soon as I said it I realized how stupid it sounded.

He looked at me with bloodshot eyes and gave me his best Valley Girl imitation: "Duh!"

"Can't we just talk about this?" I whimpered.

He shook his head and smirked, as if I just didn't get it. "It seems as though you and your aunt have already had plenty to say."

"What are you talking about?" I twisted in the seat to look more closely at him.

"A couple weeks ago I began getting these creepy phone calls from a broad who kept taunting me about what I'd done to your dad. Said she knew all about me. Said she was going to blow the whistle on me."

"How did you know it was Annie?"

"I've got caller ID. It wasn't hard to find out who she was and where she lived. So, one night, when she was alone, I paid her a little visit."

"You killed Annie?" I shrieked, a mixture of anger...and horror.

"Oh, no..." he said in exaggerated shock. "She killed herself. Carbon monoxide."

He threw his head back and howled with laughter.

"B-but how? Why?" I felt like punching him, but instead I began to cry.

"I was sitting in my unmarked outside your house, trying to decide what to do.

Not long after I saw you leave, I got a call on my cell phone. It was your aunt."

"How did she know to call you on your cell phone?" I said swiping angrily at the tears trickling down my cheeks.

"I've also got call forwarding." He grinned at his technological cleverness. "I watched her through your picture window as she read me your dad's suicide note. Said she was going to give it to some reporter." He chuckled. "That helped me decide what I was gonna do. I saw her walk with it into her bedroom and come out with her hands empty, so I knew right where to go find it."

At the western outskirts of town, Roy palmed the speeding pickup left onto Route 58. Ahead of us, an eighteen-wheel gasoline tanker truck blocked our lane. Slowly, the driver ground through the gears as he lumbered up to speed.

"B-but how did you get into the house?" I sputtered.

Roy started to pass, but a string of cars filled the other lane. Taking a deep breath, he muttered something I couldn't hear, mashed the accelerator and yanked the wheel to the right. We skidded onto the shoulder and fishtailed in the gravel alongside the big truck.

Skillfully, with only his right hand, Roy fought the wheel to keep from bashing into the guardrail on the right, or going into the tanker's wheels on the left.

As our tires chirped safely back onto the concrete in front of the truck, its driver let go with an indignant blast of his air horn.

I glanced nervously at Roy.

He turned to me…and smiled.

I was not amused. "Where are we going?"

"You'll see."

It didn't take long to answer my question. Roy swerved right, skidding onto Old 58, then crushed the accelerator to the floor. The powerful pickup lurched ahead, pressing me against the seat.

"The railroad crossing," I whispered.

"Uh huh. And it looks like we're just in time."

He skidded the pickup to a stop straddling the tracks.

I looked to my right. In the distance, just coming around the bend two miles away: the bright, white light of an approaching train.

"Dear Jesus…" I whispered.

"Trick or treat," Roy smirked.

Chapter Forty-Five

In a few minutes the train would be here.

Roy Miller turned off the ignition and sat calmly behind the wheel of his pickup, patiently awaiting death.

A panicky claustrophobic feeling clutched at me. I grabbed for the door handle, but Roy's stern voice stopped me.

"Don't do it, Lark. Either way, you're gonna die, but don't do it."

I turned to look at him.

He waggled the gun at me, and smiled. "If you stay, you get to live for a couple more minutes. If you try to leave, you die now."

As I looked down the barrel—the very large barrel—I realized the irony of the moment: Once again, I was at this railroad crossing because of this powerful, but pitiful man.

"You're drunk," I spat.

He shrugged. "Alcohol's a great anesthetic. Want a shot?" He pulled a flask out of the pocket of his hunting vest, fumbled with the cap and took a hit, then held the container out to me. Some of the liquid dribbled down the grimy salt and pepper stubble on his chin.

I turned away in disgust. "It was you who tried to run me off the road the other night, wasn't it."

"Uh huh."

"Why?"

"You knew too much. When you told me your priest might be chasing after you, I had the perfect scapegoat."

The train—a slow-moving freight—plodded closer.

"Sheriff! Don't do this."

"It's no use, Lark. It's better this way." He looked calm now, nonchalant, at peace. "She left me no choice, you know."

"Who?"

"Your aunt. She wouldn't let up. Kept taunting me. I guess she was trying to give me a taste of what I'd given your dad."

Hearing the rumble of the oncoming train—and Roy Miller's calm monologue about Annie's murder—made me want to bash in his head, wail my grief, and scream in panic, all at the same time. Instead, I strained to keep my wits. Strained to see if there was anything I could do to save myself.

"It was dark…she was alone…I put on plastic gloves…took my gas mask out of the trunk…paid her a little visit." Roy jabbered as if he had all day.

The engineer began to pump his horn in loud rapid bursts. The train kept getting closer. But there was still time to try something.

Wildly, I looked around the truck's cab, gauging my surroundings.

"Getting in was a piece o' cake. Rang the bell. 'Evenin', Ma'am.'" Roy tipped his baseball cap. "'We're investigating some burglaries in the neighborhood. I'd like to ask you a few questions.' She saw my uniform…opened the door…it was easy. Believe me, it ain't hard to overpower a broad."

The train's air brakes hissed and the thundering of the engines changed pitch.

"Put a sleeper hold on her with by forearm. No air to the lungs…no marks on the throat. Very neat. She passed right out."

The locomotive's wheels locked, throwing sparks. Steel slid on steel. Boxcars banged and bunched in syncopated explosions behind the engine.

Roy was oblivious to the racket. "Shut the drapes in front of the picture window…found her car keys in her purse…put on my gas mask…turned on the ignition.

While she was dying, I went to get the suicide note. Never thought she'd be smart enough to make a copy of it, though…"

Roy Miller, Sheriff of Bluff County, Wisconsin, casually pointed the gun at me, ignoring the noisy train. His campaign for the U.S. House of Representatives was about to come to a sudden and brutal end. He didn't care any more.

"Stuck around 'til I was sure she was dead, then laid her out for you to find."

The din from the train's horn nearly smothered his words. The noise seemed to make the truck shake. My whole body—my legs, my arms, my stomach—felt weak and watery.

Yellow-white beams from the searchlight glinted off the rails, highlighting a crack in the passenger window. The train pounded relentlessly toward me. I couldn't take my eyes off it now.

Less than a minute.

You've got to get out! You've got to DO something!

I tried to block all the noise from my mind, tried to focus on making every motion count. I was ready to make my move.

Just then, the Bronco slid to a stop behind us. Jason Jordan and his photographer—camera on his shoulder—tumbled from the vehicle. Lionel was there too, breathing heavily.

"Don't do this, Roy." Lionel yelled. "It's not worth it."

"Sheriff!" I pleaded. "You can get through this. Believe me!"

"Shut up!" He shouted at me, then glanced worriedly at the Bronco through the window behind our heads. With his right hand he slid the window open.

Lionel lunged behind the wheel of the news vehicle and revved the engine.

Jason Jordan and the photographer were off to the side, videotaping the scene.

"Don't do anything stupid, Lionel, or the girl dies." Roy pressed the cold, hard steel of the gun barrel against my temple so Lionel could see.

Lionel hesitated, then threw the Bronco into gear.

Roy yanked on the truck's emergency brake.

The Bronco slammed into the back of the truck with a loud *bang*. The impact jostled us, but Roy's pickup failed to budge from the tracks.

The crossing signals began their insistent clanging.

The train was closing fast. Frantic blasts from its horn continued to split the chill morning air.

Lionel threw the Bronco into reverse, stopped, then lurched forward again.

Roy jabbed the gun through the back window slat.

In one fluid motion, I leaned back against the passenger door, brought my left knee to my chin, then uncoiled a savage kick. The heel of my left boot hit the gun as it went off with a deafening roar.

I expected to feel the Bronco hit the rear of the pickup, but nothing happened.

Anger distorted the sheriff's face. He swung the gun toward me.

The train's horn continued to blast. The dinging of the signal bells assaulted me. Metal screamed against metal, as the train skidded toward us. The semaphore lights flashed wildly. Bells clanged incessantly.

DING-DING-DING-DING-DING-DING-DING-DING!

Before Roy could shoot again, I kicked him hard in the solar plexus. He groaned and dropped the gun.

As I clawed at the door handle, I could feel the horn's blasts.

WHAAAAAAAA-WHAAAAAAAAAAAAA

As I lifted the handle, I shoved my shoulder hard against the door. It was locked.

Chapter Forty-Six

At that moment, there was no time for fear, panic, hopelessness, or any other emotion that would paralyze and doom me. When the door didn't budge, I immediately reached for the door lock, lifted it, and yanked up on the door handle.

Meanwhile, Roy Miller, gasping for breath, made a futile swipe at me with his right hand while groping with his left for the gun on the floor.

The thunder of the train's engines, the incessant blast of the whistle, the *clang-clang-clang* of the crossing signals made me want to jam my hands over my ears. But there was no time for that. I wasn't even sure if there was any time left to escape.

I might die, but at least I'll die trying to get away.

By this time, I was too afraid to look at the train anymore, I just knew it was close. As the passenger door swung open, I jumped to the asphalt and lunged toward the rear of the truck like a swimmer off a diving board.

An instant later, while still airborne, I heard a terrific *BANG.* The wind was knocked from my lungs as I landed with a thud. My knees, left shoulder and left cheek skidded on the pavement. My glasses flew off and skittered away. Pieces of metal and rock clattered down around me.

Gasping for air, I scrambled to my knees. I found my glasses a few feet away on the pavement. When I put them on, I saw the train sweeping past the crossing. Three green, white and black locomotives pushed the disintegrating pickup along the tracks. A shower of sparks spewed from the twisted hulk. Finally, the shattered carcass slid uselessly into the ditch and a parade of boxcars slowly *thunk-thunked* past.

The Channel 15 Bronco was next to me, its grill smashed in, headlights broken—a gaping bullet hole had been blown through the windshield just above the steering wheel. I couldn't see Lionel.

"Lionel!" I screamed. I scrambled to my feet, sprinted to the driver's side, yanked on the door handle, and braced myself for the carnage inside.

Lionel lay on his side across the seat. He was covered with shattered pieces of glass that looked like small ice cubes. His white hair was disheveled. Errant strands blew in the breeze stirred up by the freight cars still clanking past the crossing. I couldn't see any blood.

"Lionel!" I cried, touching him gently on the shoulder.

He groaned.

"Lionel?"

He opened his eyes and looked at me. "Lark, are you all right?"

"Am I all right? What about you?"

He brushed the glass from his shirt and sat up slowly. "I'm fine. I'm fine, but I asked you first. You okay?" He reached for my cheek.

The honking of the engine had stopped, but the signal lights still blinked and dinged above us.

I was shaking and weak.

"You're bleeding," he said.

My cheek burned, and when I dabbed at it gingerly with my fingers, I saw the blood. "It's not so bad." I flexed my leg. "Ripped my jeans, too."

The train rattled past for at least two minutes. Jason Jordan's cameraman continued to tape the scene.

Lionel eased himself out of the Bronco and opened his arms to me. I fell against his chest, crying.

"Roy killed Annie," I blubbered between sobs. "He told me."

"Shhhh. Don't try to talk," Lionel said as he gently stroked my hair.

After a moment, I pulled away from him. "Oh, Lionel, I'm getting blood on your white shirt."

"Don't worry about it," he laughed. "I've already got eggs and hash browns on me from when Roy shoved me into the table."

"Are you okay?"

"Yeah. I'll be fine."

"How's your heart?"

"It's fine. No problem. When I saw him aim that gun at me, I hit the brakes and ducked."

The caboose reached the crossing going so slowly that the brakeman was able to easily step to the ground. He trotted to us, agitated. "Is anybody hurt?" he asked anxiously. He held a walkie-talkie in his hand.

"Some scrapes and scratches here," Lionel told him, "but," he added, nodding toward the pickup, "I'd say the driver bought the farm."

"The cops and an ambulance have already been called," the brakeman said, his eyes wide. "The engineer did that right after we hit."

He rushed off to check on the sheriff.

Lionel stayed with me.

A siren in the distance got louder as a police car rounded the curve, coming from the direction of Pine Bluff. The siren stopped and the car squealed to a stop at an angle across the road, lights strobing.

Carl Olson, the sheriff's deputy, sprang from the car. He ran to us while putting on his Smokey Bear hat. His eyes widened when he saw what was left of Roy's pickup crumpled in the ditch by the side of the tracks.

"You okay?" Carl asked me.

I nodded.

"Where's the sheriff?" Carl asked.

Lionel and I both pointed at the mangled mess. Carl ran to take a look. In a minute or two, he and the brakeman rejoined us.

"The sheriff's dead," Carl said sadly. "Killed instantly, I'll bet." From his breast pocket he took a notebook and pen. "Tell me what happened, Miss Chadwick," he sighed.

"Poetic justice," I said.

Epilogue

Lionel was right—the news media throughout the state picked up the story I wrote about my investigation into the crash that killed my parents. Once Carl Olson finished taking my statement, and after I'd caught my breath, Jason Jordan conducted a ten or fifteen minute interview with me that he used in conjunction with the breathtaking pictures of the drama that began at The Korner Café and ended at the railroad crossing.

Jason's story, because of the phenomenal pictures, was broadcast not only by Channel 15 in Madison, but was on "NBC Nightly News" that night. I was a guest on "The Today Show" the next morning. The story then went viral. Last time I checked more than fifteen million people had seen it. A week later, I was still receiving interview requests from media outlets as far away as Japan and Australia. After my appearance on several major talk shows, I got a bundle of marriage proposals, which was totally unnerving. I'm not used to—or comfortable with—that kind of attention.

A few days after the sheriff took me hostage, Jason Jordan called to invite me to dinner. I said "no way," or words to that effect. I liked Jason, but just didn't want to deal with the emotional weirdness of a potential romance. Yet every few days he'd call back, suggesting lunch, or coffee, or a movie. Each time I turned him down. Then one day Jason called me and all we did was talk on the phone for a little while. The next week I consented to meet him for coffee.

I can't say we're officially "dating" now, but we have gotten together a few other times. I like being with him. And I think I trust him.

So, we'll see where things go. He thinks I'd be great on TV and is trying to arrange for me to have an audition at Channel 15, but that idea totally freaks me.

Father Dan and Betsy got married two months ago. Jason was my guest at the wedding and reception. We had fun. I've been attending Father Dan's church, but Jason's been reluctant to go with me because he's "not into church."

Father Dan's still having a hard time convincing a lot of people in the congregation that he's not—and will never be—Father Vincent, but one by one, with Betsy's help, more people have been willing to accept Dan's ministry.

Betsy and I have become friends. It's a relationship I cherish, but sometimes I have this irrational fear Dan and Betsy will move on before the end of the year. I hope not. I pray not.

Congressman Reginald Lange, meanwhile, seems to have shed his enigmatic image. He's back in his district almost every weekend. On one of those visits, he confessed to me that when he'd learned I was investigating the deaths of my parents, he'd instructed Eugene, his aide, to keep an eye on me. He admitted that Eugene had done a "ham-handed" job and apologized for any unnecessary angst that being followed might have caused for me. I told him it was a relief simply to know that I really wasn't imagining things.

Rep. Lange has been trying to stay in close touch with his constituents by holding town hall meetings at one place or another. He's had a tough time of it because many of his critics—as well as his backers—seem more interested in discussing his sexuality than his issues. But I think if he continues to keep the focus on serving his district, the novelty about his sexuality will become irrelevant.

I've noticed another thing about myself: I'm less bitter at Roy Miller. At first, I was enraged at him for killing Annie, tormenting my father, and trying to kill me. I was glad when he died. But as the months pass, I'm surprised to find myself thinking more tenderly about him, lamenting the way he wasted his life, and wishing I'd gotten to know and understand him better. As I've come to appreciate Lionel and Dan's forgiveness, I've been able to pray that somehow Roy would be able to find peace.

I think about my parents a lot. Sometimes I dream about them. At first, the dreams were troubling, especially the ones in which I, in a sense, became one parent, or the other. In those dreams the feelings of what their struggles must have been like are so powerful, I wake up struggling to catch my breath. It's only lately I've been able to envision them as smiling and at peace with themselves and the world around them.

But those are fantasies. Rarely, I think, does anyone ever experience that sense of being properly in tune. Maybe I'm wrong.

Anyway, I wonder how I'm like my parents—and how I'm different, too. Muriel mentioned once that I have "fight and flight tendencies." I've thought a lot about that.

My dad never fought, he simply fled; Mom, it seems, was reluctant to fight and merely caved because she pitied my father.

I know I'm impulsive, and have a temper—two traits which tend to get me into lots of trouble, but if I can learn how to fight constructively, then maybe I won't feel it's necessary to disengage from a situation and run away from it. I don't know. It'll probably take me the rest of my life to sort out this stuff. But, at least I'm trying.

I still miss Annie. Every day. I always will.

And Lionel? Well, we've reached an understanding. Several hours after the freight slammed into the sheriff's pickup truck, Lionel and I were still on the scene, standing in the field about fifty yards from the crossing. My scrapes had been bandaged by the ambulance crew, which also checked Lionel's heart and found it to be ticking properly.

The tracks were deserted. The freight train had resumed its run to Chicago. The wreckage and Roy's body had been cleared away. Jason Jordan was back in Madison filing his scoop.

It was just Lionel and me.

"The sheriff told me this is where that boy found me the night my parents were killed," I said, my foot toying with a dried corn husk.

"I'm glad you survived," Lionel said quietly.

"Thanks. Me too. Now. I didn't always feel that way."

Slowly, we trudged across the field. The ground smelled rich and fertile.

"Lark?"

"Hmmm?"

"I'm sorry I got so bent out of shape about you going off the record. I let my anger over losing a good story trample all over you. And that was wrong. I should have been more understanding."

"That doesn't seem important now compared to how I hurt you." I kicked at a rock. "Lionel, I'm sorry I said what I said to you the other day about Holly."

He let out a deep sigh.

"I was way out of line. Will you forgive me?"

His jaw muscles tightened.

"Lark," he finally said, "I hope you never have to experience the loss of a child. Losing Holly was—" tears began to well in his eyes.

I bit my lip.

He battled the tears and continued. "Well, anyway, it hurts. A lot. And the ache never, ever goes away." His voice was quiet, even. "It's always there. A longing. An emptiness."

He walked slowly toward the tracks. I fell into step next to him.

"And then I met you," he continued. "Not only did you have Holly's spunk, but I noticed you had a hunger for the truth—the heart of a good journalist. When you came along, it was like having a daughter again. But I tried to guard my heart against letting myself feel that kind of father-daughter thing for you. And I thought I'd been doing a pretty good job of it, until…" His voice trailed off.

"Until I made a fool of myself?"

He nodded. "That was when I realized that I'd let myself care again. And it hurt."

We walked in silence for a few steps.

"But when you were able to confirm the story, I put all the hurt aside while we worked to get it into print. I thought I was finally in the clear, that I wouldn't be hurt again. But then, this morning, when Roy pointed that gun at you as the train was coming—" He paused, fighting to keep his composure. "I thought I was going to lose you, and I knew I was never going to be able to stop caring about you…"

Lionel couldn't finish the sentence, he simply walked a little faster.

When he got to the tracks, Lionel stopped and turned to me. "Will I forgive you?" he said. "Of course. What you said was in the heat of battle. And I said some pretty nasty things, too."

He put an arm around my shoulder and hugged me to himself.

I felt forgiven, comforted…home.

"I like you, Lark," he whispered.

I glanced at him quickly and thought I saw his eyes welling with tears again. I put my arm around his waist, then patted his back. "I like you, too, Lionel. And thanks for all your help."

"No problem." He smiled, impishly. "You needed every bit of it."

We laughed and climbed onto the railroad ties, resuming our walk toward the crossing where Muriel waited for us in the Stone's Volvo.

"Um…Lark…?" Lionel asked as we got closer to the car.

"Yeah?"

"I've got a proposal to make."

"Oh?"

"I want to hire you as a full-time reporter."

I stopped walking and looked at him, incredulous. "You do?"

"I do."

"Gee, I—"

"I've seen you at work and I think you've got what it takes. You're curious, persistent, you know how to dig, you write fast—and pretty well, plus you have guts and compassion. It's a potent combination."

I blushed, not knowing what to say.

"But there are two conditions."

"I knew there was a catch." A slight grin curled my lip as I resumed walking.

"First, you have to agree to finish school and get your degree," he called out from behind me.

"Okay," I said over my shoulder. "That sounds easy enough." I stopped and turned to face him. "And the second?"

"You have to take my journalism class next semester." He smiled, triumphantly.

"I knew it was too good to be true," I laughed. "You drive a hard bargain, Mr. Stone."

"So, do you accept?" He took a step toward me, holding out his right hand.

"How much you gonna pay?" I said, studying his hand, but not reaching for it.

"Now you're the one driving a hard bargain, kid," he laughed. "How 'bout if I buy you a cup of coffee and we'll see what we can come up with?"

"It's a deal . . . Bogie." I grasped his hand and shook it firmly.

"That's Mister Bogie to you, kid."

We walked in silence a few more steps. The morning fog had lifted and the sun was burning through the haze. It was going to be an unseasonably warm day.

In the distance, the long, sorrowful note of a train whistle echoed among the hills.

"Let's get out of here," I said, sliding into the back seat. "I've had enough of trains for one lifetime."

The crossing signal began to flash and ding. The train whistled another mournful blast, but we were already well on our way toward coffee at the middle-of-the-block Korner Café.

THE END

Excerpt from *Bluff* by John DeDakis

A Lark Chadwick Mystery

CHAPTER 1

My hand trembled as I gripped the shiny-smooth, ebony fountain pen. I took a deep breath. It's not easy signing over a treasured place I've known and loved all my life. But putting my signature on the document transferring ownership of Grampa's farm to realtor Shane L. Duran became easier when I remembered how rich I was about to become. Until now, life had been pretty much hand-to-mouth for me.

Lark Chadwick, I wrote neatly. So neatly, in fact, the name printed below my signature was unnecessary.

Shane sat across from me, dwarfed by his massive mahogany desk. "You've just become very wealthy, Wonder Woman."

"Why do you keep calling me that?" I put the cap back on the pen and slid it across the desk to Shane.

"Haven't I ever told you? You look just like Lynda Carter."

"Who?"

"The babe who plays Wonder Woman on the Sci-Fi channel."

"You watch the Sci-Fi Channel?"

"But she shows more cleavage than you," he grinned.

"You're disgusting," I scowled.

"You hide the goods under those baggy sweaters."

I grimaced.

"Keep those tight jeans, though," he smirked.

"Stop it, Shane. Your sexism is showing." I would've stood to leave, but he still had to write me a check. A big check.

"You know me all too well, Lark."

"Actually, I don't and I'd sort of like to keep it that way."

"Ah, Lark, Lark," he chuckled, "you really should go out with me. You don't know what you're missing."

"If I asked your first two wives, I bet I'd get a thorough update."

He sighed. "They never understood me."

"Or maybe they understood you only too well."

His leering had become obnoxious long before, but at least he was up front about it. We'd met a few months earlier when he approached me to see if I'd sell Grampa's property.

At first he was just flirty, but when I'd made it clear I wasn't the least bit interested, he settled into being his normal, loutish self, instead of pretending to be the charming gentleman we both knew he wasn't. To me, the relationship was purely business—he was willing to pay me way more than anyone else.

He opened the top drawer of his desk and brought out two cigars the size of calves' legs. "Join me for a celebratory stogie."

I made a face. "Ugh. Thanks, but no thanks."

He looked hurt. "You sure? They're the best. Koenigshavens—fit for a king, but priced for the common man, or, in your case, babe. Five bucks a stick, and I can get 'em at the drug store."

Shane put one of the cigars back into the top desk drawer and slid it shut after taking out a long, wood-stick match. With a flourish, he struck it on a huge rock paperweight sitting on the edge of his desk. The dark granite stone had a thick base and tapered top. It must have weighed at least five pounds.

He powered up the cigar with the match and, in no time, a mushroom cloud of thick, gray smoke chimneyed toward the ceiling.

The smell of burning rubber was making me gag. "So, tell me again: What are you going to do with Grampa's farm?" I asked, pushing my chair back to get away from the cigar stench.

"Location, location, location," he said, waving out the match and tossing it onto a glass coaster on his desk. He leaned back in his black leather throne and crossed his tasseled loafers atop his colossus of a desk. "The property is perched nicely along the banks of the Rock River." He took a drag and blew a nimbus over my head. "Gonna develop it."

"Don't forget what you promised me about the trees," I said, wagging my finger at him, then coughed and tried to wave away the cigar smoke as it descended onto me.

"Right. Don't worry. I'll keep as many of those elms, oaks, and pines as possible. At least on *that*, you and I agree wholeheartedly," he winked. "So, whatcha gonna do with the money?"

"You have to write the check first." I nodded at the pen on the desk in front of him.

"Oh. That," he snorted. "Details." He made a dismissive wave of his hand, took his feet off the desk and rolled his chair forward.

"Do it fast," I said, holding my nose. "I'm dying here."

He pulled a checkbook from the top drawer of his desk and began writing. "Geez, I haven't written a check this big in a long time," he said, guiding the pen across the pale green paper.

I watched, feeling giddy and a bit light-headed—and not only because the cigar smoke was suffocating me.

Shane blotted the ink and blew on it before tearing the page from his checkbook. As he handed the check to me across his desk, the shiny finish of the polished top reflected his French cuffs.

I accepted his check with a grin. "Thanks."

He sat back, crossed his legs, and took another drag. "So... travel? A new car? A house? Clothes? All of the above? What?"

"Not sure," I said. "Next stop is the bank. Then... well... we'll see. I'm so used to being without funds, I think I'd just like to let it sit and earn interest. Maybe invest it in something that will grow, and set aside a little bit in savings that I can get at easily for emergencies."

Shane nodded thoughtfully as he puffed a few times on the cigar. "You're a very wise young lady." His face was wreathed in gray smoke. "Not to mention being a fox."

Normally, that would have been my cue to scold him again and leave, but I wasn't listening. I was eyeing the check. Something wasn't right about it.

I sat up straight in my chair. "Hey, wait a minute!" I said, alarmed.

"What?" He scowled.

"There's something wrong here."

"What are you talking about?" He uncrossed his legs and leaned forward.

"You wrote the wrong amount on the check."

"No, I didn't."

"You did. It's supposed to be for $475,000 and change."

"No, it's not."

"Instead, you wrote me a check for $47,550. That's a big difference."

"I wrote it for that because we agreed on that." He waved the cigar at me dismissively and sat back in his chair.

"No. We didn't." I drilled him with my eyes.

"Look at the contract you signed." With his fingertips, he gave it a gentle push. It slid across the desk and came to a stop beneath my nose.

I put down the check and riffled through the document until I found the correct page. He was right. My signature committed me to accept

$47,550 for Grampa's farm, but that's not what we'd agreed upon verbally. I was sure of it.

I slapped the contract onto the desk in disgust. "Shane. How can you do this to me?"

"Do what?" He looked hurt.

"Do you think I'm just some dumb broad who wouldn't notice?"

"Well—"

"Nice try, Shane." I picked up the check for more money than I'd ever had in my entire life, tore it into tiny pieces, and poured the scraps into my bag.

"I still have your signed contract," he said, reaching across his desk for the papers in front of me.

"No. You *don't*," I hollered. I pounced from my chair and snatched the document before he could pick it up. "This contract is null and void." The pages flopped as I shook them at his face. Angrily, I shredded the closing statement with both hands, jammed the pieces into my bag and headed for the door.

"Lark! Wait!" he called after me. "You're making a big mistake."

I got to the door, spun around, and glared at him. "My big mistake," I hissed, "was trusting you, Shane Duran. But I'm over that."

I could barely see him through all the cigar smoke as he sat slumped in his chair, mouth hanging open in disbelief.

I made sure to slam the door when I left.

Acknowledgments for the 2005 Edition

Before finding a home, *Fast Track* went through no fewer than fourteen major revisions since the first draft in 1996. Along the way, numerous people read all or some of the manuscript. The constructive criticisms and encouragement of the following people helped to make the story better: Giles Anderson, Melissa Block, Doris Booth, Hugh Brown, Carol Buckland, Kim Bui, Mandy Carranza, Susan Fitzgerald Carter, Paula Cohen, Kelley Colihan, Carol Costello, Cynthia DeDakis, Dr. Emily A. DeDakis, Lauren Dembo, Dr. Paul Dobransky, Christian Duchateau, Carolyn Dudley, Dennis Dudley, Miriam Goderich, Nancy Ellis, Judy Iakovou, Beni Kurian, Chip MacGregor, Colleen McEdwards, Lynn McGill, Kathie Parks, Alison Picard, J. Mark Powell, The Rev. Elizabeth Rechter, Jay Rechter, Jacky Sach, Michael Seidman, Nat Sobel, Patricia Sprinkle, Maryanne Stahl, Andy Straka, Christine Talbott, Charles Terhune, Jeff Tickson, Karla Vallance, Judy Verbic, and Jim Vitti.

A special thanks to the ladies of the Princeton Lakes Book Club: Linda Bradigan, Ingrid Cooksey, Beth Gary, Karen Haskins, Sandra Helton, Meg Henderson, JoAnn Kilroy, Gert McNalley, Cece Meyers, Tamela Nevins, Delores Ramey, Barbara Rittman, and Pat Roth. These women helped me see that I had three subplots I didn't need. Consequently, *Fast Track* went from being a 150-thousand-word mishmash, to a tightly written 75-thousand-word mystery-suspense novel.

In addition, my thanks to Robert Ray for writing his extremely helpful books *The Weekend Novelist* and *The Weekend Novelist Writes a Mystery* (Dell); Vern Strayer for his railroading stories; Wes Pippert for his journalism stories and expertise; the late former *New York Timesman*, Bob Slosser for being a wise role model; Lowell Mays for the way he cares about people; Karen Hallacy for her train-spotting help; and Ken Talbott of the CSX Railroad in Atlanta, who let me lie down in front of his train so I could snap the picture for the dust jacket cover of the 2005 edition.

I owe a deep debt of gratitude to my agent Barbara Casey and my first publisher/editor Robert Gelinas. They helped turn a solitary creative process into a stimulating collaboration.

Finally, a big hug to my wife Cindy and our children, Emily, James, and Stephen. You put up with a lot. I love you guys.

For all of the above reasons, I am, indeed, blessed.

John DeDakis
Marietta, Georgia
August 2005

Coming Soon!

FROM THE BESTSELLING AUTHOR OF *FAST TRACK*

BLUFF

A Lark Chadwick Mystery

by

John DeDakis

Lark Chadwick is back! From the small town environs of Wisconsin to the ancient cities and mountains of Peru, the intrepid reporter for The Pine Bluff Standard is freshly embroiled in another tale of intrigue—the mysterious death of the daughter of her boss—where Lark shockingly becomes a target.

For more information

visit: www.SpeakingVolumes.us

On Sale Now!

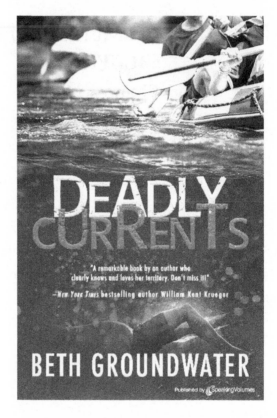

For more information
visit: www.SpeakingVolumes.us

On Sale Now!

"Irving's writing is relaxed and authentic and takes readers inside a compelling world of legal and social issues..."
—Bruce Kluger, columnist, USA Today

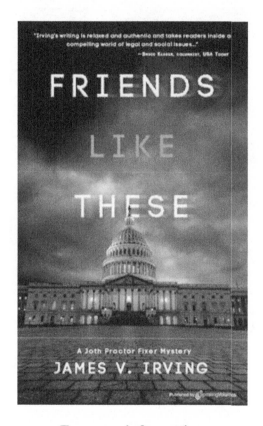

For more information
visit: www.SpeakingVolumes.us

On Sale Now!

DUTCH CURRIDGE MYSTERIES
BY
TIM BRYANT

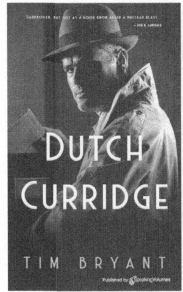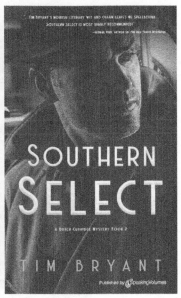

For more information
visit: www.SpeakingVolumes.us

On Sale Now!

Rat Pack Mysteries

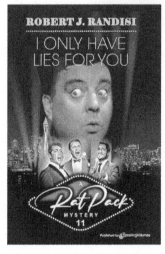

**For more information
visit:** www.SpeakingVolumes.us

Made in the USA
Monee, IL
09 July 2022